TARGETED

BOOKS BY LYNETTE EASON

WOMEN OF JUSTICE
Too Close to Home
Don't Look Back
A Killer Among Us

DEADLY REUNIONS
When the Smoke Clears
When a Heart Stops
When a Secret Kills

HIDDEN IDENTITY
No One to Trust
Nowhere to Turn
No Place to Hide

ELITE GUARDIANS
Always Watching
Without Warning

Moving Target
Chasing Secrets

BLUE JUSTICE
Oath of Honor
Called to Protect
Code of Valor
Vow of Justice

DANGER NEVER SLEEPS
Collateral Damage
Acceptable Risk
Active Defense
Hostile Intent

EXTREME MEASURES
Life Flight
Crossfire

BOOKS BY LYNN H. BLACKBURN

DIVE TEAM INVESTIGATIONS
Beneath the Surface
In Too Deep
One Final Breath

DEFEND AND PROTECT
Unknown Threat
Malicious Intent

BOOKS BY NATALIE WALTERS

HARBORED SECRETS
Living Lies
Deadly Deceit
Silent Shadows

THE SNAP AGENCY
Lights Out
Fatal Code

TARGETED

THREE ROMANTIC SUSPENSE NOVELLAS

LYNETTE EASON, LYNN H. BLACKBURN, AND NATALIE WALTERS

Revell

a division of Baker Publishing Group
Grand Rapids, Michigan

Published by Revell
a division of Baker Publishing Group
PO Box 6287, Grand Rapids, MI 49516-6287
www.revellbooks.com

Printed in the United States of America

Library of Congress Cataloging-in-Publication Data
Names: Eason, Lynette, author. | Blackburn, Lynn H., author. | Walters, Natalie, author.
Title: Targeted : three romantic suspense novellas / Lynette Eason, Lynn H. Blackburn and Natalie Walters.
Description: Grand Rapids, Michigan : Revell, a division of Baker Publishing Group, [2022]
Identifiers: LCCN 2022018322 | ISBN 9780800740283 (paperback) | ISBN 9780800742287 (casebound) | ISBN 9781493438891 (ebook)
Subjects: LCGFT: Suspense fiction. | Novels.
Classification: LCC PS3605.A79 T37 2022 | DDC 813/.6—dc23
LC record available at https://lccn.loc.gov/2022018322

To our amazing agent,
Tamela Hancock Murray.
Thank you for believing in us,
encouraging us, and championing us.
You're the best!

ON THE RUN

LYNETTE EASON

ONE

Daria Nevsky slammed the door of her Ford F-150 truck and tucked her jacket under her chin to ward off the chill of the November wind. She headed toward the front steps of her Virginia townhome, thinking how nice it would be to park in a garage. But she loved this home located in a quiet neighborhood that backed up to a park where children played, dogs chased Frisbees, and couples picnicked on warm spring days.

As she started up the steps, her phone rang. She stopped midstep to swipe the screen and turned to lean against the porch railing. "Marsha?"

"Daria, honey, I hope I haven't caught you at a bad time." Marsha McBride managed Daria's home in South Carolina. The one she abandoned seven years ago after the death of her mob-boss father and her adoption by FBI agents Linc and Allie St. John.

"Not at all." She ducked her head against the wind but enjoyed being outside at the same time. "What's going on?"

"Someone broke into my house."

Daria straightened. "What? Are you okay?"

"Yes, I'm fine, but the lock on the door is broken, and I don't feel comfortable staying there."

"All right. Why don't you stay at my father's—" She took a deep breath. "*My* house?"

"No, that place scares me too. I'll clean it, but I don't want to sleep there." She let out a self-conscious laugh. Daria didn't blame her. She didn't care for the house either. But it was hers. She just avoided dealing with it.

"What did they take?" Daria asked.

"Nothing that I could tell. I guess I came home and scared him off. I just wanted to let you know that I'll be staying with my sister until I feel comfortable going home—and I'm not sure I'm up to cleaning this week. Do you mind if I put it off until next week? I know I sound like a wimp, but I keep thinking, *What if I'd been home?*"

"Of course I don't mind. And you're not a wimp. Anyone would be shaken after coming home to that."

"Thank you, Daria. Enjoy your vacation and time with your family."

Yes, vacation—with the family who was already waiting for her in the sunny Caribbean. "I will. I'll check on you when I get back." She hung up and shivered. The temperature was dropping, and the wind cut through her coat. She was done with being outside. Her flight left at six o'clock the next morning, and she still had some packing to do.

She dug her key from her pocket and aimed it for the deadbolt.

And froze.

The door was open a fraction. A slight crack that she might not have noticed if she didn't always shut and lock her door—and arm the alarm system. Chills skittered up her arms, and she took a step back. So someone had either *been* in her home—or was still there. But why hadn't the alarm gone off?

She spun to leave, only to jerk to a halt with a gasp.

A man wearing a ski mask and a hoodie stood at the bottom of her porch steps.

"Who are you? What do you want?" She edged toward the railing.

"You. Your father sent me."

Daria froze. "My father's dead."

Eleven brick steps now separated her from trouble. He started up, lessening the distance, and she caught sight of the knife in his left hand. "But he's not gone."

Daria drew in a deep breath, trying to control her hammering pulse and . . . *think.*

He lunged.

She whirled, gripped the rail, and hauled herself over. His fingers grazed her right foot. She hit the ground hard, the seven-foot jump jarring her to the bone. She stumbled, gained her balance, and headed for the side of the townhome.

Think!

Her feet pounded the street while she searched for an escape.

"Hey! What's going on?"

Mr. Jackson. The sweet neighbor who always looked out for her had just opened his door for his evening walk.

"Get back inside and call the cops!" With a quick glance over her shoulder, Daria saw the man in the ski mask gaining on her. She cut across the street to a neighbor's front yard, hoping to go around and into the back.

"Hey! You! Stop! Leave her alone!" The man chasing her ignored Mr. Jackson's shouts.

Her foot tripped over an exposed root and she landed with a breath-stealing thud.

Move! Her body wouldn't cooperate.

He caught up with her and the knife flashed. She kicked out and connected with his knee.

"Ah!" He landed on the ground, and his pained cry gave her only a second of satisfaction before he caught her ankle in a tight grip. Daria lashed out once more with her right hand, feeling the burn of the blade on her side even as she slammed her fist into his jaw.

He jerked back and she lurched to her feet, ignoring the pain arching through her hand and just below her ribs. She kicked again. Her booted foot landed against his rib cage with a harsh crack. He screeched and rolled to his knees, his left hand clutching his side while his right hand reached for her. She grabbed it and twisted, then jammed her heel into his face. His roar reverberated in her ears as he fell to the ground once more, leaving her clutching his glove. A tattoo peered up at her from the back of his hand. Daria noted it, then covered her own bleeding wound with her right hand and ran.

"Paging Dr. Donahue. Please report to the ER. STAT."

Ryker rolled over with a groan and sat up. The lounge was shockingly quiet, and a glance at the clock said he'd managed to snag an incredible two hours of uninterrupted sleep. He'd lost track of how long he'd been at the hospital. Too long. He should have left before he'd collapsed on the bed, but he'd been too tired to risk driving home.

"Paging Dr. Donahue. Please report to the ER. STAT."

Ryker stood, went to the sink and ran cold water over his face, brushed his teeth in record time, grabbed his ever-present iPad, then hurried out the door. He rubbed a hand down his cheek and knew he needed to shave, but that would have to happen later.

He walked into the ER and Maggie, his nurse, pointed. "Door number four. Stab wound. She refused any pain meds." Maggie tapped her tablet. "Sent you the chart."

"Thanks."

He pulled the patient's chart up on the device and scanned it.

Daria Nevsky—why did that name sound familiar?—twenty-four years old, laceration to her right side under the rib cage. He knocked, then stepped inside the room.

"Daria Nevsky?"

"Yeah." She blinked up at him, face pale, jaw tight, nostrils flared. This was a woman in intense pain, yet she didn't want meds. Her gaze flicked to the door, then back to him.

"I'm Dr. Ryker Donahue. What happened? Who did that to you?"

"There was an intruder at my house. I fought him off, but he took a chunk of flesh out of my side before I could get away from him. He'd left his keys in the car, so I stole it and drove as long and as far as I— Where am I?"

"Mission Hospital."

She frowned. "What state?"

Her light accent struck a chord with him. "Asheville, North Carolina." He narrowed his gaze. An intruder had done this to her? "Where did you drive from?"

"Quantico, Virginia."

"That's quite a drive." At least eight hours.

"No kidding."

"You drove all night?"

"Pretty much."

"Did you call the police?"

She winced. "I didn't, but I yelled at my neighbor to. He probably did, so I'm sure they have a record of his account. I should probably let him know I'm okay, but I had other priorities at the time—like getting away."

"Away from the intruder."

She shot him a harsh frown. "Yes. Why do you say it like that?"

"Was he someone you knew?"

13

"No."

"Hold on a second." He backed out of the room. "Maggie?"

"Yes?"

"We need the cops. Can you get an officer in here so we can file a report?"

"Sure."

"It happened in Virginia at my home." She reeled off an address.

"They'll let Virginia authorities know," Ryker said.

"Yep. And the guy's car should be in the parking lot here." She told him where she parked, and he noted it.

"You stole his car?"

"I did."

"Gutsy." He gestured to her side. "All right if I take a look?" He pulled on gloves and snagged the rolling seat with his foot to park it next to the bed.

"Sure, why not?" She lifted the hem of her bloodied shirt to reveal a bandage.

"Did you do this?"

"A triage nurse."

"Okay, I'm just going to peel it off and see what we have." She nodded and he went to work. The wound wasn't pretty, and when he went to probe its depth, she flinched and let out a pained hiss. He stopped and sighed. "I really need to give you some meds so I can better assess this without causing more pain."

"Just stitch it up and give me some antibiotics."

Ryker frowned. "That's not how this works."

"Look, that guy came after me for a reason. I can't risk being drugged up and unconscious in case he finds me."

"Eight hours away?"

Her gaze, while pain-filled, was also rock steady. "Yes."

"Okay, well, seems to me you came this direction for a reason. Do you have anyone nearby who can sit with you? Watch out for you?"

"I do, but I don't really want to bother them."

"Then it sounds like you need some new friends. Why don't you tell me the truth? Was it a boyfriend, husband, or fiancé who did this?"

She shot him a scowl. "No, it wasn't. I don't have any of the above, so just do your job and let me worry about the rest."

"Wow, rude much?"

She groaned. "I'm sorry. I'm not usually. I'm just . . ."

"Scared and in pain?"

After a slight hesitation, she nodded. "Both are accurate. Add confused in there, and you have a surprisingly good picture of my mental state." She sighed.

Her admission touched him. "Thanks for being honest."

"I'll be honest about one more thing. I could call my family, but they're on vacation. And I don't just mean a simple trip up the interstate. They've been saving and planning for this trip for two solid years. I refuse to be the one who brings it all to a screeching halt. And . . . there are other factors in play as well."

He studied her for a moment. "All right, here's what we're going to do. I'll give you a little something to take the edge off, then I'm going to numb, clean, and stitch the wound." He held up a hand to stop her protests. "I won't give you anything that will knock you out. You'll be awake the entire time. And I'll get a security officer to stay within sight of your room. How's that sound?"

She studied him like she was trying to figure out whether she could trust him. Then she nodded. "Like a plan I can live with. Thank you."

TWO

Daria floated in and out of awareness. Each time she nodded off, she worked hard to stay awake. And for the most part, she could. But after she spoke with the security officer and saw Dr. Donahue had remained true to his word about the man staying within sight of her door, she allowed herself to relax a fraction. The events of the evening played through her mind—especially the part about her father sending the guy to attack her. Her father had been dead for seven years, and she wasn't even worried that he'd somehow managed to fake his death. No, this was something else. The security officer opened the door. "Ma'am?"

Daria rolled her head to meet his gaze. "Yes?"

"Two officers are here to take your statement."

"Sure." She raised the bed into a sitting position, doing her best not to use her abdominal muscles. It hurt but wasn't unbearable.

The officers entered, a man and a woman, and stood by the door. The woman took the lead. "I'm Officer Bailes, and this is Officer Tate." Bailes took out a notepad and flipped it open. "You're Daria Nevsky?"

"I am." She left off the FBI special agent part. Word might get back to someone in the bureau, and she wasn't ready for that to happen yet.

"Can you tell us what happened?"

Daria rubbed her forehead and debated about how much to tell them. She still needed to process and think things through for herself.

"My father's dead."

"But he's not gone."

She needed to know what the man meant by that. "My front door was cracked when I got home. I think he'd been inside and had just come out." And hadn't left. He'd been waiting for her.

"You didn't go in?"

"No. I try to be smarter than that."

A slight smile curved the female officer's lips, and she met Daria's gaze. "Good for you. What else?"

"He attacked, I jumped over the rail to run, he grabbed me, managed to slice me. I fought back, got away, and ran. I didn't get a look at him because he had a mask on. He also had gloves on. And boots."

"Well, that was a very concise summary."

Gloves. She still had one of them, which she needed to have run for DNA. "Wait." She snatched a tissue from the box on the end table and walked to her pants hanging on the wall hook. She used the tissue to pull the glove out of her pocket. "I grabbed his hand to shove him away and this came off." She passed it to the cop, who took it carefully. "There might be some prints on there somewhere—other than mine."

Tate glanced at his partner. "We'll send this off and contact Virginia PD. They'll go by and check on your home for you. You got a cell number?"

She gave it to him, then examined the other pockets of her jeans and grimaced. "But I think my phone fell out of my pocket in the struggle."

17

"If the phone's still out there and they find it," Tate said, "they'll keep it for you."

"Check with my neighbor as well. He saw the guy and yelled at him." She gave them Mr. Jackson's information.

Officer Bailes wrote on her little pad and Officer Tate stepped forward. "You said he had on a mask. What about how he smelled, words he said, his height, weight? Anything?"

"He was tall. Probably a couple of inches over six feet. I don't remember any particular smells." She didn't say anything about his words and hoped the officers wouldn't press the matter. She didn't want to lie, but she also didn't want to explain the connection the attack had to her father. Not until she did some digging and figured that part out herself.

Thankfully, they finally left. Seconds after they were gone, Dr. Donahue stepped inside. "Everything okay?"

The concern on his handsome features touched a place deep inside her. A place she'd walled off a long time ago. "I think so." She looked away, not wanting him to see her thoughts in case they were sneaking into her eyes. "But I think it's time I get out of here."

"I think you should stay the night."

Her gaze snapped back to his. "What? Why?"

———

"Because . . . because . . . someone stabbed you. We need to make sure you don't get an infection or have any other issues."

"Like?"

"Internal bleeding." He studied her, noting her calm façade. He had no idea why he felt like she was hiding something. But—

"I'll take my antibiotics and make sure I keep an eye on it," she said.

"What if he's waiting for you to go home?"

She was a patient. What she did was her business. Why was he arguing about this? Because he was drawn to her expressive blue eyes and soft Russian accent? Why was she so familiar to him?

"I have a gun and I'm not afraid to use it," she said, her words light but her tone weary.

"I assume you have a weapons permit."

She quirked a smile. "Of course I do."

"Well, I still don't think you should go home, but I guess that's your choice."

"I appreciate that. And you can rest easy. I don't plan to go home anytime soon." She shifted and winced, her hand going to her wound. "And I think I'll do my best to stay very still for the moment, though."

"Probably wise. If you pull those stitches out, I'll have to sew you back up."

She let out a low groan and closed her eyes. Ryker stood. "Since I can't talk you into some other pain meds, I've got to go check on some other patients, but I'll stop in before I leave." He wasn't obligated to, of course, but there was something about her . . . "Your name is really familiar to me, and I can't figure out why."

She opened one eye. "It's not exactly a common name."

"It's Russian, isn't it?"

"It is."

"Hmm . . . it'll come to me." He turned to leave.

"Hey, Dr. Donahue?"

He stopped. "Ryker."

"Ryker." She sighed and rubbed her eyes. "Like I said, I'm not going home. I was on my way to Columbia, South Carolina, but stopped here because I felt like I was going to pass out. I used to live on the outskirts of Columbia, and I thought I might find some . . . answers if I . . ." She bit her lip and looked away. "Never mind."

"Answers to what?"

"To why someone attacked me."

"You were attacked in Virginia. Why are the answers in Columbia?"

"I . . . don't know that they are, but I figured it couldn't hurt to go looking and find out for sure one way or another."

He smiled. "Well, I hope you get your answers soon, Daria Nevsky." He patted her hand. "Rest. I'll be back shortly."

Her eyes closed and he left her room, still pondering her name. He'd heard it before. It was distinct enough to send his memory bank spinning. But he had work to do, and he did his best to let go of the nagging at his subconscious so he could focus on his other patients.

And yet he found himself walking past Daria's room as much as possible over the next couple of hours. Twice he had to force himself to read the same information three times before he processed it. Being so distracted wasn't doing him—or his patients—any good. In fact, it could be dangerous. He sighed. He'd check in with Daria one more time to make sure she was sleeping as he'd recommended, and then maybe his attention span would improve.

He walked back down the hall, working on his reasons for looking in on her should she be awake. When he rounded the corner, he noticed a man entering her room.

Ryker frowned. She'd said she didn't have anyone to call or who might come visit, and he didn't recognize the man as a hospital worker. So who had the security officer just let in her room?

THREE

The door whooshed open and she groaned. Ryker had said to rest. If the nurses kept coming in and poking at her, she'd never get any sleep. She kept her eyes shut, hoping if they thought she was sleeping, they'd leave.

Ryker Donahue. As soon as he'd said his first name, the light went on and she finally figured out who he was. Of course she'd get the one doctor she knew—without ever having actually met him—in the state. Had she subconsciously come to his hospital hoping to find him even though it had been years since she'd heard his name?

Probably.

The hair on her neck stiffened. Seconds had passed with no movement after the opening of the door. Something was different.

She lifted her lids and found herself staring at a suppressor attached to the barrel of a Glock 17. She trailed her gaze up a man's arm to gray eyes looking down at her. His head was shaved and his full lips, encircled by a mustache and goatee, were pressed into a hard line. He had on scrubs, a name badge attached with a picture that could pass for him if someone took a quick glance at it. But it was the stethoscope around his neck that completed the authentic look. "I'm going to need you to come with me," the fake doctor said in Russian.

Daria blinked and her insides froze. "How did you find me?" She'd disabled the GPS on the car.

"There's more than one way to track a vehicle. Now come, or I will start shooting people until you understand it's better to do what I say."

So the attack at her home hadn't been an attempt to kill her? It had been an attempt to *take* her?

The wound in her side said otherwise, but she supposed the stabbing could have been an accident in the struggle with the attacker. Heart thudding in her chest, she took deep breaths in an effort to control her panic. She'd been through tough times before and kept her cool. She could do it again.

Pulling on all her training and practice at keeping her emotions hidden, Daria met the man's gaze. She thought he looked slightly familiar but couldn't place him. "Can I get dressed?"

He grimaced, backed up to the closet, and pulled her clothes —that someone had been kind enough to hang up—from the hangers. He tossed them on the bed, bloody shirt and all.

"You don't think that's going to attract some attention?"

"Change. Now."

She stared at him. "Well, I'm not changing with you standing there."

"And I'm not going any—"

The door opened and he spun.

Daria grabbed the heavy IV pole with a pained grunt and swung it. It hit him in the back, and he let out a low growl while the newcomer launched himself at the hand holding the gun. The attacker screamed and went to his knees, the weapon falling to the floor. He lashed out with a fist and caught the man— *Ryker?*—in the gut. Daria heard the air whoosh from him even as he stumbled backward and hit the closet door with a crash.

She scrambled out of the bed with a hand pressed against her wound, trying not to trip over the IV line, her goal to reach the weapon first. Her attacker twisted around to see her searching for the Glock and bit off a string of curses. He pushed himself to his feet and bolted for the door.

Ryker lunged from the closet and wrapped his arms around the man's legs in an impressive tackle. The assailant went down once again. He kicked and his heel landed on Ryker's right ear.

Ryker cried out and rolled away. The guy scrambled to his feet and fled out the door. Daria ripped off the tape holding the IV in her arm, tossed the IV aside, and gave chase. She pushed out the door and into the hallway, panting, head swimming, pain crawling through her wound, but she had to know—

"Daria, stop!"

She had no choice. It was either stop or face-plant. She turned with measured movements, praying the weakness would pass, to find Ryker at the door. Finally, the world settled and the light-headed feeling dissipated. "Are you okay?" she asked.

Ryker held a hand to his ear. "It was a glancing blow. Painful but nothing too damaging. What about you?"

"I'm fine, but he's gone." She made sure her gown covered all the essentials and looked back over her shoulder. "Where's the security guy? How did you know I needed help?"

Ryker flushed. "I saw someone enter your room. When I asked the security officer about him, he said a doctor was in here with you." Ryker paused. "And that he was going to take a bathroom break. I told him to go on, that I would watch out for you. I also wanted to know which doctor was in there."

"He was no doctor."

"Yeah, I kind of figured that out." He stepped toward her. "I need to check that wound."

"It's fine." She looked at one of the nurses standing in the hall. "Can you call security and let them know, please? They'll need to pull footage and see if they can get a shot of his face to run through facial recognition software."

The woman nodded and hurried toward the nurses' station. And while they worked on that, Daria was going to do a little investigating of her own. She returned to the room and started collecting what few possessions she had.

"What are you doing?" Ryker asked. "You were attacked—again—and the cops will want to talk to you."

"I know, but I don't have anything to tell them. The best thing I can do is start fighting back."

"Okay. So what does that look like?"

Exactly what she'd figured when she'd aimed the car toward Columbia, South Carolina.

"Like revisiting a nightmare."

"You're leaving?"

"I have to. After I make a couple of phone calls."

He studied her for a moment. "All right, my shift is over in ten minutes. No doubt security is already looking for this guy. Let's talk to the cops, do everything the right way, then I'll go with you wherever you want to go."

She gaped at him, then snapped her lips shut. "Um . . . why?"

He nodded to her side. "Because that was some of my best needlework. I'd hate to think of you doing something to tear that wound open."

A short laugh of disbelief escaped her, but he waited her out. She shook her head. "No. This could be too dangerous."

"Okay, then I'll just follow you."

24

"You don't understand—"

"I understand you're in danger and you need help, but for some reason you really don't want to ask for it. So I'm not making you ask. I'm offering."

"Insisting?"

"Semantics."

She let out a low laugh that held no humor. Finally, she nodded. "Okay."

"Now, I'm going to go check in with security and see if they managed to find the guy. Just promise you won't disappear on me?"

She sighed. "I promise."

He studied her gaze and found no hint of deception. She'd be waiting on him. "Thank you. If you'll hold on a second—or make those phone calls you mentioned—I'll find you a shirt that doesn't have a hole in it and blood on it. Then you can get dressed while I call security."

"A clean shirt sounds perfect. Thanks."

It didn't take Ryker long to find a long-sleeved scrub top that would do for now. He returned to the room and gave it to her. While she changed, he went to the nurses' desk and called security. Joe Cash answered and Ryker said, "You find him?"

"No. He ran into the parking garage and hopped on a motorcycle. We've got him on the video feed and gave photos of his face to the police along with a description of the bike, so I imagine they'll put it out there so the public can call in tips. But for now, he's not in the hospital, so you can rest easy."

If only. "Okay, thanks." He hung up and hurried back to Daria's room and breathed a sigh of relief that she was still there. "He eluded security and escaped on a motorcycle, which means you're safe here tonight. Are you sure you don't want to stay?"

"I'm sure. I need to leave while I can. Besides, the faster I get to the house, the faster I can figure out who's after me."

Ryker nodded, then paused. "I have some friends I can call. People who helped me when I needed it a few years ago. One of them is an FBI agent."

Her gaze snapped to his. "Who?"

"Caden Denning."

She nodded. "I figured that was who you were going to say."

"Why would you figure that?"

"Because he's the reason you know my name."

He raised a brow. "Obviously I've missed something. Care to fill me in?"

"I'm an analyst with the bureau. I work with Caden on a regular basis. I remember when he was helping Travis and Heather Walker when someone was trying to kill Heather. Your name came up a lot in that investigation."

Ryker couldn't believe the world was this small—literally. In fact, he was going to attribute this meeting to divine intervention. "So you knew who I was and didn't say anything?"

"I didn't at first. I put it together shortly after you told me your first name."

"Huh." It wasn't important. "Why not call him or one of your other FBI buddies?"

Her jaw tightened. "I will once I have something concrete to share with them."

"Attempts on your life aren't concrete enough?"

"Not really."

He waited for her to elaborate. When she didn't, he had a feeling there was more to the story than a lack of facts or "concrete" whatever. "You have a very hard time asking for help, don't you?"

"It's really not your business, is it?"

"And we're back to rude."

She flinched and grimaced. "Sorry." A pause. "Yes, I have trouble asking for help. I've been working on that, though." He raised a brow and she groaned. "Mostly."

He hesitated, unsure what he was getting himself into, then decided if she was a friend of Caden, Travis, and Heather, he *really* didn't want her to handle this without someone watching her back. "All right, then. Let's go."

"Do you mind driving? The car I drove here had a tracker on it and that's how he found me."

"Donahue's Limo Service at your . . . service? That's kind of redundant, isn't it?"

She started to laugh, then drew in a deep breath and let it out slowly. "Don't make me laugh, it hurts, but thank you, Ryker." She hesitated. "I really shouldn't let you do this. Like I said, this could be dangerous."

"I've kind of figured that out. And I'm no stranger to danger." He refused to let the memories of his past surface and forced a lighthearted smile. "Ready?"

"After you."

FOUR

Daria was now only fifteen minutes from a home she'd lived in for only a short amount of time and had no desire to see again.

But she would.

A little over seven years ago, her father, Vladislav Nevsky, had moved his organization from New York to South Carolina, thinking he could outrun those who were working hard to bring him down.

But the move had, thankfully, been his downfall—and the best thing to ever happen to Daria. Allie and Linc St. John, the FBI agents responsible for bringing her father to justice, then took her under their wings and showed her what it meant to have parents and a family who loved her.

She drew in a deep breath and tried to slow her uncharacteristically fast heartbeat. *Be cool, Daria. You can do this.*

"Are we at the right place?"

Ryker's question brought her out of the past to see he'd followed her directions and was now parked at the gate that would lead to the main house. She could see the front of the house from their location and noted Ryker's wide eyes on the three-story mansion. "Yeah. The code is 1104."

"The power's still on?"

"Yes."

He turned to look at her. "And how long has it been since you've been here?"

"A little over seven years."

He gaped. "What's the bill for a place like this each month?"

"You don't want to know." Money wasn't an issue for Daria. Her mother had made sure she would be well taken care of should anything happen to her. On Daria's twenty-first birthday, she'd inherited her mother's estate and never had to work again if she didn't want to. "I have one full-time staff person who keeps it clean, reports any repairs needed, that kind of thing." At his continued stare, she shrugged. "I need to keep it in good condition in case I decide to put it on the market."

"Oh. Well, that makes sense." He pulled through the opening, and the two wrought-iron gates shut behind them.

"She was one of the phone calls I made from the hospital. I wanted to make sure she wasn't here when I arrived."

"I'm guessing for her protection?"

"Exactly."

He drove slowly while Daria panned the property, her nerves on edge, senses sharp.

"Do you plan to put it on the market soon?" he asked.

"I don't know." She really didn't. She probably needed more counseling to discover why she couldn't seem to let go of the place. And yet, she'd found one good use for it, so . . .

"Okay," he said, "where do I park?"

"Out of sight of the main road. You'll come to a brick circular area with an ugly statue in the middle. Bear to the left and pull around to the back near the garage."

"Got it."

When he saw the garage, his eyes flared wide once more. "How many cars does that hold?"

"Ten. Five on this side, five on the other."

"Wow."

"I know. It's ridiculous." She paused. "I did sell six of the vehicles." And had no trouble doing so. Those cars meant nothing to her, and the money had gone to a cause near and dear to her heart. Domestic abuse victims.

"But not the other four?"

She smiled. "I like them." But she'd sell them if she needed to. At this point in time, she didn't.

"Now I want to see them."

"Anytime." She turned serious. "I didn't notice anyone following us, but that doesn't mean it's not possible."

"How long do you plan to be here?"

She shrugged. "As long as it takes."

He nodded, but the frown pulling at his eyebrows told her he was concerned. "I'm going to stay here and watch the road. If anyone turns in— Wait, you don't have a phone. How do I warn you? Honk?"

"Call the landline." She gave him the number. "If it rings, I'll know."

"You kept the phone connected too?"

She sighed. "I'm kinda messed up when it comes to my father, okay?"

"Huh. Looks like we have that in common."

"I might ask you to explain that one later." Daria liked Ryker. A lot. More than any other man she'd met other than Linc St. John. Except Linc was a father figure. She was definitely not interested in Ryker for that role.

She mentally slapped herself. Someone was after her for whatever reason. Mooning over Ryker Donahue might very well get him killed.

Clearing her throat, she headed for the little planter on the side of the garage. She'd Velcroed a key to the bottom, so even if the hiding place wasn't completely original, just moving the plant wouldn't reveal the key. And no one would suspect that the mansion was so easily accessible, especially with the code pad on the wall that blinked a steady red light, indicating the alarm system was fully functioning. But the key was faster. The code pad took several entries, and she hated waiting on it.

Quit stalling and do this.

She snagged the key and took a deep breath. Going back inside after so many years made her stomach turn. Her father's evil had driven her mother to an early death—a fact Daria still grieved. And he would have killed *her* had Allie and Linc not intervened, so needless to say, she had no love left for the man she shared DNA with. Even when he'd been killed, she hadn't mourned him, just what could have been had he made different choices. She finally twisted the knob and stepped inside.

And right back into the past.

Ryker hated waiting. Despised everything about it. He'd spent so many years of his childhood waiting for his father to come home. Waiting for the beatings to start. Waiting to be big enough to defend himself. Waiting to be old enough to escape . . .

Yeah. Waiting wasn't his favorite way to pass the time.

He gripped his phone, the landline number to the house programmed in. He'd planted himself near the edge of the garage to allow a good view of the drive but still be hidden should anyone turn in. Of course, they'd have to have the code for the gate, which gave him some comfort.

Then again, if there was another way onto the property, he'd have no warning. Comfort fled, and he wished Daria would hurry. He should have gone inside with her. He could watch the drive from one of the windows, and he'd be in close proximity in case she needed some help.

Mind made up, he headed for the door he'd seen her enter. She'd left it unlocked, so he stepped into the garage and stopped to admire the four cars she'd kept. He could see why. They were all top-of-the-line vehicles. He especially liked the Mercedes Atlas Airstream RV. Resisting the temptation to linger while danger could be stalking them, he hurried to the door that led into the house.

When he entered, he found himself in a mudroom that opened into a narrow hallway. From there, he walked into the gourmet-style kitchen that gleamed like someone had just used it yesterday and then cleaned up. He never would have guessed it had been unoccupied for seven years.

He took the first doorway he came to and walked into a dining room with a large window overlooking the front of the home. Perfect. He took up a spot to the side and looked out while keeping an ear tuned for Daria. Although, depending on where she was in the place, he might not hear her even if she yelled at the top of her lungs.

"FBI! Show me your hands!"

"It's just me!" He spun, hands held high, heart beating into overdrive. Daria stood in the doorway, holding her weapon on him.

She lowered the gun to her side and raked her free hand over her ponytail. Then she grimaced and pressed that same hand to her side. "Are you nuts? I thought you were waiting outside."

"I was, but then I got nervous you might need me and decided to come in. Since you don't have a phone, I couldn't warn you I was coming in and didn't want to call the landline because you'd think it was an emergency."

She shook her head. "Stay put, will you?"

Ryker frowned. "Yeah, sure."

"Sorry, I don't mean to bite your head off." She paused. "This is hard for me, but I don't need to take it out on my only friend at the moment."

He appreciated that. "I take it you didn't have the best relationship with your father?"

"No. The short version is, I hated him and he hated me. I've gotten past all that—or thought I had—but this place has bad memories and they keep coming at me."

Now he wanted to hear the long version. Later. "I understand. I didn't have the best relationship with my dad either."

"Bet mine was worse than yours," she muttered.

"So you're making light of my dysfunctional relationship with my father?"

She shot him a wide-eyed look. "Not at all. I . . . I'm sorry. You're right. I don't get dibs on the Worst Father Ever Award."

"It doesn't matter. What are you looking for?"

She sighed. "Come on into the study, and I'll explain a little. It's the least I can do since you're being so kind by helping me out."

"What about watching the drive?"

"I set the alarm. If anyone drives up, it'll chime."

"So me watching was just busy work? Allowing me to feel useful while you'd know ahead of time if anyone was approaching?"

"Pretty much."

Refusing to be insulted, he laughed and followed her into the study.

"Whoa. Nice office."

"This was where my father conducted most of his criminal activities—like ordering the murders of people I loved."

He blinked. "Never mind. You win."

FIVE

Daria sighed. She didn't want to "win." But she might as well tell him the truth while she searched. "My father was Vladislav Nevsky. He was with the Russian mafia here. One of the crime lords. I was a teen when we moved into this house and seventeen when Allie St. John went undercover as a cook here. She and Linc are married now, but they were partners at the time and saved my life, as my father had decided to get rid of me as well."

Ryker gaped, and she couldn't blame him. Nothing like an abrupt summary of things. Then his expression morphed into concern. "So what do you hope to find here?"

"I don't know." She opened the top drawer of the desk. Her father had always kept it locked, but after the FBI had gone through it, she hadn't bothered to lock it again. She searched and found nothing in it to help her. She pulled it all the way out and set it on the floor. "Something to tell me why someone is after me. The guy who attacked me said my father sent him. The catch is, I know good and well that my father is dead." She moved on to the next drawer and did the same thing, looking for any kind of hiding place. "But apparently, he's still calling some shots that I don't know about."

"After all this time?"

She nodded. "I know. It doesn't really make sense, but I don't have any other ideas." She opened the third drawer. Nothing. The FBI had gone over the place with a fine-tooth comb, but they hadn't let her help them. By the time her father had been killed and the majority of his minions rounded up, the feds had all they needed and more to put everyone away for a long time. They'd also shut down a human trafficking ring. "The only thing I can come up with is that they might have missed something. My father had all kinds of hiding places for stuff, and while I told the FBI about the ones I knew about, there may be others I'm not aware of."

"I see."

"Good. So, can you start on the bookcase? With two of us working, it'll go a lot faster. Just pull the books off and shake them."

"Sure." He went to work on the bookshelf. "Any idea what I'm looking for?"

"Not really. He had flash drives and he was always writing stuff down, but he usually burned any paper after he was done with it."

"What about his computer and the cloud?"

"Confiscated by the feds." She shrugged. "I know they went through this room and I'm probably just desperate, but I have to look."

"Of course."

"After you go through the books, you can start pulling pictures off the walls."

"Didn't you tell the feds to do that too?"

"Of course, but honestly, they had so much evidence on my father and those working with him that they really didn't need anything else. Not that they didn't want every shred available, but"—she shrugged—"I'm not exactly sure how well they searched." She'd given them everything they needed to put her father away—including her eyewitness testimony to murder—

and then he'd been killed when he'd tried to murder an FBI agent. The rest of his organization had been rounded up—at least the ones they could find. A few had slipped through the cracks, but not many.

"Nothing on the bookcase," Ryker said. "A few papers with some names on them. A couple of invoices for some shipments."

He held them out to her and she scanned them. "These would be related to the legal part of his business. The one he used to cover up the illegal stuff." She pointed to the name on the invoice. "That guy worked for my father on the illegal side of things, so that's kind of weird that his name would be on there. Let's hang on to that."

"Got it. That's some kind of bookkeeping system he had."

She grimaced. "He didn't care about that business. If it took a loss, it was a write-off." She shot him a look. "And yes, he actually filed taxes. Had to keep up appearances, you know. Anyway, he was an avid reader and often used whatever piece of paper was handy for a bookmark. We can just pile those on the desk to look through later. Keep looking?"

"Sure."

"Thanks."

He waded through the books on the floor and pulled the first picture off the wall. Then the next. Daria followed his actions until they were both standing in the midst of the mess with nothing to show for their efforts. She planted her hands on her hips, frustration zipping through her.

"What about the other rooms?" he asked.

"No, if there's anything, it would be in this room." She paused. "Or maybe the pool house."

"Why the pool house?"

"I spent a lot of time there. Until he did."

"What was he doing there?"

"I don't know. Once he started showing up, I stopped going. It wasn't until he died that I began restoring it back to the way I wanted it." It had been a long-distance restoration, but at least the reminders of her father were mostly eradicated from the place. A low beeping sound reached her ears and she paused. "Did you hear that?"

"What?"

"Follow me." She raced to the spiral staircase located just outside the office and went up, listening to make sure Ryker was behind her. His footsteps fell into rhythm with hers, and he was right on her heels when she reached the top. She darted down the hallway and to her room. Without pausing to take in the details, she went to the wall, removed a picture she'd painted on one of her darkest days, and spun the dial on the wall safe.

"You've been using this place as a safe house, haven't you?" Ryker asked.

She glanced at him. "I came here shortly after my father died. Allie and Linc didn't want me to, but I had to. As a way of facing my fears, I guess. In my head, I know it's just a house, but . . ." She removed the Glock and loaded it with quick efficiency, then pulled the shoulder holster from the safe and strapped it on. Next, she pulled out a cell phone. Powered it up and stuck it in her back pocket.

"What did you hear that panicked you?" Ryker asked.

"Someone entered the code to the gate and is headed up the drive."

"Who else has the code?"

"No telling."

"You didn't change it?"

She shrugged. "I changed it, but do you know how easy it is to figure those out? With a good set of binoculars and some patience . . ."

"Right."

"My father wasn't too worried about someone getting in the gate. He had plenty of warning if someone was approaching. And . . ."

She walked to the bedroom door while he continued to take in the decor. "And?" It was a teenage girl's dream room, with a large-screen television mounted on the wall across from the king-size bed. The walls were a subtle gray with white trim, and the aquamarine curtains gave the room some color.

"If it was someone he didn't like, he could kill them and say they were trespassing."

Whoa. "Okay, forget about that for now," he said. "What should I do to help in the current situation?"

"Stay with me, but don't get in front of me."

"How would someone have found you? No one followed us from the hospital."

"That's a very good question. I'll have to think on that one." She chambered the bullet and pinched the bridge of her nose. "It just occurred to me that they probably didn't follow me, which makes me slow on the uptake." Her jaw hardened. "That won't happen again, I promise."

"Then how— Oh. They figured you'd come here eventually when their failed attempt to grab you in Virginia sent you running."

"Exactly. And I should have thought of it before now. You ready to move?"

"Where are we going?"

"To the security room."

He didn't ask, just fell into step behind her. She held the weapon ready, like he'd seen others in law enforcement do. They walked down the hall past two doors. At the third, she twisted the knob and cleared the area before motioning him inside.

Monitors lined the wall on his right. "Whoa," he whispered. She flipped a switch and the screens came to life. "Do you have every area of this house on camera?"

"Most of it." She studied the monitors. "There," she said, "he's in the hallway."

A man dressed in black and carrying a weapon made his way down the hall, checking rooms as he went. Then he disappeared off camera. She leaned in and typed something into the keyboard on the wall-length table. A screen to his right flickered, bringing the living room into focus. "He's searching."

"Doesn't that mean he'll eventually find us?"

"Eventually. If we stay here."

"Where are we going?"

"Well, the good thing is, we can track him and he can't track us." She handed him the phone she'd pulled from the safe. "The battery should be fully charged. Turn on the security app and we can follow him as he moves around the house." Ryker did as instructed. "If he gets close, tap me on the shoulder."

"Got it. Oh no."

"What?"

"I forgot those papers."

"Forget them for now. They're probably nothing. Definitely not worth risking our lives for. Getting out of here is probably more important."

"Our lives? What would you do if I wasn't with you?"

"Get out."

"Liar." She'd confront the intruder.

She shot him a sideways look, then led the way to a back stairway. They went down and he found himself in the kitchen. "Through that door," she whispered, pointing to the right. Footsteps sounded in the room next to them and she picked up the pace. "Get in front of me and go through that door," she said, pointing.

Ryker opened the door and started down. She stepped through, pulled the door shut, then used the key to bolt it.

"You think that's going to buy us some time?"

"I hope so. I'd like to search the pool house."

"After you."

At the bottom of the steps, they cut through a game room and he noted the pool tables, air hockey game, and an assortment of other entertainment before she pulled to a quick stop in front of a set of French doors.

"What?" Ryker asked, barely managing to avoid running into her.

She pointed to the keypad on the wall. "He reset the alarm. When we go through those doors, he'll know exactly where we are."

"So we don't go through them?"

She hesitated, biting her lower lip.

"Daria?"

"Sorry, working out a plan. I think we'll have enough time. Are you ready?"

"I'm ready. Time for what?"

She opened the door and slipped out. The high-pitched warning sounded. They had one minute before the alarm blared full blast and alerted the cops. Ryker ignored it and shut the door behind him.

Daria grabbed his hand. "He'll shut it off before it has time to alert the authorities, and that will buy us a little time. Go to the pool house. Hopefully he'll assume we headed for the car."

Buy them time? One could hope. They reached the pool house, and she kicked over a small cement statue to pull a key Velcroed to the bottom. In seconds, after she replaced the key, they were inside, with the dead bolt latched. "Can you watch the door?"

"And what am I supposed to do when he starts coming this way?"

"Tell me." She spun from him and looked at the artwork on the far wall. "It took me a long time to replace all the pieces he burned, so I don't have to bother searching those." She whirled toward the bookcase, her desperation to find something, anything that might tell her who was after her, reaching him.

"Hurry, Daria."

"I'm hurrying, I promise."

He glanced out the door. The French doors of the main house opened and a figure dressed in black with a baseball cap pulled low stepped outside. "Daria?"

"Yeah?"

"He's heading for the car. Once he realizes we're not there, he's going to be coming this way."

SIX

just need a few minutes." Daria aimed herself at the book-shelves, ignoring the artwork on the wall. She'd learned from her father to hide small things and hang them with the artwork, but seven years ago, he'd burned almost every piece in the pool house. Gradually, she'd painted and replaced the ones he'd burned, knowing her father would hate it. After finishing each piece, she would mail it to Marsha, who hung it according to her instructions.

"He's done with the car," Ryker said. "Won't take much to shoot off the lock here."

Very true, but she still needed time to look through the books. However, she also didn't want to risk Ryker's life any more than she already had. That's why she'd left the papers behind when she really would like to study them. "Give me a play-by-play of exactly what he's doing."

"Talking on the phone and looking in this direction."

Daria started on the books in the living area. The pool house was a small home with a bedroom, two baths, and a kitchen. She'd much preferred it to the main house. Until her father started invading her space. She raked the books to the floor, hoping something would fall out.

A solid clunk, different from the sounds of the other books falling, caught her attention. She picked up the thickest book and opened it, then sucked in a deep breath. "I got it." She tucked the book under her arm to look at it when they were safe.

"Good, because if we don't do something soon, we're going to be toast."

"It's okay. I've got another way out."

"I was really hoping you'd say that." She led the way to the stairs. "We're going up?" he asked.

"Yep. I have a feeling our guy has a key."

Ryker shot her a look. "What?"

She climbed the stairs with Ryker behind her.

"How do you know that?"

"Because he broke into Marsha's home to get it."

"You can explain that later. I'm right behind you."

If Ryker hadn't been with her, she probably would have just faced down the intruder and demanded he tell her why he was after her, but . . . Ryker. Getting the handsome doctor to safety was now number one on her priority list. At the top of the stairs, she turned right and went to the end of the hall. A ladder was attached to the wall, and she scrambled up it to push open the small door in the ceiling.

"Clever," he muttered.

"My father had all kinds of escape routes," she said. "He was terrified of being trapped in his house."

"When the cops came to arrest him?"

"Or his rivals came to kill him."

"Oh. Or that," he muttered.

Once they were in the attic, she hurried to the window and shoved it open. "Now to go down." She went first, careful of her throbbing side, leading the way. As soon as her foot touched the top rung of a ladder, she heard a slam come from below.

"I think that was the door," Ryker said.

"Yep, but he didn't kick it in. Hence, the key. Hurry." She jumped the rest of the way to the ground, ignoring the blazing reminder in her side that she was wounded, and grabbed Ryker's hand when he landed beside her. Together, they raced toward the garage and darted around the side to his vehicle. "Get in," she said, then ran toward the side of the garage.

"What are you doing?"

"Putting the key back."

"Daria, I don't think you need to take the time to—"

"Start the car." She needed the key back in place so she could send someone to get the papers from her father's study without trying to explain the keypad. She slid it in place and hurried back to the car. "What's going on?"

"It won't start." He tried again, and Daria hurried back to the garage to punch in the code on the keypad to open the door.

Ryker pushed out of the driver's seat, and she glanced at him. "Grab everything out of the glove box and my bag from the back seat and come on."

He nodded and ducked back into his car.

Daria climbed into the driver's seat of the Tesla. By the time she'd shut her door, he was next to her in the passenger seat. She backed out of the garage and roared around the other side of the house to speed down the long drive. She pressed a button on the console and the wrought-iron gates swung open. A glance in the rearview mirror had her pressing the gas harder.

"He's going to shoot!" Ryker ducked, and the attacker unloaded a hail of bullets that pinged off the car. Without slowing, she whipped through the gates and spun onto the main highway.

Ryker glanced at her with wide eyes. "Um . . . what just happened? The bullets literally bounced."

She smiled. "This car is made from the same stuff as the vehicles they drive the president around in. We're good." At his stunned expression, she shrugged. "My father was a bit paranoid. All his cars were converted to have this kind of protection."

"Wow."

"Yeah."

"Daria?"

"Hmm?"

"Why'd you take the time to put the key back?"

"Because I might need it at some point in the future." She frowned. "Whoever is after us isn't going to leave a trail. He'll make sure the place is locked up before he leaves."

"Why?"

She sighed. "Because it has to look that way in case I make a report to the police. If I report it and it looks like someone was there or was trying to break in or whatever, then it becomes a crime scene."

"And they can't go back for whatever it is they're looking for?"

"Or watch the place and wait for me to return."

"Right." A pause. "But you're not going back until you catch the people doing this, right?"

She shrugged. "I honestly don't know what I'm going to do. I don't have a plan right now. And until we get somewhere safe, I'm just going to have to play it by ear."

"Play it by ear, huh?"

"Yes."

"That sounds like an invitation to all kinds of trouble."

Daria laughed, then cut it short.

He wasn't wrong.

Ryker sat silent beside her while she drove. When his heart slowed a fraction, he glanced at her. She met his gaze before turning her attention back to the road.

"Wondering what you got yourself into?" she asked.

"Something like that. What did you find in the book?"

"I'm not sure. I didn't have time to get a good look. Once I figure out where I'm going, we'll stop and I'll see what's what."

"Do you trust me to drive?"

Another quick glance. "Why?"

"Because I have a place I can take you and you can look at the book while I drive."

"What place?"

"Mine."

She hesitated. "No, that's not safe. They can track you through your license plate."

"That plate is registered to the apartment I keep across the street from the hospital. I'm talking about taking you to a place that offered me refuge when I desperately needed it."

"Travis and Heather's home? In Campobello?"

Surprised, he just stared at her for a brief moment. It was weird that she knew the same people he did, but they'd never met before now. "Yes."

She nodded and pulled off the next exit and parked. "It's all yours."

Ryker couldn't deny the electrical burst of excitement that shot through him. He had a feeling driving this car would be like nothing he'd ever experienced before. Once he was settled in the driver's seat, she grabbed the book from the back and slid into the passenger side. "Ready?" he asked.

"Go for it." She buckled up and opened the book but looked at him. "You said you didn't have a great relationship with your dad either. How so?"

"He beat me on a regular basis." Ryker didn't bother to soften his words. His childhood had been ugly, and he had no desire to make it sound like anything other than what it was. "I finally ran away from home. My grandfather had a little hunting cabin in the woods not too far from town, and I simply moved in. It was rustic, but it was safe. That's where I first met Travis and Heather. She'd crashed her car in the woods, and she and Travis were running from the guys who'd caused her to wreck." He shot her a small smile. "Best day of my life."

She blinked at him. "We have very similar stories."

"And I want to hear more of yours, but we'd better get out of here."

"Good idea." She turned her attention to the book. Ryker shifted into drive and pressed the gas, heading for the highway. Driving this car was probably the closest he'd get to piloting a spacecraft. Responsive to his slightest command, the car buzzed over the asphalt, and he wondered if the tires even touched the ground.

Thrilling didn't even come close to describing what it felt like to drive this machine. He was going to enjoy every second of it despite the reason he found himself behind the wheel.

And yet he planned to be vigilant too. The intruder at the house had gotten a good look at the car and would be searching for it. And who knew how many people the guy had on his payroll who could be helping? Ryker glanced at the woman beside him, her gaze fixed on the book in her lap. A surge of protectiveness welled up inside him, and he almost laughed. Daria was highly skilled at defending herself—and him. The thought of him protecting her bordered on ludicrous. Nevertheless, he planned on having her back and doing whatever it took to keep her safe.

Because he wanted to get to know her on a more personal level now that she wasn't his patient any longer. He quickly peeked again at her from the corner of his eye. Yeah, he definitely wanted to learn more about her. And to see those dimples flash in his direction for longer than a split second.

He glanced back at her and found her attention on him. "What?"

"Where's your father now?"

"Last I heard, he'd made his way to California and was begging on the streets."

She grimaced. "That's tough. I'm sorry."

"I am too."

"I . . . didn't mean to make the whole bad dad thing sound like a competition."

"It's okay."

"And your mom?"

"She died shortly after my sixth birthday. That was when my dad turned mean. He couldn't deal with her death."

"No reason to take that out on a kid."

"I agree. Now, look at your book and find something to put an end to all this."

"Yes, sir." She flashed those dimples at him once more and aimed her attention at the book in her hands.

SEVEN

Ryker's kind eyes lingered in her mind long after she stopped looking at him. Although looking at him was definitely more fun than trying to figure out who was trying to snatch her. Linc and Allie might have an idea, but if she called them, they'd hop on the first flight home, and there was no way she was going to do that to them. They'd be furious about it—especially if she got herself killed—but that was just the way she was going to have to play it for now.

And pray she lived to regret it.

"Daria, we're family. You don't have to do life alone. We're here for you."

Echoes from past conversations played in her mind. And honestly, if Linc and Allie had been anywhere but their present location in the Caribbean, she wouldn't have hesitated to call.

She briefly considered taking some of the other agents she worked with into her confidence, but she had no assurance that word wouldn't filter back to Allie and Linc. So . . . for now, she was on her own.

The book. Focus.

Only it wasn't a book, it was a box. Made to look like a book. Clever. And inside she found a small notebook with the binding at the top. She flipped it open and gasped.

"What?"

"It's Gerard's."

"Who's Gerard?"

"Gerard Lamb. He was my bodyguard/babysitter when I was a teenager."

"We'll revisit the whole bodyguard thing later. What's in the notebook?"

"Getting ready to find out." She started reading. "It's a description of every hiding place in the house that my father used." She skimmed them. "I knew about all of these and told the FBI about them, so nothing new there." She slowed. "He's also got some notes and some names."

"Names of who?"

"I'm not sure, but a lot of them are Russian. And one of them is . . . oh my . . ."

"What?"

"James Killian."

"Who's that?"

"A dead guy."

He frowned. "Then why do you look worried about him?"

"Not about him but about the name under his. Karl Killian."

"Brothers?"

"No, if I remember correctly, Karl is James's father."

"And that's significant?"

She shrugged. "It could be." She raked a hand over her head. "How much farther?"

"About an hour. How's your side?"

"Throbbing."

"Well, at least you're honest."

"Of course. Why lie about it?" She ignored the pain and flipped through the pages. "It's like a journal. Gerard talked about watching me grow up, some of the things I said or did." Her throat grew tight and she had to stop.

"Daria?"

"I'm sorry," she finally managed to choke out. "It reads like a father's account of his daughter's life." Her life. Gerard had loved her in spite of his professed loyalty to her father. She shut it and pressed her fingers to her lips, fighting to get her emotions under control. It had been seven years. This shouldn't impact her so much. The memories shouldn't be so strong. "He was killed—executed—when my father was in the FBI's crosshairs." Ryker's warm hand wrapped around hers, jarring her from the resurrected memories. "It's like the proverbial train wreck," she murmured. "I can't look away."

"Then don't. Think of it like ripping off a Band-Aid. Read it and get it over with."

"Good point." She opened the book once more. "'I feel torn,'" she read. "'I'm grateful that Nevsky gave me employment when I needed it most, but I wish I'd known what I was signing up for. I mean, I'm no innocent, but by the time I found out exactly what he was into, it was too late for me to get out. Not if I wanted to keep breathing. And besides, what would happen to Daria if I left her?'" She drew in a shuddering breath and swiped at a stray tear. "He was a good man."

"Sounds like it."

They fell silent, and Daria closed her eyes while Ryker drove. She must have dozed, because when she woke up, the scenery was different. They'd left the city and trees now surrounded her.

Ryker turned onto a gravel road and Daria looked around. "Wow."

"Yep. My response every time I come home."

The ranch was huge. And gorgeous. She could only pray it was safe too.

———

Ryker drove slowly, his hands relaxed on the wheel. His home had that effect on him, filling him with a peace he couldn't explain. "Tell me more about your father."

"I don't like talking about him."

"Hey, I spilled my guts to you. Turnabout is fair play." He kept his tone teasing but was hoping she'd tell him more.

Finally, after a hesitation long enough that he figured she'd decided to keep silent, she spoke. "Like I said, he was head of an organized crime syndicate."

Daria's low words swiveled his head toward her. "Yeah? And?"

"I think, for some reason, someone who used to be part of the organization—or maybe still is part of it—is after me. I just don't know why—or which goon."

"Unless they consider you a traitor for joining the FBI?"

She raised a brow and met his gaze. "Possibly. But why wait until now to do something about it?"

He shrugged. "Wish I could answer that for you."

"Yeah, me too."

"Are you sure you don't want to get in touch with Allie and Linc? Travis is here. He might spill the beans if you don't. What about Caden Denning? At least call him."

"Absolutely not. He'd get right on the phone and call Linc and Allie."

She rubbed her head, and he pulled in front of his home and cut the engine. "All right, we'll play it your way for now. In the meantime, I need to take another look at that wound—and you need to rest."

"Fine." She pushed open the door and climbed out of the passenger seat. Very carefully, he noticed. She was hurting.

"I have some pain pills inside if you'll take one."

She shot him a look and he snapped his lips shut. Fine. She could just hurt. Stubborn woman. The fact that she managed to avoid saying much more about her father didn't go unnoticed by him either. Nothing he couldn't find out with an internet search, most likely.

He led the way inside and noted her initial reaction. She loved the place. The look on her face made him smile. "You designed this?" she asked.

"Most of it. I had a little help, but yeah."

"It's incredible." She went straight through the kitchen and into the den. "It's a wall of windows."

He looked at the view, trying to see it through her eyes. "It's the highest point of the valley. Which means while there are mountains looming above us, there are also mountains below. You should see the sunrise."

"I'm sure."

"The creek you see at the bottom of the hill draws all kinds of wildlife." He slid open part of the glass wall and stepped outside onto his deck. "This is where I am every morning, rain or shine."

She followed him. "I can certainly see why."

While she didn't look like she'd mind staying out there for a while, he wanted her to get off her feet. "Let me show you to the room you'll use."

He led her through the house. "It's a simple cabin layout. I do have a bonus room upstairs that I've turned into kind of a media room. I like movies."

"What kind?"

"Anything with action. What about you?"

She shrugged. "I don't watch a lot of movies, but action is good. And happy endings. If it doesn't have a happy ending, I'm not interested."

"Gotcha. No sad or bad endings." He glanced at the small bag she'd carried from the hospital. He knew exactly what was in it. All travel-size necessities. Toothbrush, toothpaste, comb, deodorant, and a disposable razor. He blew out a low breath. "We probably should have stopped to get you a few things."

"Like a change of clothing?"

The doorbell rang and Daria froze. Ryker held up a hand. "It's okay. It's probably Heather or one of the ranch hands. I'm sure they spotted the car and came to check it out."

"You need a garage."

"I have one, I just didn't park there. I'll be happy to move it there once you're off your feet and out of pain." He headed back down the hallway to the door. Daria followed him, her hand pressed to her side.

Ryker opened the door to see Heather Walker standing there, eyes wide.

"Hi," he said.

"Whose car is that?"

Daria stepped forward. "Mine."

"Oh, hi. I'm Heather, and my husband wants to know if he can drive it."

EIGHT

A chuckle escaped Daria before she realized the woman was serious. She cleared her throat. "Um . . . sure." Men and their cars. Then again, she'd chosen to keep the Tesla, so she was the last one to throw stones. The truth was, she'd kept it more for sentimental reasons than anything else. It had been Gerard's favorite, and she'd planned to give it to him one day. Only he'd been killed before she could make that happen.

"Oh, sorry," Heather said. "Have we met?"

"Not officially. I'm Daria Nevsky. I know who you are because I work with Caden Denning on occasion. I remember when you were in danger and running from the person trying to kill you."

"You're Daria?" Heather reached out to pull her into a hug. Daria tried to cover the wince when the embrace put pressure on her wound.

"Heather—"

Daria shook her head at Ryker, and he snapped his lips shut.

"You were a big part of saving my life," Heather said, stepping back. "I'm so glad I get to thank you in person. It's been a few years since that mess, and I can't believe we've never met."

"Well, I'm not sure you'll be very thankful when you learn it's my turn to be on the run from someone and Ryker has graciously offered his home as a safe house until I can figure out who's after me."

Heather's eyes widened even more, then narrowed when she frowned. "He's absolutely right. You're more than welcome to stay here for as long as you need."

"Thank you." But she didn't plan to stay long. She just needed some time to regroup.

"Where's Travis?" Ryker asked.

"He was on his way here to inspect the car but got a call about a new client interested in boarding three horses. He decided he didn't want to chance that slipping through his fingers and sent me to get the information."

"Well, now you have it," Ryker said. "Daria was wounded in her escape and needs to rest."

"Wounded?" Heather asked with a concerned frown. "Should I take a look?"

"I handled it," Ryker said, "but if we need you, I'll come get you." He shot Daria a sideways look. "She thinks she's cool stuff because she's a surgeon."

"Then she is cool stuff," Daria said. Fatigue and nausea had hit her about thirty seconds ago, and if she didn't lie down, she was going to pass out or puke—maybe both—onto Ryker's pretty wood floors. She walked to the couch and stretched out. "I think I'm going to take a nap right here, if that's okay."

"I have a bedroom you can use."

"I seriously don't think I can move at the moment." Not unless he wanted to carry her. The fact that she would let him if he offered was too much to think about at the moment.

Ryker pulled a blanket from the basket near the fireplace and covered her with it. "Sweet dreams."

She sighed. "If only."

"We'll just move the car to the garage." Ryker escorted Heather out the door, and their voices were faint enough that they didn't stop her from dozing. After a few seconds, she heard the door shut, then the car start up. She smiled, then immediately frowned while her mind traced their dash from the hospital to this place.

Ryker had said the property was in Heather and Travis Walker's names. But that didn't mean someone with connections couldn't track them here. Somehow. Like through a power bill? Or . . . something? She probably had a few hours, then she'd have to insist on leaving. She would ask to borrow the truck in the field she'd noticed on the way up the drive and leave the Tesla with Ryker since he enjoyed it so much. Once she had a rental, she'd let Ryker know where to pick up the truck.

She was going to need more help than Heather or Ryker could offer. She faced that fact with a grimace and pulled out the burner phone she'd snagged from her father's home. Fortunately, she had all important numbers memorized and started dialing the first one.

With the plan worked out in her head and all the necessary calls made, she let herself doze. Because if she didn't get some rest, she wasn't going to be any good to anyone.

"So, tell me the whole story, please?" Heather asked, still seated firmly in the passenger seat of the Tesla. "Like with details?"

Ryker cut the engine and turned to the woman who'd been a combination of big sister and mother to him for the past eight years.

"Someone attacked her at her place in Virginia. She stole the guy's car after he stabbed her and then wound up in my hospital where I stitched her up. Then, if that wasn't enough, someone tracked her to the hospital and tried to kill her in her room. I caught him and we ran him off, then I insisted on helping her."

"Whoa."

"I drove her to her house in Columbia. Well, her father's house. He was killed and she inherited it, but instead of selling, she turned it into some kind of safe house." Heather blinked at him, and Ryker waved a hand. "Never mind. All that isn't important. What's important is that someone tracked her there too. She had the Tesla in the garage, and when my car wouldn't start, we bolted and made our way here. That's the simplified, if confusing, version anyway."

She frowned. "Are they still looking for her?"

"Probably."

"I'll alert Travis."

"I don't see how they could find us here."

"You never know. We'll need to take precautions."

She ran a hand along the dash, then opened the door and stepped out. Ryker did the same and pocketed the keys. "I didn't know where else to go, Heather. I really hope I haven't brought trouble to your doorstep."

She raised a brow. "Well, it's your doorstep too. And we've known trouble before. I guess we can face it again if it means protecting an innocent woman."

"She's FBI. I'm not sure she thinks she needs protecting."

"Even agents need someone to have their backs sometimes."

"True." Ryker led the way out of the garage and back around the side of the house. "But I'm just a doctor. I don't carry a gun unless I'm out in the woods. And that's for protection against four-legged critters who might take exception to my presence."

"And this time you might be protecting someone from the two-legged critters."

He nodded and sighed. "Well, like you said, it won't be the first time." They shared a tight smile, both remembering the time he'd saved her life. Ryker and Heather returned to the front of the house and stepped inside. The couch was empty.

"Daria?" Ryker called.

"Back here."

He frowned at Heather and walked down the hallway, only to stop at the half bath. She had her bandage off and was examining the ugly wound. She looked up at him and grimaced. "I was sleeping and turned over quickly without thinking. Not a good move. Now it's throbbing, and I think I may have pulled a stitch or two."

He looked closer. "Or four. Why don't you have a seat back on the couch, and I'll get a suture kit."

"You have one here?"

"Sure. We live out in the middle of nowhere. Heather could probably perform surgery with all the supplies we have between the two of us. I'll be right back." He retrieved the kit and returned to find her stretched out on the couch. "You ready?"

"Sure."

He pulled on a pair of sterile gloves and repaired the wound. When he finished, he sat back and nodded. "That should do it."

Daria gave a pained grunt and lowered her arm. The scrub top slid back over her midsection. "Thanks." She paused and bit her lip. "I need to go."

He frowned. "What? Why? We just got here."

"I know, but I've been thinking. These guys who're after me aren't going to stop looking. I may have lost them for the moment, but they'll find a connection. If they come here, I don't want to be here and put you all in danger."

Heather glanced at him, and he shook his head not to say anything. She nodded and pressed four orange pills into Daria's hand. "It's just ibuprofen."

"Thank you."

Daria tossed them back dry, and Heather grimaced. "The water bottle on the table is yours."

"You're very kind." Daria grabbed the bottle and downed half of it.

"Happy to help," Heather said. "But now, I'm going to check in with Travis and the kids."

"Kids?" Daria asked.

"I have a three-year-old and nine-month-old twins. They're hanging out with the sitter who comes a couple of times a week so I can get stuff done around the house."

"Nice."

"Thanks, Heather," Ryker said. "I'll keep in touch with you and make sure you know what's going on."

"That would be appreciated."

"Tell Travis he can use the car as much as he wants," Daria said. "I plan to leave it here." She looked at Ryker. "Which brings me to my next question. Can I borrow the truck I saw on the way in?"

NINE

Heather paused in her trek toward the door, and Daria wasn't sure she could have surprised them more if she'd reached out and slapped them. Ryker's deer-in-the-headlights look faded, and his frown deepened. "Daria, think about that. How are you going to protect yourself if you're all alone?" He gestured to her side. "And wounded."

She sighed. "I'm not going to be alone. I know I'm in over my head, and my desire to deal with this on my own is selfish—and could possibly get innocent people hurt. Or worse. I called Caden and left him a message. When he gets it, he'll head to meet me."

"Where?"

"At a place where he and I can talk and figure some things out."

"What about Linc and Allie?"

She nodded. "I sent them a message and let them know what was going on as well and that I'd asked for help. I did tell them that if they cut their vacation short and came home, I'd never speak to them again."

"They're going to be on the next plane home," Heather said.

She sighed. "Probably, but I can't be stupid. One thing Allie and Linc taught me is that it's okay to ask for help. It just took me a little bit to remember that lesson."

"Then don't run away from us," Ryker said. "Let us help you until the big guns arrive."

She laughed. "The big guns. Cute." Her smile faded, and she pressed a hand to her aching head. Her side continued to throb, and all she really wanted to do was close her eyes and rest. But if she brought trouble to Ryker and his family, she'd never be able to live with herself. Besides, she needed Caden and his technology to do some research and dig into the names in Gerard's book. "No, I need to go."

"Then let me at least follow you to make sure you get there safely."

Daria sighed. "Ryker—"

"Or I can just follow you anyway."

She paused, studying his eyes and the determination in them. He'd do it too. "Okay, fine."

"I mean, if you passed out or something, I couldn't forgive myself—"

"I got you, Ryker."

He laughed and she rolled her eyes. But since she felt so lousy, she had to concede that he had a valid point about the passing out thing.

"Guys, that truck isn't reliable," Heather said. "I don't know how far you'd get—or if it'll even start."

Daria shook her head. "I'd take the Tesla, but it's too noticeable."

"I have a perfectly good vehicle you can take," Heather said. "It's in the garage. I'll go get it and bring it over here." Heather stepped toward the door but paused when the doorbell rang. She lifted a brow at Ryker. "That's probably—"

"—Travis," they said together.

Ryker reached for the door at the same time Daria grabbed for her weapon. "Ryker, wait, don't—"

The warning came too late. Ryker already had the door

63

cracked. A booted foot sent it crashing inward and Ryker stumbling back.

Daria's gaze landed on Travis—then swept to the man behind him pressing a gun to his head.

"Open the door," she finished on a whisper.

Ryker froze, his gaze locked on Travis's narrowed—and furious—eyes.

The man with the gun shoved Travis inside, forcing Ryker back even farther into the room. "Get over there." Travis went to Heather, placing his body between her and the gun while Ryker did the same with Daria.

Only she stepped around him, and the man aimed the weapon at her. "You'll come with me now. No more running or your friends die." His thick accent said he wasn't a local. In fact, Ryker couldn't help but wonder if the guy's name was listed in Gerard's little book.

"Who sent you?" Daria asked.

"Does not matter. Come." He let loose a flurry of Russian, and Daria nodded. She backed up slightly, her movement causing Ryker to take a few steps back.

Then she moved. Faster than he could blink, she stepped forward and grasped the man's outstretched hand, then did something to his thumb. A harsh scream echoed through the room and the weapon tumbled to the floor.

Then Travis was there with a punch to the guy's gut that released his lungs of air and sent his knees to the floor. The Russian scrambled for the weapon, and Ryker jammed his foot on the man's tattooed hand.

Bones crunched and another scream rippled around them.

Daria pressed her weapon against the guy's bald head and he froze. As did everyone else. "Get up," she said. Then she grabbed a handful of the front of his shirt and hauled him to his feet, wincing at the effort. Ryker could only hope she hadn't undone his recent stitching.

Clutching his injured hand and breathing hard, the Russian glared at her. The look in his eyes sent shudders through Ryker, but Daria was in full-on professional mode. "Travis, can you call Caden, please?"

"Yeah. I've got cuffs at the house."

Daria shook her head. "He was planning on taking me. He's got zip ties or something on him."

Ryker lifted a brow when Travis stepped forward to search the seething man.

"They are out there waiting for me," their captive said. "If I don't come back with you, they will come and shoot everyone on this property who is breathing." His eyes lifted to Ryker's. "Everyone."

Ryker walked to the coat closet and opened his gun cabinet. He pulled out three rifles and leaned them against the wall before he turned and met the man's gaze. "Then I guess it's a good thing we have plenty of weapons and ammo to shoot back."

Travis pulled two zip ties from the man's front pocket. "Well, well. Daria called it." He glanced at the woman who hadn't so much as twitched while Travis searched the man. "Hi. I'm Travis, by the way."

A ghost of a smile curved Daria's lips. "I figured. I'm Daria."

"I figured." Travis shoved the man onto the couch, and Daria kept her weapon trained on him.

She narrowed her eyes. "I recognize the tat on your broken hand. You tried to grab me from my house."

The man's nostrils flared. "I did."

"And you said my father was involved in this. How?"

His hard gaze never changed, but his lips lifted into a smile that had death written on it. "If you come with me, I'll tell you everything you want to know."

TEN

For a moment, Daria actually considered the man's offer. It would get him away from the ranch peacefully.

"Daria?" Ryker said. He must have noted her hesitation. "No."

"If I go with you," she said, ignoring him, "will you leave these people alone?"

"*Da.*"

"That's not an option, Daria," Travis said. "Caden is on the way."

Still, she hesitated. She couldn't let Ryker's family get hurt, and she didn't know how far away Caden was in relation to the murderous army she felt sure would descend on this place if her captive didn't show up or check in at his appointed time.

Ryker caught her gaze. "Why are you even thinking about this?"

"She wants to protect us," Heather said. "We don't need you to sacrifice yourself for us, Daria. Let us help you put an end to this."

"I need to know what they want," she said. "I can't end it until I have that knowledge."

The man shifted and Daria tensed.

Travis caught her eye and shook his head. "No." He sounded just like Ryker.

Helicopter blades beat the air, and Ryker blew out a low breath. "That's Caden."

Daria nodded. She should have known he'd arrive in a bird. She went to the window. The chopper hovered over the open pasture a football field's length away and started its decent. A shot rang out and pinged off the side of the aircraft.

Heather gasped and Travis flinched. The chopper pulled away and whirled out of range.

Daria spun to eye their captive, and he smirked. "Guess it's too late now, eh? Better to surrender to me than your friends die, yes?"

Ryker snorted. "No way."

She grabbed her phone and punched in Caden's number.

"Daria!" His shout-answer reverberated in her ear. "Are you okay?"

"Don't get shot down," she said. "We have one of them in here. Right now, he's under control. They want me alive, Caden, but I don't think they care about collateral damage. So I'm going to be on the run. Try not to lose me."

"What?" Caden, Ryker, Travis, and Heather shouted the word as one voice.

"I have to lead them away from here. Heather and Travis have kids on this property." She had a plan. An incredibly stupid one, but it was better than nothing. She hoped. "Can I get to the Tesla?" she asked Ryker.

"The garage is detached," Ryker said.

"They'll have someone guarding it," she murmured.

"You stay put," Caden said. "Reinforcements are on the way."

Ryker's front kitchen window exploded inward, and all four of them hit the floor.

Flames danced from the Molotov cocktail that had rolled

under the table. Travis grabbed a blanket from the couch and threw it over the burning mess. "That was a warning!" A voice came from just outside. "Saw some kids at the other house. I have a guy waiting to go in and grab them unless she comes out."

Heather gasped and bolted for the door. Travis snagged her arm, his face pale. "Hold on, Heather."

"Caden?" Daria strode to the door. "I have to do it. I can't let them hurt those kids."

"Daria . . ." Caden's voice came as though from a distance.

"Don't lose me!" She met Travis's and Heather's eyes. "I'm so sorry. I never should have agreed to come here."

Heather's jaw hardened. "No, we'll figure something else out. The FBI will have this place surrounded shortly."

"Maybe, but their guy can get in your house faster than the FBI can get to him, and then we're going to have a hostage situation. I need to leave before that happens. They want me. I'm going to give them a good chase, and I'll be in communication with other agents the whole time. Since I can't get to the garage, I just need the keys to the truck I saw near the first pasture on the way in."

"They're in it," Travis said, "but getting to it is a long shot."

"I know. But it will pull them away from this place—and right now, that's my goal." She flicked a glance at their smirking captive and wanted to wipe the look off his face. Instead, she pressed a hand to her side. "All right, they're expecting me to go for the garage. Instead, I'm going to go out the back and hope I can slip past whoever's watching."

"How do you know they won't shoot you?" Caden demanded.

"They won't shoot me. They want me alive or I'd already be dead." She looked at Travis and Heather. "Give me a thirty-second head start and then tell them I'm running."

Ryker's gaze darted back and forth between her and the others, and she wished she could read his mind.

"Now, Daria!" The voice outside the house sounded closer. Travis nodded. "Go."

"Leaving you on the line, Caden."

"Be careful, Daria. Linc and Allie will kill me if something happens to you."

She slipped out the back door and took off in the direction of the truck. Five steps in, she heard footsteps behind her. When she turned, she saw Ryker lunge and tackle the man chasing her. Ryker landed a hard punch to the guy's nose. Blood gushed, he yelled, and one more hard hit from Ryker's fist stilled him.

Ryker grabbed the rifle from the ground, looked up, and hurried to join her. "Let's go."

His fist throbbed, and he wondered if he'd fractured a bone, but he couldn't let her do this alone. They might have a better chance of getting away if they worked together.

He could only pray that was the case.

It took her about half a second to recover from the shock of his appearance, but she didn't bother to argue with him. She took off toward the truck with him two steps behind her.

Ryker kept an eye on their backs. They were ten yards from the truck.

A shout from his left pulled his attention to a man in a Jeep about fifty yards away. He lifted his rifle to his shoulder. "He's got a gun aimed this way!"

"Keep going!"

The first shot kicked up dirt in front of Daria, and Ryker put on a last burst of speed to reach the truck and throw himself into the driver's seat. A split second later, Daria was in the passenger side. "Go, go, go!"

"Going."

He cranked the engine and it sputtered. She stared at him with wide eyes and a "you're kidding me" look. He twisted the key again and it caught. Another crack sounded beyond the windows, and he glanced in the rearview mirror to see the Jeep bearing down on them.

Ryker shifted into gear and pressed the gas. The engine died. "Unbelievable," he muttered.

"Now would be a good time for this thing to start."

"I told you—"

"I know." She glanced back. "But if you don't get it started—" *Please, Lord, we could use some divine inter—*

The engine roared to life and he pressed the gas once more, shooting them forward across the pasture and toward the driveway that would take them onto the main highway.

"Thank you," she whispered.

"Where are we going?" Ryker asked.

"Anywhere that will allow us to lose these guys."

"There are lots of hills and curves between here and there."

She pressed a hand to her forehead and glanced in the side mirror. "Why didn't you just stay back? You would have been safer."

Ryker shook his head. "Not in my nature to dodge trouble if I can do something to help the situation."

"They're gaining on us."

"I see them."

"Do you know what you've done?"

"What do you mean? What have *I* done?"

She shot him a look from the corner of her eye. "As soon as

we get out of sight of these guys, I need you to drop me somewhere and then you disappear."

"What? No!"

"Don't you get it? If we're taken together, they'll use you to get whatever they want out of me!"

Ryker blinked. "Oh. Like torture and stuff?"

"Yeah, Ryker. Like torture and stuff."

ELEVEN

Daria leaned forward, her eyes bouncing between the mirrors and her surroundings. She needed a place for Ryker to swing into, let her out, and keep going. "Cade? You still there?"

Silence. She glanced at the screen. The call had dropped. Of course it had. She tried dialing him back, but it wouldn't go through. "Ugh. No signal."

"Yeah. If I'd had time, I would have grabbed the SAT phone. Sorry." Ryker glanced at her, then behind them. "Hold on."

"What?"

"I have an idea."

"Care to share?"

"No time."

He whipped the wheel to the right and onto a dirt path. For a brief second, the Jeep behind them disappeared from view. Another quick turn, then another, and they were off the path and dodging trees, branches scraping the roof and sides of the truck. Daria held on to the handle above her head.

"Stop," she said.

"I will. Almost there."

"Where?"

He rounded one more curve, then kept driving straight for a wall of trees. "Um . . . Ryker? You see those trees, right?"

"Yep, watch this." At the edge of the leaves, he drove straight through them and brought the truck to a stop. "Get out."

"What in the world?" Daria glanced around and realized that as long as the guys in the Jeep hadn't seen them drive through the leaves, they might be safe.

"Found that spot a couple of years ago. The tree on the right was struck by lightning and one limb dropped parallel to the ground. The leaves grew . . ." He shrugged. "It won't fool them forever. If they have any tracking skills at all, I'll have bought us only a few minutes."

"That's more than what we had before." She pushed open the door and met him at the front of the truck. "What are you doing? Get back in the truck and get out of here."

"No way. I have another hiding place, but we can't take the truck." He grabbed her hand and took off. Daria had no choice but to follow him, her gaze scanning the skies for the chopper. Where was Caden?

"I need to find a way to signal to Caden where I am without letting the guys after us know."

"How do you want to do that?"

"I have no idea. I guess I just need to get to a spot where I can pick up a phone signal."

"We can head toward town," he said. "After we hide from these goons and they give up."

"Fine. Where's this hiding place?"

"Up. If you can make it." He pointed. "You see that ledge between those rocks and shrubs?"

"Yeah."

"There."

She blew out a low breath. "Up, huh?"

"Up."

She scanned the mountain wall visible above the tree line and studied the path leading up to the ledge. It wasn't horribly steep, and if she wasn't hurting so bad, she could scale it with no problem, but with her side . . . She looked back and spotted a figure in dark clothing heading their way. "They're coming," she said. "Just lead the way. I'm right behind you."

Daria's side throbbed a painful beat, but she pressed on and followed him through the trees to the base of the mountain, shooting glances over her shoulder every so often. "I guess someone was a tracker," she muttered.

"Yeah. I didn't expect to see someone that soon." He hesitated. "On that note, can you climb?"

She looked back and didn't see anyone. In the distance, she could hear the helicopter, which meant Caden was most likely nearby. "I suppose it's too much to hope for a cell signal up there."

"There's a signal, but not in the way you mean. There's a small cave in the side of the mountain. At the back of the cave, there's a sharp drop-off and it's super dangerous. Travis's nephew disappeared one day and was found in the cave. After that, Travis installed a camera with motion detection. If we can get to it, it'll signal to Travis where we are and he can send in those big guns."

"Let's go." She'd make it. She had to.

Ryker could tell she was struggling. "It's not that much farther." He looked back and gasped. "Got one getting closer on our tail."

"I saw him," Daria said. "Go faster."

"You can't go any faster."

"It's either go faster or get caught."

75

Ryker picked up the speed and reached back. "Give me your hand."

"You can't climb and pull me too."

"I got you. Now, grab my hand."

She did, her firm grasp surprising him. Reminding him that while she might be small, she was strong. Stronger than he might think.

Good. He'd help her all he could, but she was right. He couldn't climb for both of them. He hoisted himself to the next rock and swung his leg over a small overhang. "Just a little more, Daria."

"Yeah." Sweat stood on her brow, and her breaths came in quick pants.

"You haven't ripped that wound back open, have you?" He looked over her shoulder. The man on their tail was climbing too.

"No. Not yet. Now, quit talking so I can—" Her foot slipped. A yelp slid from her, and Ryker grabbed for her.

And missed.

"Daria!"

She slid, spun on her back, and headed straight for the man waiting for her twenty yards down. Ryker started after her, then she caught herself on a rock and jerked to a stop with a pained moan. "Ryker, no!" Her yell froze him, and he caught her eye. "Go! Get Caden!"

The man below her latched onto her ankle and pulled.

Then lifted his weapon and aimed it at Ryker. Daria threw herself forward and tackled the man. The crack of the gun firing echoed all around, and Ryker held still, expecting to feel the bite of a bullet. Instead, debris rained down over him. The bullet had gone high.

Ryker glanced at the top of the ridge, then back toward Daria in time to see her roll to her feet. She looked up one more time. "Go!"

The man whipped something out of his pocket, pointed it at Daria's face, and sprayed. She swayed, then crumpled.

"Daria!" Ryker shivered. He couldn't do anything to help her at the bottom of the cliff. The best thing he could do would be to get to the top.

Another man dressed in jeans and a dark long-sleeved T-shirt appeared from the brush and looked up. He lifted his gun and Ryker climbed.

TWELVE

Daria blinked, her gaze blurry but sharpening the more she returned to consciousness. She raised a hand to her aching head, not even wondering what had happened. The events returned in full technicolor flashes of remembered terror.

Her foot slipping.

The gun firing.

Ryker's start down the mountain.

Her terror that he would try to save her.

The spray of something in her face.

Unconsciousness.

Now questions tumbled over one another in her mind. Where was she, and how long had she been out?

Waves of nausea warned her not to move, so she lay there long enough for the feeling to fade. Finally, she swallowed hard and dared to lift her head. When her stomach stayed put, she rolled to her side, noting her hands were zip-tied in front of her but her feet were free. She curled her fingers. They were stiff, but she could feel them. So . . . good circulation. That would help.

Next, aches and pains battered her, and she bit her lip on a groan before taking a physical inventory. Her shirt stuck to her back. The back that burned like someone had lit a match to it. Okay, so she'd acquired a few scrapes and cuts during her slide down the cliff. Yep, those hurt. The fact that the blood had had time to dry told her she'd been out for a while.

She had an assortment of other bruises and sore muscles that would hurt worse tomorrow. Assuming she lived that long. What else? Her head ached, but that was probably from whatever they'd sprayed her with, as she didn't think she'd hit it on her tumble. And then there was her side. She pressed her bound hands to it and was surprised they came away clean. No blood meant she hadn't ripped open the stitches. Again. So her back had taken the brunt of her slide. That was probably a good thing.

Her ears picked up the faint sound of voices somewhere in the building. As she studied her surroundings, her immediate priority was escaping.

Without the use of her hands, that was going to be a challenge. But she had to do something. Footsteps pounded her way, and she rolled onto her back and shut her eyes, hoping they wouldn't realize she was awake.

Seconds later, a foot nudged her. "Come on, girl," a deep voice said. "Get up. I know exactly how long that drug lasts, and you've had time to get over the nausea by now."

Daria opened her eyes and swallowed her gasp with effort. Karl Killian stared down at her, his blue eyes hard chips of ice. His lips curled into a smile that did nothing to comfort her. "I see you recognize me."

"I do."

"Good. That should save us some time. Tracking you down and getting you here has been a lot of trouble for me. I should make you pay for that."

"So I should have just gone willingly with the guy at my home? The one who had the knife?"

He shrugged. "Would have made things easier on all of us."

She was tired of playing games with him. "What do you want, Killian?"

"Your computer skills. Your father often praised your technological expertise."

"He knew?"

Killian scoffed. "Of course. It infuriated him that you outsmarted him so many times."

"Huh. That's good to hear."

He grabbed her arm and pulled her to her feet. "Come on." She swayed, a wave of nausea and dizziness sweeping over her while fire burned along her back. "Hold still. It'll pass."

She did as he instructed, and within seconds the sensation was gone. She met his gaze and gave a slight nod. He pointed to a room with glass walls. "We're going in there. Walk."

Daria obeyed once again, noting the goons with guns. Her gaze skirted the perimeter, taking in the details, including the nearest door—the *only* door in sight—with the deadbolt on. Then she stepped inside the state-of-the-art office. The office included motion sensors above the door, with lights and a sprinkler system. In the corner was an impressive computer system setup with a very professional-looking printer. "What's this?"

"Your next project."

She raised a brow. "Project? What kind of project?"

"There are five of us here." He pointed to the men and named them one by one. With each name that passed his lips, her heart chilled and fear shook her.

Every person in the room was on the FBI's most wanted list.

"I see you know who we are," Killian said, amusement glinting in his hard eyes.

"Yeah."

"And we all worked with your father in some capacity. But the last seven years have been very hard."

"Because you're on the most wanted list?"

"Exactly."

"So what do you want me to do?"

"Take us off the list."

She blinked at him. "Okay, but they'll just put you back on it."

He shrugged. "I don't mean literally. You're going to give all of us new identities." He held up a badge that looked very familiar.

"Where'd you get that?"

"It's not so hard to re-create. But the identity to go with it? That's much harder. That's where you come in."

"You want me to give you legit new identities so you can pass yourselves off as FBI agents?"

"Your father always said you were brilliant."

Yeah, brilliant enough to know that they would kill her once she'd done what they'd asked.

Nausea churned once more. A sickness that had nothing to do with the drug and everything to do with the thought of unleashing these men on the world with legit Bureau credentials. "I'm going to be sick. I need a bathroom. Now."

He looked at her, obviously wondering if she was stalling. The bile continued its climb up the back of her throat and her fingers curled into fists. His eyes widened and he pointed. "Go."

She ran.

Ryker sat across from Caden in his smoky-smelling cabin. Fortunately, Travis and Heather had managed to put out the fire from the Molotov cocktail, and he had minimal damage to repair—which was the absolute least of his worries.

"How are we going to find her?" he asked.

Ryker had made it to the ledge on the side of the mountain, and just like he'd told Daria, the motion sensor camera had pinged Travis's phone and the man had come to get him. When they'd returned to his home, Caden and the other agents were waiting. They had two of the men in their custody. The one who'd held Travis at gunpoint and the one Ryker had knocked unconscious in the yard. He flexed his fingers. His knuckles were swollen, but nothing was broken.

When Caden didn't answer, Travis frowned. "Well?"

Caden ran a hand over his dark hair. "I don't know."

"Not the answer I was looking for."

"Not the answer I wanted to give." Caden sighed. "We have the locals searching for her. We have choppers in the air, roadblocks at every part of the town, agents looking, and one of our best analysts trying to track her cell."

"Wait a minute. She doesn't have her Bureau cell. She grabbed a burner when we were at her father's house."

Caden's head snapped up. "Her father's house?"

Ryker pressed a scraped hand to his head. "Let me start from the beginning."

"That's a good idea."

The beating of helicopter blades interrupted them, and Ryker opened the door to watch the chopper hover over the empty field, then touch down with a light bounce. Two people scrambled from the bird and ran, heads down, toward his cabin.

He raised a brow when they approached with outstretched hands. "Let me guess, Allie and Linc St. John."

Allie's lips curved in a tight smile. "And you're Ryker?"

"Yeah. Nice to meet you. Sorry it's under these circumstances. Come on in."

They followed him inside and nodded to the other agents there. "Holt's on his way. The bureau chopper was tied up, so Penny's flying him in."

"Holt and Penny?" Ryker asked.

"Holt's another agent. Penny's his wife. She's also a chopper pilot for Life Flight."

"Right. Well, right now, Daria needs all the help she can get. And so do I."

They took seats, and Ryker readied himself to tell the story so everyone was on the same page. Speaking of pages, what had Daria done with the little book of names?

"She left it in the car," Ryker muttered.

Linc frowned. "What?"

"There was a book with a list of names in it. Daria knew a bunch of them. Maybe you could look at them, see if you recognize one or something. It might help figure out where they'd take her."

"Get the book."

Ryker darted out to the garage, praying he was right. He opened the Tesla's passenger door. The seat was empty. He opened the glove box. Empty. Checked under the seat.

Also empty.

"Come on, Daria, please don't tell me you have that book on you."

He started to shut the door when something in the side pocket caught his attention.

The book. With a relieved "yes," he grabbed it and headed back inside.

THIRTEEN

Daria hated puking, but right now, she was grateful for the reprieve it bought her. Someone had handed her a ginger ale and some stale crackers. She ate them and sipped on the soda while her mind flipped through escape ideas.

First, she needed to know where she was. And she could figure that out via the computer in there, depending on how closely they watched her. She grimaced. Someone would be keeping an eye on her. Which meant she'd just have to be more clever than they were.

"Come," Killian said. "It's time."

She nodded and stood, not bothering to protest. She was feeling decidedly better but hoped she could hide it for a while longer. "What did you spray me with? That stuff is potent."

He frowned. "You're fine. Time to work."

She held up the can of ginger ale and the last two crackers in the pack. "Can I bring these?"

"Of course. Just get in there."

She followed his orders and settled into the comfortable chair in front of the monitor. She wiggled the mouse and waited for Killian to type in the password. All numbers and two letters at the end followed by three dollar signs. She repeated it three times until she was sure she had it memorized.

The fact that he didn't care that she watched him enter it said a whole lot about his plans for her.

He shoved her shoulder and she winced. "What are you waiting for?"

"I need you to tell me exactly what you want. I'm not stalling. I need to know. And I need you to write down the names."

"You are not fighting very hard." He narrowed his eyes at her. "Why are you making this so easy?"

A low laugh slipped from her. "Seriously?" She waved a hand at his goons. "I'm feeling a little outnumbered at the moment." She wasn't going to be able to fight them and win. Not in a physical fight anyway. The only way she was going to get out of this alive was by being smart—and figuring out how to let Caden or someone know where she was.

She placed her hands on the keyboard and clicked through all the security protocols and passwords that would grant her access to her private Bureau account. She could only pray someone was watching it and would notice she was logged in. Then they could track her.

She frowned. Maybe. "Where does it look like I'm logged in from?"

"Singapore," the nearest goon said. She looked closer.

Of course. But still not untraceable. She'd have to do her best to leave some footprints to follow.

"She's online," Annie said. Ryker looked up when the young woman's voice came through the speaker. Linc stared at the phone as though he could see straight through the device and into the office Annie occupied at Quantico.

"Where is she?" Allie asked. The agent leaned forward, her gaze as intense as her husband's.

"It's being routed in so many different directions," Annie said, "it's going to take me a while to figure it out."

"Daria may not have a while, Annie," Caden said from his spot in front of the door. He held the book Ryker had retrieved from the Tesla and was slowly flipping through the pages.

"I'm aware," Annie said, "but I also don't want to go so fast that I miss something."

Other agents had hauled away the two prisoners when they'd clammed up and refused to talk while in custody on Ryker's property. Caden had waved them away, stating he didn't want to waste time trying to get information from them when Daria needed Caden's attention focused on finding her.

Annie didn't speak again, but the click of her fingers on the keys said she was working as hard and as fast as she could. A frustrated growl came through the speaker. Linc and Allie exchanged a frown.

"Annie?" Allie said.

"Whoever set up the security on the computer she's using is good. I'm pulling out all the tricks in my white hat, but I'm not making much progress."

Ryker had only heard about Annie through the grapevine—mostly from listening when Caden talked about his work—but knew she was one of the best tech agents in the bureau. Caden credited her with solving most of his cases and often referred to her as a white hat hacker. She used her skills for the good of the country, and she'd trained Daria to do the same.

"Why is she online?" Ryker asked. "Why would they even allow her access to a computer?"

"Because they want something from her," Caden said. "They need her skills."

Duh. He should have figured that out.

"Hey, I might have something," Caden said.

"What?"

"Annie." Caden glanced at the phone. "You listening?"

"I am. What did you find?"

"There are names in here that I recognize. Every single one that I'm familiar with is on the most wanted list. Not sure about the others. But if they have anything to do with the ones I do know, then they probably *should* be on the list."

"Okay."

"Gerard Lamb made this list in the book, so I'm sure the names have something to do with Daria's father, but what?"

"Read them off to me. Spell the ones you can't pronounce."

He did so.

"All right," she said. "I'll get to work on finding out who these people are. I think that might be the best way to go while my software to find Daria's location runs in the background. Stay tuned. As soon as I know something, you'll know it too."

She hung up, and Caden pressed his thumb and forefinger to his eyes. Ryker frowned, something niggling at him. "One of the names you said, Ivan Stasevich, I've seen that one somewhere."

Caden's head snapped up, his eyes narrowed. "Where?"

"At Daria's house when we were searching it. It was on a paper that fluttered out of a book. An invoice."

"For what?"

He shook his head. "Not sure, but we piled all the papers on the desk in the office to go through later. I set a book on top of them." He shrugged. "Only, we never got to later. We had to run."

Allie nodded. "We need those papers."

Caden was already tapping his phone. "I'll call in a favor

and get a search warrant fast-tracked. Then I'll have an agent go over there. Hopefully, he can get in."

"There's a little statue by the garage door. A key is Velcroed to the bottom."

Caden raised a brow but passed on the information. "All right, someone is on the way. Let's all pray there's something in those papers that can lead us to Daria."

FOURTEEN

Daria's side throbbed, her head ached, and her stomach rumbled.

Surprisingly enough, the hunger was what bothered her the most. She ate the last two crackers and finished off the can of ginger ale, then looked up. "I'm in my Bureau account," she said, "and I've looked for a way to get into the website page you're talking about. It's impossible. Annie writes the code for it, and the firewall is top-notch. I simply don't have access to it. Which means I can't remove you from it."

Killian centered the bullet end of his weapon on her forehead. Daria closed her eyes and swallowed hard while she pulled on every inch of courage and acting ability she'd acquired as a teen with an abusive father.

"Let's get one thing straight, Daria Nevsky. I know you can get into that website." He paused but didn't lower the weapon. "Your father left a plan behind. Did you know that?"

"No."

"Well, he did. In this very warehouse that used to belong to him. When I was rebuilding his empire, do you know what I found?"

"What?" Daria was listening, but she was also using the moment to think.

"Plans. A whole book of plans about how to circumvent

89

the FBI and other law enforcement. Very good plans that mentioned your expertise in all things computer related. So . . . here we are."

Well, that explained a lot. Mostly the timing of this little situation. "Yes. Here we are."

He rested the weapon against the area just above her right eye. "I also know you're scrambling to figure out how to contact someone and let them know where you are." He jerked his head to the man seated on the couch behind her. "He's very good with a computer, and he's watching everything you do. In other words, if you do something you shouldn't, he will know."

Then what did they need her for?

"Got it," she said, biting her tongue on the words she wanted to say. But at least she now knew how her father was involved in the whole thing.

He lowered the weapon, and Daria sucked in a shaky breath. Her eyes locked with the man on the couch. Tadeas. The name popped into her head. Definitely on the most wanted list. He looked like a clean-cut college graduate ready to go on a date with his girl. But his eyes glinted with a darkness she'd seen only in those who'd worked closely with her father.

He might know computer stuff, but she was going to have to bet on the fact that she knew more. Otherwise, why was she there? "Okay if I walk you through exactly what I'm going to do so you don't think I'm doing something I shouldn't?"

Those cold eyes narrowed. "Okay."

She launched into her explanation, making it as technically difficult to follow as she possibly could. About five minutes into her monologue, his eyes flickered, widening slightly before returning to their blank state. Exactly the kind of reaction she was hoping for. "Don't you think that's the best way for me to do this? It will allow me to go in the back door of the site, and if someone is working on it, they'll never notice I'm there. I'm effectively writing a program that overwrites whatever anyone else may put on the website. This keeps your information off the site—and changes your pictures so that when someone does a search for you, it comes up clear. Does that make sense?"

He nodded. "That's an excellent idea."

At his approval, Killian relaxed a fraction. "Then do it." He turned his attention away from her and to his phone. "I need to take this. Watch her."

"I'm watching her. I don't need a reminder."

Killian paused, his hand tightening around the grip of his weapon. Then he shook his head and walked out of the office, lifting the phone to his ear.

Daria met her watchdog's gaze once more, then spun the chair back to face the computer and settled her hands on the keys. *Please, God, let this work.*

Ryker paced the damaged floor of his home while the agents discussed plans and waited for Annie to get back to them. She'd already confirmed the identities of the two men taken into custody and the fact that they had connections to the Russian organized crime ring.

They were being questioned but had, thus far, not been willing to talk.

"Hey, Cade?"

"Yeah, Annie." Caden strode to the phone and waited.

"Agents are inside. You should be getting a picture of that invoice in just a few seconds. And I've been doing a search on Stasevich."

"What'd you find?"

"He was one of Nevsky's rivals. When Nevsky died, Stase-vich slowly but surely took on Nevsky's lowlifes—the ones who didn't get arrested because they weren't really on the radar or they managed to slip through the cracks. And just to clarify, there weren't many."

"Okay. Any idea what he'd want with Daria?"

"The first thought that comes to mind is her computer skills. She's an agent. She has access to all kinds of information."

"And the know-how to get it."

"Exact— Wait! I just found her . . ."

"Where?" Caden's snapped word threaded tension along Ryker's shoulders.

"Not her physical location, but she's . . . on the FBI website."

"Doing what?"

"I don't know. She's . . . created some kind of back door. Give me a few minutes, and I might be able to give you her physical location."

Ryker stood back and watched the group so intent on find-ing Daria. Why had her initial reaction been to go it alone? As soon as the thought crossed his mind, he smiled. He and Daria were alike in that respect. He hoped he had a chance to find out what else they had in common.

Please, God.

FIFTEEN

Annie's message came in the form of a pop-up ad, but Daria managed to see it before her babysitter ordered her to shut it down. "Not much I can do about those," she muttered. She hadn't had time to answer Annie as to her location, but she breathed a fraction easier knowing everyone was looking for her. So far, she'd managed to keep her sneakiness undetected, but she noticed her babysitter leaning in and looking closer.

The frown on his face sent her adrenaline spiking. "Pull that ad up again," he said.

She looked at him. "I can't. I've already closed and blocked it."

"You can. Do it."

She shoved the keyboard at him. "You do it. I don't have time to do that kind of thing and get this other stuff done in the time frame Killian has given me."

Killian stuck his head in the door, his perpetual scowl even deeper. "Problem in here?"

"Ask your goon," she said, feigning irritation to cover the fear that he would actually take her up on her challenge. "A pop-up ad is making him paranoid. If you want this done anytime soon, I suggest you let me get back to work."

"Show me what you've done so far," he said, stepping into the room.

Daria pulled up the cloned website page she'd managed to

create in record time and showed him the first two new faces in place of his and one of the others. She'd found the images from stock photos and had inserted them. Of course, she never planned on letting the images go live. "I'm getting there."

"It's taking too long."

"Well, I can hurry it along, but I can't guarantee I can cover my tracks."

His gaze flicked to her watchdog. "Is this true?"

The man sighed. "Yeah. Probably."

Killian studied her for a brief second. "Just get it done."

Daria pulled the keyboard back in front of her and let out a low breath. If Killian's computer "genius" really did have more skills than the average person, he probably could have found the fake pop-up ad.

The fact that he didn't bother trying made her suspicious. Whatever the case, Daria wanted to know where she was being held and felt a little better about sneaking in a search. She slid a glance to her babysitter. He was still watching, so she focused on doing what she'd set out to do. Make it look like she was complying with Killian's orders.

With as many pages open on the screen as possible, she hoped to disguise her search for her coordinates.

"Dude, what's Killian's deal? I'm starving."

The babysitter looked at the new man in the doorway, and Daria let her fingers change course. She shifted in the chair in a subtle move that allowed her to see the men's reflection in the glass window to her right. Watchdog's attention was diverted for a split second and she got what she needed.

"Hey."

Her stomach flipped, and she ignored his attempt to get her attention. With the window closed, she focused on one of the others.

He jabbed her in the back with his weapon. "Hey."

She dropped her hands and spun. "What?"

"Gimme the keyboard."

Uh-oh. That glint in his eyes didn't look good. She tapped a box in the righthand corner, then Enter.

"I said give me the keyboard!" He jerked it from beneath her fingers and shoved her from the chair. She landed on the concrete floor with a hard thud.

Pain stabbed her side. She had about ten seconds and needed to be ready. *Nine, eight, seven . . .*

While he fumbled with the keyboard, Daria backed toward the door. She'd have to make a run for it and pray anyone in the vicinity was a bad shot.

. . . three, two, one.

The sprinklers turned on and water rained down.

Daria darted out of the office door and beelined toward the warehouse exit. Water sprayed around her, and she could only pray the sprinkler system overrode the locks on the door.

"You know, they tried to grab her in Virginia, so wouldn't they have a location in that area where they would have taken her had they been successful?" Ryker said.

Caden nodded. "Of course. Already thought of that. Annie's looking into that too."

"Of course."

"But here . . ." He rubbed his chin and shook his head. "They don't have anywhere to take her."

"They'd take her to Columbia," Allie said.

Linc nodded. "I'll call Holt and have him be on the alert that we may need him to move in if we get a physical address."

Allie raked a hand through her hair and redid her sloppy ponytail. "Okay, I think we need to head toward Columbia." She glanced at Linc, who had his phone pressed to his ear. "See if Holt will get permission from his SAC for us to be a part of whatever goes down."

"Already crossed my mind," Caden said.

"Then let's bolt to Columbia."

"Hold on a sec." Ryker darted down the hall, grabbed his medical go bag from the closet, and hurried back to the den. "I'm ready."

Caden frowned at him. "You need to stay back."

"Happy to do that while you do your thing, but I'd really appreciate it if you'd let me go. If she's hurt, she's going to need medical attention."

"There are doctors in Columbia," Caden said.

Allie sighed. "He's right. Let him come. Having a physician on-site might not be a bad thing for a lot of reasons." She shot Ryker a fierce frown. "But you can't drive. Not at the speeds we'll be going. Linc will drive you in your vehicle. If he can keep up."

Linc scowled at his wife. "Allie . . ."

Ryker could see the protests forming. "We'll take Daria's Tesla. It'll keep up."

Linc's scowl faded. "Keys?"

SIXTEEN

Daria huddled inside an empty train car. She'd made it out of the warehouse and found herself in a train yard. She suspected it was the one just outside the Columbia city limits. Columbia was the only place that made sense. The setup inside the warehouse indicated they had been planning this for a while. If they'd snatched her in Virginia, they would have transported her to this very spot.

Which contained a lot of empty train cars and open spaces. But it couldn't be too far from the city limits. Which meant help.

Footsteps approached and Daria tensed. She'd grabbed a rusted wrench for a weapon, and her fingers spasmed around it.

"Search each car. She's around here somewhere. There's only one way in and out of this yard, and the guards at the exit said they haven't seen her."

Well, that was helpful information. No going out the exit. Daria stayed silent until the footsteps faded, her stomach twisting with each passing second. She wasn't sure if her coordinates had gone through to Annie. She thought so but couldn't trust that was going to save her. She *had* to get away, find a phone. But how?

She listened to them searching. Soon they'd reach the car she was in. She crept to the open door, careful not to make a sound.

Peering around the edge of the metal door, she glanced out into the darkness. With no streetlamps and only a sliver of a moon overhead, the dark was an inky blackness that pressed in on her. Then again, it could work to her advantage. Just ahead, a light flashed, bounced off the ground, and then swept an area, the beam lighting everything in its path.

Daria pulled back, trying to figure out the best course of action. She needed to stay on the move. If she could get to one of the searched cars, that would give her some time to come up with a plan. Not knowing the layout of the train yard was a big disadvantage, but she'd manage.

As soon as the beam passed over the opening of her car, she slipped around the edge and dropped to the ground with a soft thud.

She froze, praying no one had heard.

When no attention came her way, she crouched low and scurried to the next car, staying behind the searchers, using the darkness to cover her and the bouncing beam of light to focus her and keep her bearings. She crawled inside and slid to the floor, noting she at least had two ways out of this car. There was another open door opposite of the one she'd just crept through. She shoved aside a used syringe and grimaced. Looked like she'd found one of the "good time" cars. Probably a former hangout for local drug addicts or teens who liked to party. No doubt Killian and his goons had chased them off.

"I heard something. In there!"

Daria froze at Tadeas's cry.

Footsteps came her way and she sucked in a deep breath, ignoring the smell of rotting trash and other debris she had no desire to identify. But the footsteps passed her hiding place, and she dared to peer around the edge of the door. One of the men climbed into the rail car opposite her. He let out a sharp cry and stumbled back out. "There's a whole pack of rats in there!" The flashlight beam cut across him, and Daria saw him shudder. "I'm done with this."

"Better not let Killian hear you say that," Tadeas said.

"He's on the other side of the yard. This situation is out of control. It was just supposed to be a 'grab, get what we needed, and kill her' job. I'm done."

"He'll kill you."

"He'll have to find me first. Nevsky never would have let this happen."

"Nevsky's dead."

"Because his daughter got the best of him."

"Betrayed him."

"Whatever."

Daria swallowed. She hated thinking about those days. Dark, depressing days. She'd known her father skirted the law, but she hadn't realized he was a killer until she watched him murder a friend. A boy she'd had a crush on. Granted, the kid had worked with her father and had probably done his share of bad deeds, but that didn't matter to her at the time. In that moment, she'd vowed to bring her father down. And she'd done it, with Linc's and Allie's help.

Now she'd have to survive long enough to do the same with these guys.

Sirens in the distance reached her, and she desperately wanted to believe they were coming this way, but she couldn't depend on that.

"Find her!" Killian's enraged scream sent chills dancing along her arms. "And someone get some lights out here!"

"She sent out our coordinates," Tadeas said, his voice so

close she could reach out and touch him. Thankfully, the sirens were closer too. "They know where we are."

Everything except the approaching sirens fell silent while Daria's heart raced with fear and hope. Her efforts had paid off. Daria pressed her palms against her eyes and prayed. If she could just stay hidden a few minutes longer, she might actually get out of this alive.

When Linc pulled the Tesla to a smooth stop an hour and fifty minutes later, Ryker sat still, knowing he'd get yelled at if he attempted to exit the car. Instead, he rolled the window down, hoping to catch any information he could via eavesdropping.

Linc walked over to Holt. "Any sign of them?"

"Yeah. SWAT is in place, but we haven't been able to get eyes on Daria. However, there's lots of commotion going on in the yard. We're lying low for the moment until we can get a handle on what's happening and locate Daria."

Of course they wouldn't want to rush in and risk her getting killed. For that, Ryker was grateful, but each passing second that she was in the hands of those killers meant she was that much closer to death. He pinched the bridge of his nose and prayed for this woman he'd known for only a short time but felt like he'd known forever.

"Okay," Holt said, "here's the setup. Two guards at the entrance gate. We can take them out easy enough, but as soon as the others realize we're here, it's very possible they'll just kill her."

Ryker winced.

"Can we sneak someone in there with the equipment to get us eyes and ears?" Linc asked.

Caden nodded. "I'm already ahead of you. I've got a team digging under the back of the fence. Fortunately, that part crosses a portion of a grassy field."

Holt raked a hand over his hair. "Cameras?"

"None detected on that side."

"That doesn't make sense," Linc said, his voice low enough that Ryker had to strain to hear it. "This was part of Nevsky's old stomping grounds. He'd have more security than Fort Knox."

"Maybe so," Holt said. He paused. "But it's been seven years, right? Could be the cameras weren't even working and they were taken down."

Ryker thought the man had a point. Caden must have too, because he gave a quick nod. "All right, so what's the plan?"

"As soon as our guys are inside the fence, they'll do their best to locate Daria. Once we have her location, we grab the guards and close in on the others. Quietly. We need to take them by surprise."

Caden nodded. "I like it."

"Good."

Two gunshots sounded, and Ryker gasped. He jumped out of the car in time to hear Holt yell. "Shots fired! Get the chopper in the air and light on the ground! And someone give me a status report. Now!"

SEVENTEEN

At the sound of the gunshots, Daria's breath caught. Killian and another man had been arguing. The first wanted to run and Killian demanded he stay.

"No one goes anywhere until we find her," Killian said. "Anyone who tries to leave dies. Got it?"

"You've lost it, Killian. I'm not going down with you. You're on your—"

Two gunshots cut off the man's words. Daria froze, heart pounding, a hard ball forming in her stomach. She waited to hear if there would be any other loud pops.

"What was that?" Tadeas asked, sounding out of breath.

"Someone who disagreed with me."

"FBI is at the gate, Killian. We have to get out of here."

"Not without the girl." A sliver of desperation coated his voice. "Have the other two hold off the FBI as long as possible while we search."

Blades beat the air, and she figured that was the FBI chopper. *Please, God, let it be them.*

"Killian, we—"

"Do it!"

"Yeah. Okay. I'll tell them."

"I thought you might. Then you can start checking all the cars again. She's still here somewhere."

The man had lost it for sure. What was he going to do when

he found her? Law enforcement would have him surrounded by now.

She'd be his hostage. His way out. Which meant she had to remove herself from the picture to avoid that scenario.

Before she could come up with how to do that, a beam of light flashed into her rail car and her stomach dipped in fear. *No, no, no.* The light crossed her face, and she blinked and bolted for the opening across from the man with the light.

"Found her!"

Floodlights from the overhead chopper lit up the yard.

Daria hit the ground and raced away, desperate to get out of the light and back into the safety of the shadows. She spotted the entrance to the yard and the FBI logo on the jackets of the agents at the gate. Familiar faces sent hope surging. "Linc! Allie!" And Ryker leaned against the front of the Tesla, arms crossed, chin jutted.

Linc's head jerked up, and his eyes locked on hers. Ryker straightened and pointed.

"Daria!"

She wasn't sure who had called her name, but something slammed into her back and she went down. Hard. Pain arched through her side and hip, and for a stunned moment, she couldn't move.

It was enough time for her attacker to grab her and yank her to her feet.

And jam a gun against her temple.

"You're dead."

More gunfire erupted behind the fence. Agents ducked and readied their weapons. Radios and comms went off in a squawk of noise and codes. Another crack sounded. The window on a nearby SUV shattered and an agent cried out. Ryker grabbed his medical bag and raced toward the woman.

"Ryker, get down!"

Unsure who shouted the order, he ignored it and dropped beside the injured agent. She clasped a hand against her thigh, and he pictured a worst-case scenario.

"Jess!" Another agent settled beside them and shoved Ryker out of the way. "Jess!" The agony in his voice told him the woman was more than a coworker to him.

Ryker placed a hand on the man's shoulder. "I'm a doctor. Let me help her."

His stricken gaze met Ryker's and he moved.

"I got you, Jess," Ryker said, his voice soft. "You're going to be fine, but I need to take a look."

Her frightened gaze locked on his, and he moved her hand. And breathed a relieved sigh.

"What?" the other agent said. "What is it?"

"It's not pumping, just bleeding. I think she'll be just fine." He met her gaze. "I'm sure it hurts, but I'll get you fixed up for the time being until you can get to a hospital. They won't let an ambulance in here until it's safe."

"I know."

"It's possible the bullet could have done some damage on its way out. Won't know until you can get some scans done."

"Right." She closed her eyes and a tear leaked down her temple. "Thanks."

Ryker bandaged the wound and let his mind go back to Daria. Where was she?

Activity inside the fence ratcheted up to a near ear-shattering decibel level. Now that he'd done what he could on this side of the fence, he could only pray for those on the other side.

Had they found Daria?

The chopper blades continued to pound overhead, and the spotlight was still on the yard.

But where was Daria? Ryker's gaze swept the scene. Linc and Holt were nowhere to be found. He glanced at the other agent. "You got her?"

"Yeah."

Ryker raced back toward the Tesla and took cover behind the passenger door he'd left open when he'd grabbed his medical bag. The chopper kept its steady beam on the ground. Agents inside the fence stepped backward, weapons aimed.

Ryker's heart thudded when Daria came into view. A man walked behind her, his arm wrapped around her throat, gun held to her head. "I need a vehicle. Now!" His gaze landed on the Tesla and a cruel smile curved his lips. "That one."

Ryker dropped down out of sight, then slid the passenger seat forward and slipped into the back seat. Working quickly, he rummaged in his medical bag and closed his fingers around the item he'd been looking for.

Now to pray no one had seen him get in and that whoever had Daria would be in a hurry and wouldn't glance in the back.

Assuming they made it into the car to begin with.

If not, his plan was worthless.

And Daria might wind up dead.

EIGHTEEN

You're not going anywhere," Holt said.

"Well, it's either that or she dies."

"Come on, man, we have everyone else in custody. Give it up, and let's end this peacefully."

"We're getting in that car and driving away. If you don't give me a hard time, I'll let her go when I'm safe."

Daria ground her teeth and focused on the scene before her. The whole area was lit up like Christmas Day. Part of the fence was gone, and law enforcement was ready to act.

But the one thing that stood out to her was her car.

The car Killian wanted to take.

Wait. Why was her car here?

It didn't matter. They'd never let Killian get in it.

But they weren't stopping him either.

The gun to her head was a good deterrent to action. He had her directly in the line of fire. Her head pounded every time Killian pressed the gun into it. Which was often.

Holt stepped out from behind the protection of the bureau's SUV and planted himself in front of them. "Let her go, Killian."

Daria winced. What was he doing? Trying to get himself killed?

Killian stilled, but the weapon never moved from Daria's temple. "So you know who I am?"

"Of course they know who you are," Daria said. "They're not stupid. How do you think they knew to come here?"

"Shut up, unless you'd like a bullet in that brilliant brain of yours. There's still a way out of this for me."

Daria snapped her lips shut and blinked when a light flashed into her eyes. It was so fast, she might have imagined it.

The light flashed again. Right into her left eye.

What in the—

Someone was trying to get her attention.

From inside the Tesla.

She focused on the car and noted Ryker peering at her from around the open passenger door. What was he doing? Seriously? Who had allowed him to come?

Did he just wave at her? Gesture her to come toward him?

This time he simply jerked his head.

Trust him.

The thought echoed in her mind.

Trust him.

He'd stuck with her this far, had gotten her out of the hospital, protected her as best he could at his cabin on the ranch. Taken her into his home when he'd known being around her could be lethal. He had to have a plan of some sort and was asking her to trust him—to let him help. But did she dare? She was scared to death she was going to get him killed if she went along with his plan, but what choice did she have?

Killian was out of patience and edging her toward the Tesla.

Holt hefted his weapon. "Don't move!"

"Holt," Daria said, "it's okay. Back off."

"Daria—"

"Do it! Linc, make him!"

Holt frowned, his displeasure abundantly clear. Her gaze

107

flicked back to Ryker. She couldn't see him. Had she misunderstood?

Holt backed up a few steps, and Daria allowed Killian to move her closer to the vehicle.

The agents clearly didn't like this and closed in. "Holt! Please! Back off or you're going to get me killed!"

He ordered the others to stop, his frustration evident. "What are you doing, Daria? This isn't how we do things!"

"Yeah, well, when you're on this side of the scenario, then we can talk. But for now, please play it my way!"

Linc met her gaze, and she tried to convey her thoughts. That she had a plan. Well, Ryker did, but . . . "Please," she mouthed.

Linc laid a hand on Holt's bicep. "Let her do it."

His words reached her despite the noise from the chopper. Holt shot a confused look at Linc but must have seen something in the man's face, because he said something into his radio and the agents fell back even farther. They didn't lower their weapons, though.

"Smart girl," Killian muttered. "I might just let you live if you keep this up."

Right.

She let him guide her. "How are you thinking this is going to work?" If he climbed in first, she'd run. If she went first, they'd shoot him. Maybe.

"I'm going to hold on to your wrist and climb in and over the console. You're driving. You try to get away, you die. Understood?"

"Understood." She understood there was so much wrong with his plan that her hope rose. She was going to have a fraction of a second to act, end this, and keep Ryker out of danger.

Please, God.

Killian backed toward the driver's-side door, keeping the weapon at her temple and his eyes locked on hers.

And if his attention was on her, it wasn't on Ryker.

"Open the door," he said.

She did so, and he stepped back and put himself between her and the car. With his left hand gripping her right wrist, he started to lower himself into the driver's seat. Which meant the gun was no longer pointing at her temple.

"Three minutes, Daria."

Ryker's voice came from the back seat, startling Killian enough that Daria found her split second to act. She shot her palm out and into Killian's nose. The man screeched and released his hold on her wrist. Ryker jammed something into Killian's neck, then wrapped his forearm around his throat and held on.

Killian still held his weapon, and Daria grabbed his wrist, keeping the barrel away from her. Behind her, she could hear the commotion of descending agents and local officers and just prayed they would let her finish this. She kept a grip on the hand with the weapon. "Two more minutes," Ryker said through gritted teeth.

"What's the countdown for?" Daria asked between pants. Killian struggled, but his strength seemed to be lessening.

"For the drug to kick in."

Killian let out a string of Russian curses. The weapon tumbled from his grip and fell to the floorboard of the car.

"You're crazy," she said. "Five thousand officers in the area, and you take the guy out with a shot." She didn't know whether to laugh or yell at him.

Killian finally went limp, and Ryker relaxed his hold. Her ears tuned in to Linc and Allie and others calling her name.

With two hands, she grasped the front of Killian's shirt, and pulled him out. He rolled to the ground and lay still. Ryker shoved open the back door and joined her while agents swarmed them. Almost before she could blink, Holt had Killian's wrists cuffed. He looked up at her. "You okay?"

She nodded and glanced at Ryker. "Thanks to him."

"That hurts," Linc said, coming up to wrap her in a hug. "Allie and I were here to save the day, and all you needed was a doctor."

NINETEEN

Ryker pulled into the drive of Daria's home in Columbia, noting the manicured lawns and the floodlights that made the place glow. He and Daria had spent as much time as possible together over the past three months. Which hadn't been nearly enough for him. Between his shifts at the hospital and her work at Quantico, it had been difficult to manage.

But not impossible. They'd met in person and FaceTimed when they'd been apart. They'd even fallen asleep during one of the calls where they watched a movie together. He'd awakened to the sound of her cooking breakfast before they'd cut the connection and gone about their day, only to do the same thing that evening.

Sure, he was tired, but he'd do it all over again if it meant time with her. She fascinated him. Not just because he was attracted to her physically, but he found himself constantly trying to figure out how her mind worked. She was compassionate and strong, goal-oriented and fearless. She'd discussed her plans to use this house to do good in the world and invited him to share in the first look now that the construction crew had done its job.

Ryker knew he'd found the one he wanted to spend the rest of his life with. The funny thing was, he never thought he'd be one for a whirlwind romance.

And yet, here he was.

He was pretty sure Daria felt the same, but they hadn't exactly gotten to the "I love yous" yet.

Soon, he hoped.

Daria's Tesla sat in front of the house at the top of the circular drive, parked behind a newer-model SUV. Ryker pulled in behind the Tesla and cut the engine.

The moment he stepped out of his vehicle, the front door opened and Daria raced down the steps to throw herself into his arms. "You're here!"

He squeezed her to him, relishing the feel of her next to him once again. When she stepped back, she smiled up at him, looking like a woman who was thrilled with something. "Come on in. There's someone I want you to meet."

Ryker followed her inside, the tantalizing smells coming from the kitchen making his stomach growl. She led him through the massive foyer and into the kitchen. A woman in her midfifties stood at the stove flipping burgers. "Ryker, this is Marsha McBride. Marsha, this is Ryker Donahue, the man I told you about."

The woman put down her spatula to turn and wipe her hands on a towel. She shook Ryker's hand, and her blue eyes glinted. "Thank you for saving this girl."

Ryker laughed. "It was a team effort." He turned his attention to Daria. "So, fill me in. What's the plan?"

"The girls will be here shortly, so I need to give you the tour."

"Lead on." He nodded to Marsha. "Nice to meet you."

"You too, Ryker."

Ryker followed Daria out of the kitchen and stepped into the great room that looked like when he'd seen it last, but now it sported two additional couches for more seating. "Nice."

"I left this floor pretty much the same. Marsha and her

husband are certified foster parents and approved for emergency placement. All the bedrooms have been divided in half to make two rooms, so now we can house ten girls. Mr. and Mrs. McBride have agreed to move in and take the master bedroom. We have one other couple—a husband-and-wife team of psychiatrists—who've agreed to move into the pool house and will alternate with the McBrides when it comes to caring for the girls. One of the 'rules' for staying here is that the girls have to agree to daily counseling sessions. Weekends and holidays off."

"Wow. Impressive."

She continued the tour, and he realized she'd kept the house a home. It might have more bedrooms and baths now, but the house itself didn't feel like an institution. It could be a home to those who desperately needed one.

"The security system has been updated, the pool area safely enclosed with access granted by someone in authority." She drew in a deep breath and clasped her hands together at her chest. "It's happening, Ryker."

"I know."

"This has been a dream for a long time."

"I know that too."

"I know you know. It just feels good to say it."

"How are you going to manage this and your job at the FBI?"

She shrugged. "I won't live here. This isn't where I belong. That's why I've got people in place who can do everything that needs doing. I'll check in and come visit, but for the most part, I won't have to do much of anything else."

"You're amazing, Daria."

She hugged him, and Ryker kissed the top of her head. "I think you're the amazing one. You've supported me all the way through this."

He nodded. "If there'd been a place like this with people like you're describing when I was a kid, I might have been more willing to go into the system instead of running away."

"The system is flawed for sure, but there are good people in it. We just have to make sure they're able to be found."

Ryker pulled her closer in the middle of the hall, standing outside the bedroom that used to be hers. "Daria, can I be blunt?"

She blinked up at him. "Sure."

"Okay . . . here goes."

"I'm listening."

"I think I'm falling in love with you."

TWENTY

"Oh. Wow."

He clutched his heart. "Ouch."

She chuckled. "Stop, you goof. You just took me by surprise, that's all."

"Good surprise? I hope?"

"Definitely a good surprise. I feel the same about you, Ryker, but . . ."

This time his flinch was for real. Then he stiffened like he was steeling himself for a blow.

"But," she said, "I just don't see how there can be an 'us' with the physical distance of our careers." She bit her lip. "I've racked my brain trying to figure out a solution, but even halfway is a three-and-a-half-hour drive one way."

"I know. That's why I did . . . a thing."

She paused and raised a brow. "You did . . . *a thing*?"

"I did."

"Details, please?"

"I applied to Inova Alexandria Hospital and was offered a position there."

She gasped. "You what?"

He shrugged. "I can be a doctor anywhere." He reached out to trail a finger down her cheek. "I haven't accepted the position yet. I told them I needed to check with someone before saying yes."

Her heart pounded at the thought of him being so close. "But your home is in Campobello. The one you built. Remember?"

He laughed. "A home is what you make of it. That house will always be there. If I decide to move, Travis and Heather will rent it out for me as an Airbnb or something." He glanced at their clasped hands, and she hadn't even realized he was holding hers. "I guess what I'm trying to say in my fumbling, bumbling way is that I'm willing to do what it takes to see where this relationship might go. If moving and working near you is the way to do that, then why not?"

Tears filled Daria's throat and made their way to her eyes. She blinked and sniffled and blinked some more. "I don't know what to say."

"Say you're okay with that, and tell me I should accept the job."

"I'm so okay with that." She reached up to plant a kiss on his lips and then wrapped her arms around his neck and hugged him. "Oh, Ryker, this makes me so happy."

He kissed her again and again. Then pulled back to cup her face. "Making you happy is making me happy. This could be addictive."

She laughed. "Well, I can't say I'm glad I was attacked and stabbed, but I sure am glad I landed in your hospital."

"That was a divine appointment. God had a plan. What some-one meant for evil, God took and turned it into something good. And I, for one, want to see him do that over and over again. With you."

"I'm okay with that."

"Then I'll accept the job."

The chime sounded, indicating someone was on their way up the drive. Butterflies swarmed in her stomach, and she gripped his hands. "That's them," she whispered. "The girls are here."

"Then let's go welcome them home. I'm looking forward to watching your dreams play out."

She kissed him one more time, then pulled him toward the stairs, her heart full. Joy exploded as she looked around the home. A home that had been used for evil but would now be open for those seeking shelter and love.

A home for the lost.

Finally, her father's nightmare legacy was being erased and a new, honorable one was just beginning.

Lynette Eason is the bestselling author of *Life Flight* and the Danger Never Sleeps, Blue Justice, Women of Justice, Deadly Reunions, Hidden Identity, and Elite Guardians series. She is the winner of three ACFW Carol Awards, the Selah Award, and the Inspirational Reader's Choice Award, among others. She is a graduate of the University of South Carolina and has a master's degree in education from Converse College. Eason lives in South Carolina with her husband and two children. Learn more at www.lynetteeason.com.

DEADLY OBJECTIVE

LYNN H. BLACKBURN

ONE

Emily Dixon nodded at the Secret Service agent standing post inside the front door of the vice president's home. She handed him her bag and waited for him to examine the contents, the same way she had three times a week for the past six months. Before he finished, another agent approached from the long hallway to her right. Red hair, blue eyes, freckles, and a baby face that made him look like a college student and not the seven-year-veteran agent he was.

He stopped well into her personal space, crossed his arms, and loomed over her. "You're early today, Ms. Dixon. This is going to mess up the schedule."

Her Southern accent usually lingered around the edges of her voice, but she layered it thick on every word as she replied, "Good morning to you too, Special Agent Harper."

Liam Harper developed an immediate and intense fascination with his shoes, but not before she caught the twitch of his lips. He made no reply until Emily's bag had been returned to her and they were behind the closed doors of the small room designated for her to treat the vice president's son. She and Liam had been on a first-name basis for months, but not in public. The only person who'd picked up on the way their relationship had been sliding from professional to personal was Mason Lawson. Her patient. Liam's protectee.

"You really let the East Tennessee fly this morning." Liam

grinned at her, his words coming in a slow, low-country drawl that she didn't ever get tired of hearing.

"My East Tennessee can take your South Carolina any day, and we both know it."

"All kidding aside . . ." He leaned against the door, arms crossed, ankles crossed, accent gone—well, mostly. "Do you need me to get Mason early?"

She dropped her bag onto the octagon-shaped table to the left of the door and pulled out the exercise bands and massage gun she needed for today's session. "There's no rush. I hit the traffic jackpot today. I've never managed this trip in under forty-three minutes. Today was thirty-five."

Liam waggled his eyebrows. "Right. That's your story, but I know the truth."

"Which is?"

"You couldn't wait to see me."

Emily made a show of pondering his words before giving her head a slow shake. "No. That's not it." The words were true enough. She'd been lucky with the traffic today. But they were also a whopper of a lie, because somehow over the past few months, her three-times-a-week therapy sessions with Mason Lawson had become the highlight of her week.

And it certainly wasn't because of Mason. The teenager could be a nightmare when he was in a mood. Emily and her twin, Gil, had gotten into their fair share of trouble as children, but Mason Lawson was like a Tasmanian devil in three-hundred-dollar khakis and four-hundred-dollar polo shirts.

For the most part, the press left the VP's kid alone, but that didn't mean Mason hadn't earned a nickname. It was unclear who'd started it, but rather than referring to Mason as a royal pain in the rear, someone had dubbed him His Royal Hiney.

It was ridiculous, but it stuck. Probably because while the VP was on the campaign trail during the previous election, four different agents were assigned to Mason on a one-week-on, one-week-off rotation. No one could put up with him for more than a week at a time.

Enter Special Agent Liam Harper. The only agent on the VP's detail who could keep Mason in line. He'd been assigned to the VP's son for almost a year, and while Mason could still be moody, he reined it in when Liam was around. And after a rocky start, he'd also settled in with Emily. She suspected Mason might have a wee bit of a crush on her. She suspected the same of his favorite agent.

Liam pulled his phone from his back pocket and tapped on the screen. "I'll have him come down. Do you want him longer or to finish up early?"

"How's his mood?"

Liam cut his eyes to her but didn't respond to the question before returning to his text. Awesome. Mason was in a mood.

She hadn't fully appreciated the "Liam effect" until her third week of working with Mason. Liam was on vacation, and by the end of the last session that week, Emily told her practice manager she "would never see that brat again unless Liam Harper was available to run interference."

Her displeasure had been communicated, and since then she'd never seen Mason without Liam being present. Over the past few months, she'd discovered that she and Liam were polar opposites. He was an outdoorsman. In fact, the week he'd been on vacation, he'd been in Wyoming. Hiking, camping, living off the land, with the frequent use of a compass to navigate.

Emily, however, had never met a hotel, mall, or nail salon she didn't like. The only time she wanted to be outside was when the temps were in the low seventies, humidity was nonexistent, and there were no bugs. Or dirt. So, basically, she had about a five-hour window in spring and another in the fall.

If she'd been interested in pursuing a relationship with Liam, they might have been able to get past that. But she was not interested. At all. He was an agent who would literally take a bullet for someone else. She didn't date agents. Ever. Some women were attracted to men like that. Not her.

Liam frowned at his phone as he spoke. "I'd say let's get it over with. The family has an appearance this afternoon." Mason hated public appearances. "If he has a few extra minutes before that, he'll be happy to take them."

"You make it sound like he'll be happy or there will be consequences. And based on the length of the text you're sending, I'm suspicious that you might be laying out those consequences in detail."

Liam grunted but continued texting.

Not for the first time, she caught herself staring. With his head bent over the phone, she had a perfect view of his thick red hair. Before she met Liam, if anyone had asked her if she found redheads attractive, she would've said she'd never thought about it. But Liam had great hair. It suited him.

"Emily, I would never threaten my protectee."

She waited.

"I would, however, remind him of promises made and the rewards coming his way if he holds it together, but that will be lost to him if he screws up."

Liam had a great voice that made her name sound like music. He was quick to laugh, but he never laughed at anyone, only with them. And when he cared about something, or someone, his devotion was off the charts. He cared about his job. He cared about his family. He even cared about Mason Lawson, and unfortunately, unless they were a blood relative, not many people did.

All those things would've made Liam someone she would at least entertain the possibility of considering. But he was an agent, so she'd friend-zoned him on day one, a move she didn't regret. Much. She understood the life. Her brother was up to his eyeballs in it. It had almost gotten him killed several times, and worrying about Gil was all her heart could handle. Gil had had her heart from the womb. Caring about him and for him was literally in her DNA, so she'd learned to live with the constant fear.

But there was no way she could hand her heart over to someone else and risk losing them.

Liam finished his text and pushed away from the door. "Mason's en route. How can I help today?"

Emily flashed him the smile he liked to think she reserved for people she really, really liked, but he reminded himself, as he did every time she was here, that the only reason he was in this room was to protect Mason Lawson.

"I'm good, thanks. Just need the man of the hour." She pulled a few more exercise bands from her bag. "Did you try the Thai place I told you about?"

"I did." They spent the next ten minutes in easy conversation. Everything about Emily was easy. She was easy to look at. Easy to talk to. Easy to make laugh. The one thing that wasn't easy? Getting out of their easy camaraderie and into something . . . more.

The kind of more where they'd be trying new restaurants

together as opposed to telling each other about them and trying them separately.

Mason slouched into the room. The agent with him didn't say a word, but her eyes spoke volumes before she touched her fingers to her head in a small salute. Liam acknowledged it with a chin lift. Mason was now his responsibility. And he knew everyone in the house breathed a collective sigh of relief.

Mason knew the drill, and he took a seat in the chair while Emily asked him questions about how his shoulder felt and if he'd done his exercises yesterday.

Mason grumped a few words, and Liam cleared his throat. Mason sat up straighter and spoke politely.

Better.

At only sixteen, the kid could be a handful. There was no way around it. Mason approached all new relationships with bluster and attitude, and most people let him get away with it because they didn't think it would be appropriate to correct the vice president's son.

Liam had no such issues. It wasn't his job to correct the kid, but it also wasn't his job to be his best friend. It was his job to protect him, and he'd made that clear to Mason on their first afternoon together.

He'd also figured out fast that Mason Lawson was like those yappy little dogs who talk a big talk but have nothing to back it up. Establishing boundaries and enforcing them had been huge.

"So, is everything a go for your camping trip?" Emily asked the question right as she pulled Mason's arm into a stretch the kid hated. She had a knack for finding the right time to ask a question that would give Mason something to think about other than the discomfort.

"All packed." Mason hissed the words between clenched teeth.

"The weather looks good for it." Emily counted a slow ten count before releasing Mason.

Liam couldn't agree more. "It should be perfect. Chilly mornings, pleasant afternoons, sunshine."

"When do y'all leave?" Emily continued to move through what Mason dubbed the "torture routine."

Mason glared at Emily but managed to say, "Tomorrow."

"Mason here tried to get out of all his classes tomorrow, but Mrs. Lawson vetoed that. She did approve an early dismissal, so we're hitting the road after lunch."

"Trying to throw your rabid fans off the scent?"

Mason flushed bright pink at her question.

The press left Mason Lawson alone. But that didn't mean he didn't have a devoted, some would call it obsessive, following of teenage girls who made it their mission to track Mason everywhere he went. It was an overly excited group of teenage girls that led to his shoulder injury.

Liam knew the torture routine well by now, and he grabbed a small green exercise band from the table. "That would be a bonus, but it's mostly so we can get there and set up before dark." He handed her the band with a wink.

Emily took it with a nod of thanks, their private choreography having settled into a comfortable pattern at this point. Her expression altered, and Liam braced for what was coming. He knew that look. It was her "I'm up to something" look.

"I don't know." Emily nudged Mason until he looked at her, then wrinkled up her face and shook her head. "Mason, weren't you here when Liam told us he could put a tent together blindfolded?"

Mason's expression cleared of pain, and he nodded with overdone solemnity. "You know, Emily, I do believe I heard those very words come out of his mouth."

"Must not be true." Emily's eyes were wide, and she shook her head sadly as she dropped her voice to a stage whisper. "Go easy on him this weekend, Mase. This may be why he's held off on taking you. He claimed it was because your shoulder needed to heal. But the truth is going to be revealed. I'm going to need a full report from you on Monday, so maybe you should take notes."

Mason sucked in a deep breath as Emily twisted him up like a pretzel, but he managed to gasp out, "I'll do that."

"If I were you," Emily continued in her stage whisper, "I'd make myself scarce during the tent setup. That way he won't be embarrassed."

"Oh no." Liam gave them both a wide and completely fake smile. "I think Mason needs to be there every step of the way. So he can document this and report back to you later."

Emily released Mason and gave him a small shrug. "I tried."

Mason grinned, actually grinned, back at her. "It was a great effort. I appreciate it."

The session continued for another twenty minutes, and now that the worst of the treatment was over, Mason gabbed about hiking, fishing, and the potential for animal sightings. He was particularly hoping for a bear.

"Liam, please tell me you're not going anywhere near bears. Or mountain lions." Emily didn't sound like she was joking.

"Yes, ma'am."

That earned him a spectacular eye roll, complete with a head shake and hands raised in a "What am I going to do with him?" gesture. Mason rolled his eyes at Liam and muttered,

"Man, you keep poking the Tiny Tyrant with that ma'am stuff. When she finally snaps and attacks you with a massage gun, I'm taking her side."

Emily wasn't large, but she also wasn't tiny. After one particularly tough therapy session, Mason had referred to her as the Tiny Tyrant and the nickname stuck, although now it was said with what Liam knew was genuine affection, not belligerent exasperation.

"I wouldn't bother with the massage gun." Emily positioned the gun on Mason's shoulder and moved it in tight circles. "I'd grab some of the massage balls out of my bag and take him down."

Mason snorted. "You think that would work?"

Emily's expression grew smug. "It worked for David against Goliath. And I have excellent aim. My brother almost went pro in baseball, and I learned to pitch right along with him."

"No way."

"I assure you, it is the truth."

Now it was Liam's turn to share an exaggerated eye roll with Mason.

"Right." Liam reached for Emily's arm and squeezed her bicep. "You know how to pitch?"

Her back went straight, and her voice was frosty when she said, "Are you doubting my skills?"

Mason laughed, and Emily winked at him.

"Why didn't your brother go pro?" Mason asked the question with a hesitancy that surprised Liam. Maybe the kid was learning some tact. Finally.

"Injury."

Mason's entire body reacted to that one word. His injury had threatened to end a promising golf career. "How old was he?"

Emily didn't make eye contact with anyone as she spoke. "Seventeen. Senior year. Scouts had followed him for years. He was going to be drafted straight from high school."

"That must have been awful." The total absence of sarcasm in Mason's voice testified to how strongly he was responding to this revelation.

"It was." Emily continued to work Mason's shoulder. "He was devastated, and he was in a dark place for a while."

"Is he okay now?"

Was Mason genuinely concerned?

Emily smiled at Mason. "Oh yeah."

"How—" Mason cut himself off with a frown, and Emily gave his arm a gentle squeeze. It must have given Mason what he needed to continue to ask his question. "How did he get better? I mean, from being depressed about it?"

"It took a while. But he found other things he enjoyed doing."

"Like what?"

"Guitar, music, cooking."

"Cooking?"

"Yep. He's amazing. His coworkers buy groceries so he'll cook for them."

"What does he do?"

Liam watched the interaction, fascinated by the way it was playing out. Emily continued to drop crumbs. And as she did, Mason continued to follow them.

"He's an agent."

"What kind?"

She shrugged and glanced at Liam. "Secret Service."

"What? Do I know him?"

"No. He's in Raleigh. If he stays in, he'll probably be on a protection detail in a few years."

"Why wouldn't he stay in?"

Liam lost the thread of the conversation. Emily's brother was a Secret Service agent in Raleigh? That would explain how easily she'd adjusted to the protocols and extra hoops she had to jump through to take care of Mason and meet the strict safety measures he lived under.

"Why wouldn't he stay in?" Mason asked again, oblivious to the tension that now emanated from Emily.

"He has a woman in his life now. They're solid, but her job will keep her in Raleigh."

That wasn't the real answer. It wasn't a lie, but it wasn't the whole truth. Mason didn't know what Liam knew—that the Raleigh office had nearly been decimated the previous spring. Of the five surviving agents, only two had avoided injury. Then last month they'd had a major malware case that somehow had led to a shootout in an agent's house.

The Raleigh office was small enough that there was no way Emily's twin hadn't been involved, at least at some level. It wouldn't be surprising for an agent to want to find safer employment after surviving that. And if her brother had been injured recently, that might also explain why she kept Liam at arm's length.

A sharp rap on the door interrupted his thoughts. Liam opened the door, his body blocking the view into the room. The Second Lady's chief of staff, Lisa Goldman, glared at him from the hall. "Are they done yet?"

"No."

"I heard she was early."

"Emily was. *He* wasn't."

Lisa frowned at her iPad. "I need him ready for the road in thirty minutes."

"They'll be done in fifteen. He won't need more than fifteen to change. His clothes are already prepped."

"If he's late, it's on you."

It took all Liam's restraint to keep his face still when every muscle itched to contort into a grimace. But this new chief of staff had a reputation. She tolerated no dissent, no attitude, and no disrespect, especially from anyone she deemed beneath her. And those beneath her, in her mind, included the agents assigned to protect the Second Family.

"It won't be a problem." Liam moved to close the door.

Before he succeeded, an explosion shook the house.

TWO

The room rocked, lights flickered, and Emily dropped the massage gun. She pushed Mason forward as part of the ceiling crashed behind her. Another part to the left. Something slammed into her elbow.

Before she could process what was happening, Liam roared into her space. He grabbed her arm with one hand, Mason with his other, and hustled them from the room. "Let's go."

The next few minutes were a blur of yelling, squawking alarms, and someone screaming. The only constant was Liam's grip on her elbow.

He didn't release her until they reached a small SUV, and he put both hands on Mason to push him into the back seat. The moment Mason was in, Liam shoved Emily into the seat next to him and then followed, squeezing her even closer to Mason as he settled beside her. This was not the typical Secret Service Suburban, and the three of them in the back seat made for a tight fit. But when the vehicle peeled out of the drive a nano-second after Liam closed the door, she was thankful the snug fit kept them from being tossed around.

Emily had so many questions, but the look on Liam's face warned her that now was not the time.

Mason wasn't looking at Liam or out the windows. He was looking at his phone. Leave it to a teenager to hang on to his phone in the middle of an attack. Liam reached across her and snatched the phone from Mason's hand, powered it off, and tucked it into the pocket of the seat in front of him. He ignored Mason's grumbling. "Get your seat belts on." He barked the order just as his own phone buzzed. In such close proximity, Emily could feel the vibration. He pulled his phone from his pocket. "Harper."

Mason managed to twist enough to grab his seat belt, but Emily had to squeeze herself closer to Liam for Mason to have enough room to snap it in place. When she did, Liam's hand pressed into the small of her back, flat at first, then with more pressure and a definite squeeze of his fingertips.

"Yeah." He spoke into his phone, but his hand didn't move.

When Mason shifted back into his seat, it was her turn. She had to sever the connection to Liam, so she twisted her body and leaned into Mason's space to get her seat belt latched.

She tried to shove the clasp in, but her hands were trembling and she missed it twice. Liam wrapped a hand over hers, then gently eased the seat belt from her hand and clasped it for her.

"Got it." He was still on his phone. "We're three minutes out."

Three minutes from where? She didn't bother asking. It was clear no one would answer anything. Whatever had happened, her best shot at keeping herself and Mason alive was to stick with Liam.

So she tabled her questions. For now.

But as far as she could tell, the vice president's home had been successfully attacked.

The Secret Service had a zero-mistake policy. They didn't need to be successful 99.99 percent of the time. One hundred percent was the only acceptable success rate.

And today had not been a success.

Liam didn't take a deep breath until Mason and Emily were secured at the rendezvous point. A safe house in DC, not far from the VP res, this spot had never been intended to be a long-term stay. It was designed to be a location where they could regroup, analyze the threat, and determine their next steps.

This concept was good in theory but had one glaring flaw. They'd had to make this run in broad daylight. The driver had taken a circuitous route, and they didn't think they'd had a tail.

But this was Washington, DC. There were cameras everywhere. There were people everywhere. And they couldn't assume that at this moment, whoever had initiated the attack on the home wasn't regrouping and preparing to attack them here.

Still, they were off the road and in a location with a bunker and secure communication equipment, so for now, it would do.

"Emily."

At his call, she turned to him. On the outside she appeared mildly interested in the goings on around them.

But he knew better.

He'd felt the shudders running through her body in the car, seen her hands tremble. Emily Dixon was scared. And the thing that gutted him was . . . she had every reason to be. "Let me see your elbow."

"Why?"

"You're bleeding."

"What?" She twisted to see the back side of her arm.

Liam grabbed her wrist. "You're going to make it worse."

"She's hurt?" Mason joined them, taking what couldn't be mistaken for anything other than a protective stance at Emily's other side.

Liam pulled the sleeve of her sweater away but didn't respond. The blood dripping to the floor spoke for him.

Mason's gaze traced the trail of blood. "Does she need a doctor?"

"Mason, honey." Emily reached for his arm with her free hand. "I'm okay."

"That doesn't mean you don't need a doctor."

Liam fought back a grin at Mason's bullheadedness.

"Fair enough." Emily acknowledged Mason's comment and spoke in a serious tone. "But I don't think I'm in danger of losing this arm. It doesn't hurt."

Liam pulled the bloody sweater farther up her arm and she flinched.

Mason alternated between glaring at her and at Liam. "Right."

"Well, it doesn't hurt when no one's touching it." Emily turned her baby blues on Liam. "What's the verdict?"

"We need to clean it. Thoroughly. It might need stitches, but for now, we'll use some butterfly bandages and—"

"Mason!" Heather Lawson, the Second Lady of the United States, otherwise known as the SLOTUS, and the darling of the press and most of the country, rushed toward them. "Are you all right?" She reached for Mason, and he allowed her fluttering hands to skate over his arms and back as she checked him for injuries.

"I'm fine, Mom. But Emily's bleeding."

Emily's hand clenched in Liam's, and he squeezed it back while pulling her slightly closer to him as the full force of Heather Lawson's scrutiny flowed over them. "Agent Harper, explain."

"The best we can tell, a piece of the ceiling caught her elbow."

"She was protecting me." There was a low growl in Mason's

voice that Liam had never heard. "She pushed me down. I didn't know what was happening. It would've hit me if she hadn't done that."

Mrs. Lawson sucked in a breath.

"I'm fine, ma'am." Emily spoke in a rush. "I've just been telling Agent Harper and Mason that it doesn't hurt. It's nothing to get worked up over."

"Emily, when someone is injured protecting my son, it is absolutely appropriate for me to get worked up over it."

Mason didn't miss a beat. "Mom, do we have a doctor around here?"

"One is en route. I'll be sure he sees to Emily first when he arrives. Agent Harper"—Mrs. Lawson turned to him—"you'll be sure she cooperates." It wasn't a question.

"Yes, ma'am."

"As for you"—Mrs. Lawson's entire face gentled as she looked at Emily—"you've been a blessing from the first day you stepped into our home, and I can't ever thank you enough for protecting my son. With that said, don't argue with Mason or Agent Harper about this. I know you're trying to keep them from worrying, but they'll worry regardless, so you might as well roll with it." She squeezed Emily's hand, then patted Mason on the arm. "Come with me, sweetheart. Your father's calling. He wants to see your face."

Mason turned to go but met Liam's gaze. "The doctor?"

"I've got it, man. Go with your mom. She needs you close."

Mason allowed his mom to wrap her arm around his waist, and Liam waited until he was out of sight before turning his attention back to Emily. "Let's find you a place to sit."

"I'm fine."

"I'm glad to hear it, but you'll be more fine sitting down."

She glared at him. "I don't need coddling."

"Mrs. Lawson and Mason disagree, and you know I always try to do what they ask."

She snorted. "Right."

"You don't believe me?" He kept his tone light as he guided her to a high-backed chair in the corner of the room.

"Two weeks ago I heard you tell Mason that when he was an adult and paying taxes, he could have some say in the matter, but until then he could do what you told him to do, when you told him to do it, and have a good attitude while doing it."

"That was a unique situation."

"In what way? I distinctly heard him mumbling along with you toward the end, which means that's a speech he's heard many times before." She sat in the chair and rested her head against the back. "He's changed because of you."

"He's changed, but I can't take credit for it. He's growing up."

"And you're helping him grow up well. In this environment, he was desperate for someone to call him on the stunts he was trying to pull. His parents love him, but they spend so much time away from him, they tend to indulge him when they're together."

She was spot on, but Liam wasn't sure how she knew that. She rarely saw Mason interacting with his family.

Emily winked. "People talk, Liam."

"I don't."

"I didn't say agents. I said people. I received an in-depth briefing before I took him on. My boss was afraid he'd be assigning therapists the way the Secret Service used to have to assign agents. He actually offered me hazard pay." The humor faded from her eyes. "Although this wasn't the kind of danger he thought I'd be in."

"Hey." Liam knelt beside her, placing one hand on her knee. When her hand covered his and squeezed, he couldn't stop himself from squeezing her knee in response. "You're doing great. Mrs. Lawson will probably nominate you for sainthood."

"I'm no saint."

"You put your body between Mason and danger. In her mind, you are."

"What about you?"

"It's my job."

She groaned. "Yeah. I know. Trained to run to the danger, not away."

"You say that like it's a bad thing."

"Agents who run into danger sometimes don't run back out."

She wasn't wrong. Her brother had obviously survived the drama in Raleigh, but it dawned on him that if she was as close to her brother as she seemed to be, then she'd probably known the agents who'd been killed.

She straightened in the chair and flexed her hand on his before moving it away. "Sorry. No time for melodrama. I know it's your job. And I know your training means that you run to danger, and you're so well trained that there's an excellent chance you'll not only survive but also save everyone around you in the process."

"None of us have a death wish, Emily. The ultimate goal is to shut down any threat before it ever manifests so we never need to respond to any danger."

She gave him a tight smile. "I know. But I wonder if you know how hard it is to love someone like you."

THREE

At Liam's raised eyebrow, Emily ran back over the words she'd just said. Oh no. No, no, no. She scrambled to explain. "I mean, agents in general. Hard for your families."

A slow chin lift. "Right." The word indicated agreement. The tone indicated that she was in for some epic teasing. She needed to switch gears—and fast.

"Please don't take it personally. Lots of people are difficult to love for any number of reasons. Trust me on this. Being hard to love because of your job is far better than being hard to love because of who you are."

Liam's hand clenched on her knee. "Emily, did someone actually tell you that you're hard to love?"

Uh-oh. She knew that tone. That look. Liam was ready to dispense justice on anyone who'd ever said that to her. But there was no way she could tell him the truth.

Time to defuse the situation.

"My twin points it out on a regular basis."

"Your twin?" Liam wasn't buying it.

"Oh yes. He's a bossy, overprotective, thrill-seeking know-it-all." Liam frowned, concern etching his features, so she hurried to finish the description. "He's also loving, compassionate, gentle, hilarious, a scary-good cook, and my favorite person in the world."

As she spoke, Liam's expression shifted from concern to amusement to something that hinted of jealousy. "Your favorite person in the world? Does he feel the same way about you?"

"He used to, but as of a month ago, I'm officially in second place. It's a close second, but his allegiance has shifted, and I'm completely okay with that. She's one of my best friends, and I'm thrilled."

"You have a generous heart, Emily. Not everyone would be okay with being bumped off their pedestal."

She couldn't stop herself from laughing. "Gil has never had me on a pedestal. He knows all my dirty secrets and loves me anyway."

"As he should." Liam spoke with such certainty and finality that even though she was trying to pull the conversation to lighter, less personal topics, she couldn't leave the remark alone.

"Why would you say that?"

"Say what? That he should love you for who you are, without trying to change you? Isn't that what love is supposed to be for everyone?"

"Hmm . . . yes . . . I guess it is."

"So why would you think you're hard to love? If someone is struggling to love you, then they aren't doing it right."

Whoa. Yeah. They were solidly back in the deep end with this conversation. She swam for shallow water and gave him what she hoped was a teasing smile. "You may not have picked up on this, having only interacted with me professionally, but in my real life, I'm a lot."

"Define 'a lot.'" Still not relaxed.

She winked at him. "I'm not sure you're ready for that. It's already been a traumatic day."

"Try me." There was no amusement in the command, and it was definitely a command.

"Okay. You asked for it. I—"

Her words were swallowed by a scream as the air around them filled with the staccato rhythm of gunfire.

Before Emily could process what was happening, she was on the ground, Liam's body solid on hers, his head tucked beside hers, his arms wrapped around them both. She had no idea how much time had passed—it could have been a few seconds or a full minute—before an eerie silence descended.

"Regular breaths, baby. I've got you."

At Liam's words, she focused on her ragged breathing and fought to find a normal pace. Gil had taught her this trick. Deep breaths weren't always the best option. Measured breaths did a better job of regulating anxiety and stress. She counted. Three beats for the inhale. Three beats for the exhale. Repeat.

Liam hadn't moved, but she could sense the muscles in his arms relax. "Good. Keep doing that."

His head stayed pressed against hers, but he turned his face toward the door, then back toward her, his lips against her ear. "We need to get out of here."

"Okay."

He didn't sit up but slid off her so their bodies were side by side. "We're going to army crawl to the doorway. You with me?"

She nodded.

Something flickered in his eyes. Approval. The warmth of it cloaked her in a delicious heat that, for a few moments, chased away the chill of terror.

"Okay, follow me."

Army crawls, as it turned out, were a lot harder than they

looked. Every time her injured arm touched the floor, a sharp bite of pain lanced through her. She was fighting for air and dripping with sweat by the time they reached the door.

"Hold on." Liam mouthed the words as he pulled his phone from his pocket and typed something on the screen. She lay there, still attempting to get her breathing under control and wishing there was an Off switch for her sweat glands. She'd counted to sixty before he turned the screen to her so she could see the words on it.

> Come into the main living area. We have everything locked down. No casualties.

He nudged the door open and peered out before slowly climbing to his knees. When she moved to follow him, he held a hand up. "Wait here." Then he disappeared.

She fought back the unreasonable panic that threatened to overwhelm her. He wasn't leaving her. He was making sure everything was safe. She knew that. But her emotions were riding an out-of-control bullet train by the time he returned, a mere thirty seconds after he'd disappeared. He knelt beside her. "Are you okay?"

Of course she wasn't okay. So far today she'd been nearly blown up and then shot at. Nothing about this was okay. But what came out of her mouth was, "Peachy. How are you? You're holding your neck like it hurts. Did you land funny?"

"I'm fine. Just a little tight."

"I want to check it later."

"I'm good."

"Then it won't be a problem for me to make sure."

Liam's lip quirked. "Fine. Let's join the others. Looks like we're moving. Again."

Liam helped Emily to her feet, and even though she was steady, he kept his hand on her elbow. She didn't pull away. It could have been his imagination, but she might have leaned toward him as they made their way through the house.

Emily paused, and he came to a stop with her. She leaned closer, definitely not his imagination this time, and came up on her tiptoes. "Do you know what will happen when we get in there?" The words were more breath than whisper.

He lowered his head and spoke directly into her ear. "Not precisely. In this scenario, my job is protection, not strategy. In the short term, we'll put the entire family in a safe house, probably one outside the city, and basically barricade them inside until we can figure out what's happening."

Emily pulled back enough to look at him and nodded. "Thank you. I like to be prepared."

Liam drew her closer, and this time when he spoke, his lips brushed her ear. "I'll do whatever I can to get you out of here and safely home. I promise." Then he pulled back and tugged on her uninjured elbow. She fell into step with him, and when they approached the living area, neither of the agents at the door made any effort to stop him as he walked through with her at his side.

"—but Mason has been planning this trip for weeks."

Liam fought back the groan that ached to find release. Most of the time, the SLOTUS was relatively easy to work with. She was well aware of the threats her family lived under, and she wasn't one to try to circumvent the protective procedures put in place to keep her child safe.

But every now and then . . .

"Ah, Emily. There you are, dear. I need to speak with you privately. Come." Mrs. Lawson beamed at Emily.

"Of course, ma'am." Emily's Southern manners were on full display as she joined the SLOTUS in a corner of the room.

Jesse Sanderson, one of the agents on the SLOTUS protective detail, caught Liam's eye and motioned to the opposite corner. Liam didn't waste time joining him, then cut his eyes toward the conversation happening on the other side of the room. "Do you know what that's about?"

"Oh yeah. Brace yourself, man. SLOTUS wants the cute PT to come with us to the house in Maryland."

Liam closed his eyes and took a few deep breaths before he trusted himself to respond. "Is she out of her mind? There's no reason Emily can't return to her home." And she'd be safer if she were away from whatever entity had wreaked havoc today.

"The word from above is that they want the family to stay there for a week, maybe longer. There's no way they can go home tonight, and probably not next week, but hopefully by next week we could bring them back into DC."

"That doesn't explain why Emily needs to join the party."

"SLOTUS doesn't want Mason's therapy to be interrupted. And she's"—at this point, Jesse pitched his voice higher and adopted the Jersey accent Mrs. Lawson hadn't completely eradicated from her voice—"sure Emily won't mind coming along and helping."

"Please tell me we aren't considering this."

"Sorry, man. But there's some chatter that it will be easier to run the investigation and keep tabs on everyone if Emily stays with us."

"Who said that?"

"Goldman."

As Emily had said, this was just peachy. Mrs. Lawson leaned far too heavily on her chief of staff. The woman annoyed the ever-living daylights out of Liam, and Mason despised her with the kind of intensity only broody teenage boys could manage. Liam attempted to push his personal dislike of the woman to the side and think rationally. Goldman had never been anything but annoyed by Emily's presence. Why would she want her to come now?

The SLOTUS stepped back into the circle of agents and administrators. Emily, with a look on her face that told Liam she was both flattered and confused, caught his eye and shrugged.

Liam tried not to frown at Emily. It wasn't her fault. She was caught up in the whirlwind along with the rest of them. He'd assumed it had been a fluke that she'd been there.

Now, with the SLOTUS and her chief of staff mounting an all-out offensive to be sure Emily stayed in the middle of the storm, he wasn't so sure.

FOUR

Emily made her way to where Liam stood beside another agent. She recognized him but had never spoken to him before.

Liam took care of the introductions. "Emily Dixon, Jesse Sanderson."

Emily took the hand Jesse extended. "Pleasure to meet you."

"Likewise. You're Gil Dixon's sister." It wasn't a question.

"I am."

"How's he doing?" The way Jesse asked the question made Emily think he knew about the issues in Raleigh.

"Great."

Jesse winked at her. "I heard he fell in love."

"He did."

"Do you approve?"

"I do. We've known her since we were kids."

"He's happy?"

"Deliriously."

"Couldn't happen to a nicer guy. Is he going to take my head off when he finds out you're caught up in all this?"

"No." Emily felt her entire body wilt at the thought, and as nice as Jesse was, she couldn't stop herself from looking to Liam for some support. "Do we have to tell him?"

Liam didn't try to stop his grin. "We don't have to. But if you don't, don't blame us when he loses his mind. I don't know your brother, but if my sister was in this mess, I'd want to know."

"Oh, he'd want to know," Jesse confirmed. Someone called his name from across the room and he held up a hand, then turned back to her. "It was great to meet you. Tell your brother I'm keeping an eye on you, but now I won't be doing it from afar." Another wink, and he was gone.

Emily stared after him. "I'm going to kill him." She hadn't meant to say the words out loud.

"Jesse? What did he do?"

"Not Jesse. Gil. I knew he was way too nonchalant about me working with Mason. He's had Jesse keeping an eye on me."

"Ah." Liam pinched his lips together but didn't succeed in hiding his smile.

"It's not funny, Harper. My brother has no business messing with my professional life."

Liam's smile broke out in full. "Oh, come on, Em. He didn't. I've known Jesse for years, and he didn't mention anything to me. My guess is your brother was fully aware of the scuttlebutt regarding your patient, and he wanted to be sure you weren't being railroaded by the patient or the patient's family. Sounds to me like all he did was ask Jesse to keep an eye on you."

"Yeah. And report back. And not let me know Jesse was doing anything." She could almost feel steam coming from her ears.

"Em."

Since when did Liam call her Em? And since when did the way he said her name calm her? She couldn't bring herself to look at him, because who knew what he might see in her expression. "What?"

"Baby, look at me. Please."

He'd called her baby earlier, but that had been in an intense situation. She'd assumed it had slipped out. But there was no way it was an accident this time. And when she looked at him, there was no way she was going to be able to hide how much she liked it.

She should have been less worried about her expression and more worried about his. There was tenderness in his eyes. Amusement on his lips. And a bit of drama going on with the way he had one eyebrow raised. She couldn't speak, but thankfully he didn't seem to need her to.

"Please allow me to speak on behalf of brothers everywhere. The good ones will never leave you alone, will always stick their noses in your business, and will hold a secret desire to wrap you in Bubble Wrap. And with everything your brother's been through lately, you can't blame him for looking for ways to protect the people he loves. Especially his sister."

"How am I supposed to argue with that?"

To his credit, Liam didn't gloat or laugh. "You can't. And you should probably shoot him a text that says, 'No matter what you hear, I'm fine.' Because"—he inclined his head in Jesse's direction—"you'll want to beat Jesse to the punch."

Emily pulled her phone from her back pocket. "Fine. I'll text him. But he's going to lose his mind. He'll drive to DC tonight, and I won't be home, and it will get messy."

"Why won't you be home?"

"Mrs. Lawson asked me to stay with the family."

"And you agreed?" This was hissed more than spoken.

"How could I not? I can assure you, my boss falls all over himself to accommodate the family. Whatever they ask for, they get. And that means everyone else on my patient list just got booted to other therapists or asked to wait."

"Emily, you should take the opportunity to go home. Whatever this is, it isn't going to go away by tomorrow."

"I know. But I like feeling useful. And this is a way for me—"

"To get hurt or killed when a ceiling crashes into you or the room you're in is razed by bullets."

"I'll be fine. You'll protect me." Liam's eyes widened, and Emily ran the words back over in her mind. She'd done it again. What was wrong with her? Why did she lose her ability to speak in coherent and logical sentences whenever she was alone with him? "I mean . . . you know . . . you, as in all of you, all the agents. Because you aren't going to lose anyone in the family, and I'll be with the family, so . . ." She shut up because all she was doing was making it worse.

Liam leaned toward her, and once again, his lips brushed her ear as he whispered, "Just so we're clear. I'm fine with you trusting *me* to protect you. I'm *not* fine with you trusting any of the rest of these yahoos."

It was entirely possible that her ear had caught on fire. And now he was looking at her like he was expecting a response.

"O-Okay."

"Good. With that said, I think this is a mistake and you should go home. Being protected from danger is great. Not being in danger in the first place? Much better."

He had a point. But Mrs. Lawson had been quite convincing. Emily wasn't naive or desperate enough to believe all the things Mrs. Lawson said. She was the Second Lady, but everyone knew the VP wouldn't be the VP if it wasn't for her. The woman was a consummate politician, and she knew how to get her way. But despite the fact that Emily knew full well she was being played, she couldn't deny the delight in feeling like she could make a difference. It was a small thing, but Mason Lawson needed people around him who would help him heal—physically and emotionally.

"I have to help, Liam."

"You don't."

She hadn't been able to stop her brother's decline into depression and darkness after his injury. Hadn't been aware it was happening until it was almost too late. But she could make sure Mason Lawson healed and went on to play golf and live a full life.

"I want to."

"Why?"

"I have a pathological need to be needed." She spoke flippantly, but the words weren't far from the truth.

Liam didn't argue further. What he did do was keep her within arm's reach for the next thirty minutes, and when they once again loaded into an SUV for the drive to the safe house, she found herself sandwiched between him and Mason.

Both of them wearing matching frowns and emitting a vibe that could only be described as "seriously ticked off."

———

Liam glanced at the phone Emily held in her hand. He wasn't trying to read over her shoulder, but he couldn't help but see the text stream. The date stamp indicated it was from this morning.

> Give her a hug for me.

What about me?

> I'll be there in 3 days. I'll hug you then.

Too long.

> I love you too.

Liam had never met Special Agent Gil Dixon, but he could tell from that tiny snippet that the man adored his sister.

Tell me you are safe in your office.

Emily?

???

Based on the last comment, time stamped ten minutes earlier, he'd already heard about what was happening in DC.

Emily was typing in a message.

I'm safe. I'll send more when I can.

Three dots appeared immediately. Gil Dixon had obviously been waiting on her reply.

Who are you with?

My client and his agents. I know you're worried. I'm sorry. But that's all I can say.

Do whatever they tell you to do. I mean it, Em. If they tell you to hit the floor, you do it and you'd better not worry about getting dirty or breaking a nail. I'll pay for the manicure.

Emily stuck her tongue out at her phone.

Liam bit back a chuckle. Mason laughed outright. So he wasn't the only one who'd been reading Emily's texts.

She flipped her phone over and turned to Mason. "It's rude to read someone's phone."

"I couldn't help it. You had it out there for us to see. What did you expect me to do?" Mason's teasing didn't hold his usual belligerence. This was gentler and more cajoling.

Emily turned from Mason to Liam. "You were reading too?"

"Kid has a point, Em. It was hard not to see it."

"You like manicures?" This came from Mason.

"Yes." Emily's response was curt. A smart man would've left it at that. But Mason was young, and he hadn't yet learned what that tone meant.

"Why?"

Emily's response was three long, slow inhales and exhales. "Mason, there are a lot of different women in the world. Some love to be outdoors in nature. They love hiking and kayaking and sleeping under the stars. Some women are athletic. They love to swing a bat or a racket or dribble a basketball. They get a great deal of enjoyment from it even though they are hot and sweaty and their bodies are screaming for mercy."

"Okay." Mason threw a glance to Liam, eyes wide. Yeah. He'd figured out that he'd messed up. There was nothing to be done now but to let it ride.

"Those women are lovely. I'm friends with several of them. I"—Emily waved her hand from her head to her knees—"am not that type of woman. I like soft things. Warm things. Comfortable things. I like to look nice, whether that's my hair or my nails or my makeup or my clothes. My idea of a great day is waking up in the morning, then sipping my coffee while reading for a few hours. After lunch, I'd love to go shopping, followed by a nice dinner out. When I get home, I'd curl up in my coziest pajamas in my cushiest chair and read a book until bedtime. Please note that almost all of this takes place in a climate-controlled environment, which means the only time I'm in danger of sweating is when I walk from my car to the restaurant."

"So," Mason summarized, "you don't like to sweat and you really like to read."

"Essentially."

"I hate to have to tell you this, Emily, but all that reading? Sounds boring."

Emily was gentle when she replied. "Some people—a lot of people, actually—think golf is boring."

"Golf is awesome."

"Reading is awesome."

Liam kept his mouth shut throughout this exchange, but his mind was whirling. Did she think he only wanted to be with someone who shared his love of the outdoors and would want to go hiking with him all the time?

If that's what she thought, she couldn't be more wrong.

"Do you read?" The question came from Mason and was clearly directed at Liam.

"Yeah."

"A lot?"

"Define 'a lot.'"

"How many books have you read this year?"

"I don't know off the top of my head. I'd say thirty to forty."

Mason and Emily both turned to him. Mason was shocked. Emily was . . . pleased?

"You'd have to be reading close to a book a week to have read that many." Mason wasn't buying it.

"That sounds about right. It's probably more. While my ideal day wouldn't quite match Emily's, I also enjoy starting my morning with a cup of coffee and some reading. And if I'm home, I read in the evenings and usually before bed."

"Why?"

"Why not?"

"I hate to read."

"You just haven't found the right book." Liam and Emily

said this at the same time, then Emily turned to him, eyes wide with wonder and that something else Liam kept seeing from her. He wanted to believe it was affection, but he wasn't certain yet.

"New mission parameters, Agent Harper." Emily said this with a wicked grin that she shared with him before turning it on Mason. "*You* keep him alive. *I* fix his shoulder. But *we* turn him into a reader."

Liam nudged her shoulder. "What would you suggest he read first?"

The rest of the hour-long ride was spent tossing out book suggestions, asking Mason about his likes and dislikes, bonding over childhood classics they both enjoyed, and arguing through laughter over the ones they disagreed about.

By the time they pulled through the iron gates that blocked the half-mile driveway, Liam had learned more about Emily Dixon than he'd been able to glean in the past several months. He owed Mason big-time.

FIVE

Emily took the hand Liam offered and climbed from the SUV. There was no time to admire the house because she and Mason were hustled inside and all but shoved into the interior of the home, then left standing in the middle of an opulent living room while Liam, Jesse, and the other agents secured everything.

Ten minutes later, Mrs. Lawson, Mason, Lisa Goldman, and several staff members were settled on sofas and chairs when Jesse and Liam returned to the room. Emily had declined to sit and instead leaned against the back wall. Liam joined her as Jesse addressed the group. "Your rooms are ready, and your agents will show you where you'll be sleeping tonight. We have a fully stocked kitchen but no chef, so for tonight you'll be on your own. Feel free to use whatever's available. Please stay inside the house at all times, and please do not share this location with anyone."

While the others talked among themselves and spoke with the agents who continued to stream into the room, Jesse made his way to where Emily stood and gave her a smile. "Emily, I talked to Gil on the way here." That explained why Gil had stopped pestering her via text. He'd found a more reliable source of information. "He's not happy, but he won't be bugging you."

"Am I supposed to thank you for your collusion in this matter?" Emily didn't try to hide her annoyance.

"Nope. Gil told me you'd be ticked. Also told me he didn't care, and that you flamed huge and flamed out fast."

Emily gave Jesse what she knew was a fake smile. "There are rules about murdering your twin. Right?"

"'Fraid so, beautiful." Jesse grinned broadly.

Liam stood to her left, close enough that their shoulders brushed. "Enough, Sanderson. You're in touch with her brother. We get it. Don't you have work to do? Maybe a SLOTUS to protect?"

Jesse winked at Emily before he backed away to rejoin the others. "You get tired of hanging around with Trusty Rusty, come find me."

Liam didn't move, but Emily got the distinct impression that Trusty Rusty was not a nickname he liked. She could leave it alone, or she could be nosy and try to figure out what was going on. Once Jesse was out of earshot, she whispered, "Trusty Rusty?"

His response was a grunt. "Let's get you in a room."

Mason joined them as they moved to the stairs. "Mom says your room is beside mine." He gave her a tight smile. "You should also know that she thinks the best use of my time would be intensive physical therapy."

Poor kid. "Does your mother realize that PT isn't a particularly pleasant experience?"

"No. She equates it to having a massage."

"Ms. Dixon?" There was no mistaking the command in the voice of the SLOTUS. Everyone stopped moving.

Emily had to lean around Mason to make eye contact with Mrs. Lawson. "Ma'am?"

As Mrs. Lawson approached, Mason and Liam both closed in on Emily as if they were protecting her from the Second Lady.

"Since you're here," she said, "one of the agents is in some pain. His back and neck were wrenched pretty significantly. I was wondering if you'd be willing to take a look."

"Of course, ma'am."

"Lovely." Mrs. Lawson turned to Liam. "Agent Harper, can you get a room secured for Ms. Dixon to work in? And then let the agents know they can come see her if they're having any discomfort."

Emily called on years of practice in staring contests with Gil and Ivy, contests she usually lost, and kept her expression neutral despite the audacity of Mrs. Lawson's request.

"Mom." Mason hissed the word. "Emily isn't here to treat everyone in the place."

Emily risked a glance at Liam and wished she hadn't. His neutral expression told her more than he probably realized. She knew that look. That was the look agents got when they were intentionally shutting down their emotions and personal feelings about a situation. Gil did that. Always annoyed her when he did. But she'd learned that when she saw that look, it didn't mean he didn't care.

It meant he cared so much that he didn't trust himself not to explode unless he locked himself down.

Liam Harper was currently locked down.

Mason Lawson, however, was not.

"Mom, she's not our personal physical therapist. She's been scooped up in all this mess, but she has a job and a life that I'm sure she would like to return to as soon as possible. While she's here, she shouldn't have to take care of everyone with a mild twinge."

"Mason Lawson." Mrs. Lawson's tone said she brooked no argument. "I'm not asking her to take care of everyone in the building. Just the ones who would otherwise be seeking medical attention but are currently unable to do so because of their presence here."

"Yes, Mom. I realize that." Mason's patronizing tone set Emily's teeth on edge, but Mrs. Lawson either didn't notice it or was so used to it that it didn't faze her anymore. "But maybe you should have asked Emily before you assumed she would do this. You shouldn't take advantage of her."

Before Emily could respond, Mrs. Lawson was called by Goldman. "We'll discuss this later."

Emily looked from Mason to Liam. Liam bumped Mason with his elbow. "Well done."

"It won't change anything." Mason stared after his mother. "She thinks everyone will do whatever she says to do because she's—"

"The Second Lady." Emily placed a hand on his arm. "It's okay, Mason. Let's go locate the rooms and then find the agent with the tweaked back. Your mother may have gone about it wrong, but she was right about one thing. If there are injuries I can help ease, I'll do it and do so gladly. It would be selfish of me to sit in my room while people are hurting."

"You're too nice, Emily." Mason held out his arm, a gesture he'd undoubtedly learned in the etiquette classes his mom had insisted he participate in.

She tucked her hand in the crook at his elbow and gave him a grin. "I'll remind you of that in a few hours when I get ahold of that shoulder."

Mason finally gave her a real smile and Liam relaxed, marginally, as they found the rooms they'd been assigned, then went in search of the injured agent.

Three hours later, Liam brought Emily a bottle of water. Since word had spread that a physical therapist was in lockdown with them, she'd had a steady stream of patients.

Some of them, Jesse Sanderson included, had not one single thing wrong with them. They just wanted a chance to talk to the pretty PT who'd been coming in for months but had never given anyone a second glance. Mason had set himself up as Emily's personal bodyguard, and Liam had no plans to dissuade the young man from his mission.

"Thanks." Emily took the bottle and drank half of it. "Unless you know of someone with a legit injury, I think it's time to close the clinic. I'd like to finish Mason's session from earlier today." She exchanged a meaningful glance with Mason before casually adding, "And your neck needs to be checked, Agent Harper. Don't think I've forgotten."

Oh no.

Mason groaned, then laughed. "Can I stay in here while you work on Liam?"

Emily straightened and looked down her nose in a prim and proper expression. "That's up to Agent Harper, Mr. Lawson. A patient has a right to be treated privately."

Mason scoffed. "He sits in on all of my treatments."

"That's different." Emily narrowed her eyes and pursed her lips, the effect making her look like some type of angry teacher, except for the twitching lips that gave away her humor. "I could hurt you, and Liam's job is to be sure I don't."

Mason cowered in mock terror. "Now it's clear to me. But all the more reason for me to stay close. I'd hate for you to damage my favorite agent."

The words hit Liam in a soft spot he didn't realize he had,

and he turned quickly to close the door. It wouldn't be appropriate for Mason to realize how his words had landed.

"Since he's your favorite, I'll be gentle with him." Emily's vow was solemn and sincere, and then she burst into laughter. "Come on, you two. Let's get everyone treated and call it a day."

Liam stood at the door as Emily guided Mason through the exercises and stretches she'd planned for him that day. The kid winced more than once. Emily never failed to acknowledge Mason's pain, but rather than stopping, she encouraged, teased, and whispered goofy comments that often had Mason grinning through the grimace.

Then it was Liam's turn.

"I'm fine."

"Special Agent Harper. Sit down." Emily pointed to the chair Mason had vacated moments earlier.

Liam sat. But he wasn't relaxed. How could he be with Emily standing mere inches away and preparing to put her hands on his neck?

He forced himself to sit perfectly still when her fingers brushed his shoulder, but then her breath tickled his ear. If he didn't take his mind off the heat he could feel coming from her body, there was no way he wouldn't pull her into his arms and kiss her until he no longer cared about his neck or that someone had attacked the VP res or that they were currently in a safe house or that Mason was standing three feet away watching him with a knowing smirk that did not belong on the face of a sixteen-year-old.

Mason's presence gave Liam willpower and an infusion of energy. Enough that he managed to draw Emily into a conversation about the anatomy of the neck, which seemed like a safe enough body part to discuss.

And for the next twenty minutes, he followed Emily's instructions and kept his focus on her words, not her touch.

Then Mason's phone dinged. The SLOTUS had sent a text and requested that Mason join her for a FaceTime with the VPOTUS. "Emily"—Mason pointed a finger at her as he left the room—"he needs to be in one piece when I get back."

"I'll do my best."

And then they were alone.

Emily's strong hands slid from his neck to work a tight muscle in his back that she'd already explained was part of the reason his neck was so stiff. He couldn't see her face, but she let out a frustrated grunt and mumbled, "This would be so much easier if we had a bed."

Her entire body went solid beside him, and then the words tumbled out. "I mean, because your back, your muscles are so hard, and it's difficult to get the muscles to cooperate when you're sitting and . . . oh, oh, just forget it."

"I'm never going to forget this." Liam couldn't help but laugh, not at her but at the obvious discomfort his teasing had caused her. Maybe she wasn't as ambivalent about touching him as she appeared.

She returned to her attempts to make his muscles cooperate, but he heard her low chuckle followed by a slow inhale and exhale, as if she was trying to pull herself together.

She succeeded and kept their conversation focused on the intricacies of the nerves in the back and neck until she stepped away from him ten minutes later. "I'll need to work on you again. Tomorrow. First thing. But you'll be fine."

Under her watchful gaze, he slowly rotated his neck in a circle, then shrugged his shoulders up and down, then twisted his back a few times. Everything felt loose and relaxed. "You're amazing."

"Don't sound so surprised."

"I'm not." He'd been serious and didn't like the way she kept forcing things to be fun and light between them. He cleared his throat and held her gaze even as he dropped his voice low. "I just never imagined I'd be on the receiving end of your touch."

Her eyes flashed with something that wasn't humor. It was something much worse. Unless he was mistaken, it was fear.

Not the reaction he'd been going for. Why would she be afraid of him?

Emily recovered from whatever she'd been experiencing and gathered her things. "I need to go freshen up before dinner." Her words held a distinct note of false casualness. "Mrs. Lawson informed me that I'm expected to dine with the family even though I'd much rather eat in my room. I don't know wh—"

"Emily." He wasn't sure what he was going to say. He just needed her to look at him and give him a chance to bridge the gap he could almost see forming between them.

"I'll see you later, Liam."

Short of grabbing her, which he would never do, there was nothing he could do to stop her as she slipped around him and out the door.

That had not gone well. Not at all.

SIX

Emily leaned against the door and closed her eyes. She would give just about anything right now to be able to talk to Ivy.

Gil would lose his mind.

Ivy would commiserate.

"I don't date agents." Emily whispered the words again as she ran her hands over the base of the lamp in search of the switch. "Agents get hurt." She found the switch, and soft light filtered over the bed. "Agents are lovely people. Dedicated. Focused. Salt of the earth. Some of my favorite people are agents." She turned off the overhead light in preparation for bedtime.

"But agents are also overbearing, type A, overprotective workaholics who will literally put themselves in front of a bullet for someone else and who make terrible partners."

Guilt shot through her patently false words.

Being with an agent had its challenges. Long hours. Frequent travel. Moving all over the country for new assignments. It wasn't an easy life.

But the agents she knew made wonderful partners. Gil would turn the world upside down for Ivy. Luke Powell, one of Gil's best friends and an agent in the Raleigh office, was engaged to an FBI agent. Both of them dedicated and driven, they had taken that same level of intensity and poured it into their relationship, and it had been beautiful to watch them become the couple they were now.

Then there was Zane and Tessa. If those two ever sorted themselves out, they would be amazing together.

And the new guy who was probably transferring soon. Benjamin North. He and his fiancée, Sharon, were so sweet together, it almost made her teeth hurt to be around them.

So, no, agents did *not* make bad partners. They made fabulous partners. The problem here wasn't Liam.

She was the problem. She wanted to be loved with the same type of intensity and devotion she saw from Gil, Luke, Benjamin, and even Zane.

She also didn't want to be constantly afraid her man wouldn't come home at the end of the day.

"No one who leaves their house is guaranteed a return trip." That's what Ivy had reminded her one night when Gil was working. *"I'd rather love Gil for however many days we're given than not have him at all. If I lose him again, I might not survive it. But"*—Ivy had flashed a wicked grin—*"when he's holding me, when we're dancing in the kitchen, when we're curled up on the porch swing talking about our days, I know there is nowhere else I want to be. The joy of having him is worth the risk of losing him."*

Emily flopped onto the bed. Liam Harper had been wriggling his way into her heart and mind for months. But her "no dating agents" rule had held, and she'd mostly convinced herself that he wasn't interested in her as anything more than a friend.

But today. Tonight. What he said. The way he looked at her. The way he called her *baby* when she was scared.

Was there any going back from this? Could they be just friends? More to the point, did she want to be just friends?

Or did she want to know that, when this situation was over,

he'd call her. They'd go out after work. They'd visit all the dives in the DC area until they found the best burger, the best pizza, and the best chocolate pie. Together.

Could she take the risk?

Could she live with the regret if she didn't?

Would it even matter tomorrow? Liam had inched that door open, and she'd slammed it shut. Would he try again? Or would she have to open the door and risk having him close it on *her*?

She ran her hands through her hair and groaned. Why was she so weird? She didn't have an answer when she slid into the lush sheets thirty minutes later. Before she could stop herself, she grabbed her phone from the nightstand and pulled up her last text with Liam.

> I've found the best sheets in the greater metropolitan DC area. They are on this bed. I must have them. How many weeks do you suppose I'll have to work to buy a set?

Based on the "Read 10:27 p.m." that flashed under her message, Liam saw it immediately. But there were no flickering dots to indicate that he was typing a reply. And an hour later when she switched the damp pillow she'd been using for the one on the other side of the bed, there'd been no response.

At 1:00 a.m., Liam stifled a yawn and took another lap around the perimeter of the house. He'd volunteered to take the first round of outside security. It wasn't ideal, but he'd be relieved soon and then he'd crash.

He enjoyed the protective detail. He even enjoyed Mason Lawson. But he missed the investigative side of this work. It chafed at him not to have a clue about what was happening with these attacks. Why had someone come after them? It was unlikely the attack was intended to take out the VP. The man worked twelve-hour days. Yesterday the family was going to meet him at a museum in DC for an appearance, and then he'd been scheduled to fly to Minnesota, so there would have been no reason to believe he'd be in the residence.

That left the SLOTUS. Or Mason. Injuries to either of them would definitely get the VP's attention. Liam disagreed with most of the VP's policies, and he believed the man was a workaholic who was sacrificing his family for his political aspirations.

Liam preferred the concept of both quality and quantity when it came to time with those he loved, and the VP fell short on quantity. But he excelled at quality. He brought Mrs. Lawson breakfast in bed on the weekends when they were home. And he'd made heroic efforts to be present at Mason's golf tournaments last year.

And Liam had seen the man break down when the doctors told him about Mason's injuries—a mixture of relief that they weren't more serious and heartbreak for his son.

If the objective was to put pressure on the VP or force him to resign, attacking the SLOTUS or Mason could get the job done.

Liam blew out a long breath as he scanned the area to the rear of the house and tried to shove the questions from his mind. A host of agents were investigating the attacks and hunting down the perpetrators. Liam's job was to keep Mason safe.

It wasn't to solve the crime.

It wasn't to get the girl either.

He'd seen Emily's text, but he'd had no idea what he was supposed to do with it. Was she trying to be funny? Was she apologizing for running away from taking their relationship to a different place? Attempting to pull them back to the casual friendship they'd been building?

What had he been thinking? He hadn't known her brother was an agent until yesterday. For all he knew, she might have a boyfriend. Or be planning to move to France in six weeks. How was he supposed to know?

He knew a lot about her, but did any of it matter? How important was it that he knew she was an Atlanta Braves fan and had been to games at most of the major league stadiums, that she'd never met a mall she didn't like, that she'd never said no to eating a burrito, that she had not one but four favorite yoga studios in DC, that she got a manicure every Wednesday at 5:30 p.m., and that her manicurist had invited her to her wedding in November?

Except it told him so much. She loved the Braves because her dad and her brother loved the game, and she'd wanted to be with them. And she still did. The three of them went to a game a few weeks ago—the three of them because family traditions mattered to her.

He knew about the burritos because she'd told him how she was mentoring a high school student and they went to the same Mexican restaurant every week, so she'd made it her mission to try every item on the menu. That's how she'd discovered that burritos were her favorite.

The yoga was because she loved deeply, and because of that love she carried a lot of worry for others and needed to release the stress.

The manicures. Okay, there wasn't much on that one, except for the fact that she'd been so friendly with the manicurist that they'd become fast friends.

Emily was beautiful, inside and out. Complicated. Maybe high maintenance. Absolutely worth it.

"Harper, got something on the east perimeter." Jesse Sanderson's voice came through the earwig, and Liam picked up his pace. "Colson and I are checking it. Stay close to the main house."

"Copy."

The radio was silent for two minutes.

"Harper. Back door. Now." That didn't sound good.

"Copy."

Liam wasn't surprised to find Mason Lawson slumped in a rocking chair on the porch and Jesse standing nearby. "Seriously?"

"I needed some fresh air."

"Do you realize that every agent on the property is on high alert?"

"Yes, but I didn't expect anyone would shoot me."

Liam couldn't do this right now. He was exhausted beyond belief, and all he wanted was sleep. "Mason. Get inside. Go to bed. Do not be surprised when I open your door in three minutes to be sure you're where you're supposed to be."

Mason rose and left without a word.

Jesse slapped him on the back. "Don't know how you do it."

"He's acting out."

"He's sixteen. Old enough to know better."

"True, but nothing about his life is normal. And I do think sometimes he needs fresh air. A little space. That was the whole point of the camping trip. To give him room to breathe."

"You're a good man. We've got everything covered. Go catch some z's."

"Roger that."

He went inside, and his first stop was Mason's room. He opened the door and walked all the way in. "That wasn't cool."

"I know."

"I want your word that you'll stay in this room until daylight. I need to sleep, and I can't do that if I'm worried about you roaming the grounds."

"I promise."

Fifteen minutes later, Liam closed his eyes on a prayer that everyone would survive the night and tomorrow would bring him a solution to the Emily situation.

SEVEN

Liam meant his prayers. He did. But he was utterly unprepared for the way God chose to answer.

At 6:30 a.m. he was awake and standing in the small room Jesse Sanderson had chosen to use as an office.

"You want me to take Mason and Emily camping?"

Jesse sat behind the desk he'd commandeered and grinned. "The car is packed and ready to go. You can leave this morning."

"You can't be serious."

Jesse held eye contact, and there was so much there. Worry. Anger. Frustration. Fatigue. Determination.

"You're serious."

"Think about it. This gets His Royal Hiney out of the picture, away from the social media followers, away from the danger. And"—Jesse's expression darkened—"we don't have to worry about him doing stupid stuff, like wandering around the property in the middle of the night. It makes SLOTUS happy, which makes everybody happy, and we can get on with the business of figuring out what is going on."

Liam couldn't argue with any of what Jesse said. But . . . "Why Emily? If Mason's not here, Emily could go home for the weekend."

Jesse's eyes cut to something behind Liam, his gaze tracking something—someone—and he didn't speak until whoever was back there left the room. "I don't have an explanation other than that my gut says if we send her home, we put her at risk. Which means I have to put someone on her. I don't have anyone to spare. But if I send her with you, she's protected while we get to the bottom of this. Not only that, but it will make SLOTUS happy, and it's obvious Mason has a crush on her, so he'll love it."

Liam absorbed Jesse's words. "What if she refuses? I won't force her to do anything, and this is not something she would enjoy. Emily's not the camping-and-fishing type."

"How do *you* know?" Jesse cocked his head to the side.

"I know."

"I'll get Mason to ask her." Jesse grinned. "Or better yet, I'll mention it to SLOTUS."

Liam clenched his jaw. If the SLOTUS asked, Emily would say yes. And part of him, a big part of him, wanted this. He'd been hoping for coffee, dinner, a date—anything that would give him more time with Emily. Jesse was offering him a weekend with her. But this wasn't how he had wanted it to happen. "I don't want her manipulated."

"I'll manipulate her every day and twice on Sunday if it keeps her alive." Jesse's tone was a honed blade, slicing through all arguments and effectively closing the discussion.

"Fine. If she agrees, I'll take her."

"You won't have the full complement of agents we'd planned. But the area has already been cleared, and the three agents in place will remain there through the weekend."

Liam held Jesse's gaze. "What if we're putting her *in* danger rather than protecting her *from* danger?"

"Why would she be in danger? You'll be in the middle of a forest. I guess she *could* get eaten by a bear . . ."

"Not funny."

Jesse grinned. "I don't have another agent better equipped to protect Mason, or Emily, in the wilderness. I have every confidence that you can handle whatever nature throws at you. And while you're doing that, we'll get to the bottom of this. Whatever this is. The investigative teams are losing their minds. This came out of nowhere. No chatter. Nothing that would give them reason to suspect an imminent threat. No one has claimed responsibility."

It was the worst-case scenario. The Secret Service followed up on all threats, no matter how insignificant they seemed. Agents watched social media feeds, internet posts, videos, and chats. Most people who wanted to take out a politician didn't have the good sense to keep it quiet.

But Vice President Lawson was the most popular VP in decades. Midway through his second term as senator and five years after the death of his first wife, he'd met a Maryland lawyer, Heather Carver. Their romance was a political strategist's dream come true. Fifteen years younger, the feisty attorney was neither impressed nor intimidated by Senator Lawson and turned him down five times before finally agreeing to a date.

Six months after their first dinner, they were married. Mason came along a year later. Seventeen years had passed since their wedding, and the vice president was a shoo-in for the presidential nomination. Reporters and investigators had tried to find dirt on the man. There had to be some. He was a politician, after all. But if the Lawsons had skeletons in their closet, they were hidden behind a façade of love and laughter. With his approval ratings at an all-time high, it appeared nothing could stop him from attaining the highest office in the land.

Was that what this was about? An attempt to shake up the

political power structure during an election cycle? Or was there something else? Something personal. Something deadly.

Emily woke from a dream so random that it could best be described as the love child of Cirque du Soleil and NASCAR. She climbed from the bed, took several long pulls from the bottle of water on the nightstand, and dropped into her morning stretching routine.

As her mind cleared, she listened for sounds coming from the rest of the house, which had to have been built well and probably didn't allow for much sound to carry. A scraping sound that might have come from the kitchen. Low murmurs of conversation too muffled to understand.

Firm steps in the hall that stopped outside her room.

She waited for a knock, but it didn't come.

She'd slept fully clothed, and now she reached for her shoes and slipped them on. Then she pulled her hair into a low ponytail, securing it with the hair tie that had remained on her wrist since yesterday.

A definite creak of floorboards on the other side of her door.

She should have brushed her teeth before stretching. Too late now. Whatever was coming, she was as ready to face it as she could be.

The knock, when it finally came, was three firm taps. She opened the door to a frowning Liam. "Good morning."

"Morning."

He sounded . . . off. Definitely not his normally enthusiastic and teasing self. "What's wrong?"

Liam's lips twitched. "Seriously? Should I give you a list?"

She didn't dignify his sarcasm with a response, but she did

step back, and he entered the room. "Aside from the obvious, you look mad."

"I'm not happy."

"Care to share?"

He dropped his head. "I probably shouldn't be here, but I couldn't let you be blindsided."

"That sounds ominous."

Liam gave her a fake smile. "It is."

"Give it to me straight, doc. Don't sugarcoat it."

He fought the battle with his lips and lost. This time the smile he gave her was reluctant but real. "Are you always such a smarty pants?"

"No, but it comes out a lot when I'm nervous. I default to making jokes or snide remarks because I'm avoiding reality."

"You're incredible."

The two words, spoken softly but fervently, made her insides fizz. She didn't need fizzy insides. Not around Liam. But she couldn't stop her reaction, and when he reached for her hands, she met him halfway.

"When you get downstairs, the SLOTUS is going to ask you to go on the camping trip with us."

This was too much. Sweet words. Holding hands. And then a request so far out of left field that Emily couldn't make any sense of it. "I'm sorry?" She'd heard him wrong. She was dreaming. That's what this was. Another bizarre mashup her subconscious was doling out in that weird place between sleep and waking.

"The camping trip. It's on. And the SLOTUS is going to ask you to go with us."

"I don't . . . what?" It was too early for confusing conversations. Why would anyone think she would want to go camping? "Is *she* going?"

"No. It would be you, me, and Mason, with a few other agents nearby providing security."

"Does she hate me?"

Liam's response was a quick shake of his head.

"Then what?"

"We're stretched thin. Under the circumstances, my bosses aren't comfortable sending you home without protection, but we don't have any spare agents. If you come with us, you'll be safe, and—"

"Gil can—"

"I mentioned that. It was a no."

Wait a minute. "You don't want me to go?"

"Em." Liam's thumbs made slow sweeps across her hands. "I would love to go camping with you."

He sounded like he meant that.

"But, baby," he said, his voice gentling further, "you don't like to be outside. You don't like to be cold. You don't like dirt."

"True."

He wasn't done. "We're backpacking to the campsite. Carrying everything in—tents, sleeping bags, food, etc."

"Right."

"That means no electricity. No toilets. No showers."

EIGHT

No toilets. Lovely." Emily tried not to let her distaste show. "Tell me again why you do this?"

"If you say yes, I'll show you."

"I have a choice?"

"Of course. It's a free country. You can't be forced to do this."

"I can survive anything for three days." There was one big problem, though. "I don't have anything to wear."

Liam didn't try to hide his amusement. "I see how it is. No toilets. Yuck. But the wrong outfit? Horror!"

"I'm dressed for fall in DC. Indoors. Not three nights in the woods."

"We'll find you some clothes."

"Awesome."

"And shoes."

"Great." She couldn't meet his eyes. How could she explain her roiling emotions? It wasn't that she didn't want to go camping, although she could have easily gone the rest of her life without adding that to her list of experiences. Not only would Liam think she was a pampered princess, but she would be nothing but a hindrance. How could she be helpful when she had no clue how to pitch a tent or start a fire or . . . anything!

"Em?"

"Hmm?"

He squeezed her hands.

"You okay, baby?"

"Peachy." She caught herself before she burrowed into his chest. What was she doing? She pulled her hands away and took a step back. "I'll pretend I'm surprised when she asks."

"Em—" His phone buzzed. "Sorry. A second." He answered the call. "Harper."

Emily took the opportunity to increase the distance between them and grabbed her phone from the nightstand, but in the small space she couldn't help but hear the male voice on the other end of the phone. "Need you down here for a few minutes. Gotta get everything finalized."

"Yeah," Liam grumbled into the phone. "Be there in a sec." He disconnected the call.

"I'm guessing this establishment doesn't have room service." Emily tried to smile through her lame joke. "Is there coffee downstairs?"

"Yes." Liam slid his phone into his pocket, then put his hands on his hips. "Emmy, baby. It's going to be okay."

The way he said her name and called her *baby*. The way he looked at her like he knew her and liked what he knew. All of it melted her from the inside out. If she could freeze this moment, she would.

Because after this camping fiasco was over, he would never look at her the same way again.

Liam fought his instincts and kept his hands at his hips even though what he wanted to do was pull Emily into his arms and hold her until she trusted him with whatever was eating her up inside right now.

He couldn't get a read on her, but something was very wrong. She wasn't thrilled about the camping. No surprise there. But this was something more.

He didn't yet have the right to know all her secrets.

But he wanted that right. And he was tired of waiting to see if she would give him a chance. "When this is over, can I take you to dinner?"

Emily's expression went from confused to amused to something else. That something else had acid churning in his gut.

"Maybe you should wait until this is over to ask that."

"Why?"

"Spending three days in the woods with me might change your mind."

He closed the distance between them, crowding her but not touching her. "Not gonna happen."

"We'll see."

"You still haven't answered my question." It would have soothed his ego if she'd smiled radiantly and said, "Yes!" Instead, the only woman he wanted to spend time with looked like she was preparing for battle. Her shoulders were tense. Her mouth tight, lips pulled into a flat line, eyes wary.

She shook her head, and on the heels of the crushing realization that she was going to turn him down came the alarming awareness that he wasn't going to give up.

She studied the carpet. "I'll hurt you."

If she was worried about hurting him, she cared. "I'm tough." He reached for her hands, and when she allowed him to hold them, he kept going. "Give us a chance."

"I won't hold you to this, Liam. But when this is over, if you do ask me again, I'll say yes."

He released one hand and used his free hand to tilt her chin up. "I'm not as magnanimous as you. Don't say it if you don't mean it, because I will hold you to it."

That earned him a flicker of a smile. "Good."

Good? So she wanted him to hold her to *her* promise, but she wouldn't hold him to *his*? This woman was full of contradictions and mysteries. She would drive him bonkers.

He couldn't wait.

NINE

Six hours later, Emily twisted in the passenger seat to grin at Mason.

"What?" he half snarled, half laughed at her.

"Just checking on you. You've been without your phone for thirty minutes. I was afraid you might be experiencing withdrawal symptoms."

She was stunned that Mason had agreed to Liam's rules for this trip. No cell phones. No electronics. He had agreed to battery-powered flashlights, but otherwise everything was manual.

"Two and a half days living with nature. Nothing else." Liam's eyes had glowed, and if she hadn't been joining them on this trip, she would've been delighted to see him so happy and content.

She glanced at her wrist, again. She kept forgetting she'd left her watch, along with her phone, with Talia, the female agent who had been her personal camping fairy. After a brief phone conversation where Emily had given up her height, weight, and clothing sizes, Talia showed up at the safe house with well-worn boots, hiking pants, thermal shirts, sweaters, a jacket, and gloves. She also brought new undergarments, still in their packaging, and new socks because, *"Nobody should have to borrow that stuff. They're going to drag you into the woods for three days, they can make sure you have clean drawers."*

True that.

The clothes weren't anything Emily would wear.

Ever.

But they were comfortable. They also fit, and they appeared to be rugged enough to handle whatever Liam had planned for them.

If Liam still wanted to go out with her when this was over, she would never need to wonder if he was only with her for her looks or fashion sense.

But one thing refused to stop niggling at her. An incessant worry worm burrowing through her mind. What if he did like her this way? With boots and thermal shirts and hair all disheveled, as it surely would be tomorrow? Because that wasn't who she was.

"What's on your mind?" Liam cut his eyes to her, then put them back where they belonged. On the road.

"Nothing much."

"Liar."

"I beg your pardon."

"You let out a huge sigh. Which I chose to ignore. But then you did it again."

"You did," Mason chimed in from the back seat.

She hadn't meant to sigh. "You'll both have to be patient with me. I'm not an expert outdoorswoman."

"I'm not an expert outdoors*man*." Mason didn't sound upset about that. "That's kind of the point. Liam's the expert. It will be different. We might hate it. We might like it. Either way, we aren't at home, we aren't dealing with the fallout from whatever the heck that was yesterday, and we don't have to see Lisa Goldman for three days."

Emily couldn't let that go. "You really don't like her."

"How could you tell?" Mason shrugged. "She's creepy. I can't figure out why Mom and Dad hired her."

Emily didn't like her either, but she couldn't fault the woman for her ability to manage the day-in, day-out schedule of the Second Lady. "She's excellent at her job."

"I don't trust her."

Liam hadn't moved, but Emily could sense his focus funneling straight to the back seat.

"Can I ask you why?" Emily intentionally gentled her voice. "Is it because she's not Macy?" The previous chief of staff, Macy Williams, had been with the SLOTUS for a decade. She started out as an assistant, and her responsibilities had increased along with the Lawsons' political power. She was very much part of the family. But she'd gone on leave six months ago after the discovery of aggressive breast cancer. Two months later, she resigned. She was now receiving hospice services and not expected to live to Christmas.

"Please don't try to do some kind of mental therapy on me now, Tiny Tyrant." Mason ran a hand through his hair. "Of course I miss Macy. But Lisa is up to something."

"I think at this point, anyone associated with your family has their eyes on the White House. Some political posturing is to be expected."

"Yeah, maybe." Mason pulled a small book from his backpack. "How much longer? An hour?"

"Ninety minutes." Liam tapped the GPS. "Then we hike."

"Awesome. I'm going to try to read this and see what all the fuss is about," Mason said. Emily had found an entire set of The Chronicles of Narnia in the living room of the safe house. The three of them had divvied up the set and stashed the books in their packs.

The fact that Liam was a reader and loved C. S. Lewis had done a number on her. How was she supposed to resist a man who loved Narnia? It was too much.

Mason opened the book and focused on the pages.

Emily turned back to the front and settled deeper into her seat. Mason didn't need to say "I don't want to talk anymore" for her to get the point. But that didn't mean she planned to let it go.

She had questions for Liam, but she couldn't ask them now. She closed her eyes. *Lord, I'm so far out of my league right now. Please help me not to make a fool out of myself. To find a way to contribute this weekend and not be a drain. Be with the agents in DC who are trying to get to the bottom of these attacks. Protect everyone involved.*

Liam pulled into the parking lot at the trailhead. The two-hour drive had gone without incident. He didn't think Mason or Emily realized they hadn't been alone on the road. They wouldn't be alone on the camping trip either. The VPOTUS and SLOTUS wanted Mason to get the experience of roughing it for a few days, but that didn't mean they didn't want him protected in every way possible.

Mason leaned toward him and whispered, "Should we wake her?"

They both looked to the passenger seat, where Emily had nodded off an hour earlier.

"I think she'll wake up when we start unloading."

With that, he and Mason exited the SUV and pulled their packs from the back.

Emily joined them a minute later.

"Hey, sleepyhead." Liam winked at her.

Emily's response was a scrunched nose followed by a yawn. Then she raised her arms above her head before bending at the waist and touching the ground. When she was upright again, she gave Mason an appraising look. "You need to stretch too." Her gaze moved to Liam. "Wouldn't hurt you either. I don't want all my hard work going to waste."

Was it his imagination, or was there some genuine affection in her grumbly demand? "Yes, ma'am."

Mason snorted. Emily rolled her eyes.

Liam set a small backpack on the ground beside a quiver and bow. Emily's eyes lit with surprise. "What is that?"

Mason grinned. "We found it at the house and thought you'd like to shoot some while we're out here."

Emily's smile, which Liam had rarely seen in the past twenty-four hours, stayed in place as they unloaded the SUV and settled backpacks on their shoulders.

Seeing her delight, he was tempted to correct Mason's use of the word *we*, but he kept his mouth shut. His restraint was rewarded a few minutes later when Emily nudged his shoulder and whispered, "Thank you for bringing the bow."

"You're welcome."

She shifted under the weight of her pack. "I promise not to be a burden. I don't have a clue what to do, but I won't be in the way, and I won't complain."

"You could never be a burden."

"You say that now . . ." Her words were light and teasing, but there was an undercurrent of anxiety Liam couldn't ignore.

"If you keep worrying, I'm going to start to think you don't trust me."

"I trust you plenty. But I'm the interloper in this scenario. I'm crashing your boys' bonding weekend, and I'm not pulling my weight. This pack"—she bounced the pack on her back—"is way too light compared to the behemoth you're carrying. Mason's pack is double the size of mine. And he has the bow."

"Mason is a sixteen-year-old boy. He's an athlete. He has energy to spare. If we don't load him up and wear him out, he'll be going wide open tonight and we'll be listening to him ramble about golf, video games, golf, the NFL, and did I mention golf?"

"Valid point." She walked to the front of the SUV. "Let's go camping!"

They took a few minutes to look at the trail map, and Liam explained how he would use the compass and what they could expect to see over the next few hours. "We're going to be on a well-traveled trail for the first hour, but then we'll be headed to a primitive camping area that isn't heavily used." He didn't mention that on the off chance anyone decided to hike in their direction, they would respectfully but firmly be encouraged to find a different spot.

"Have you been there before?" Emily asked as they approached the trailhead.

"Of course."

"When?"

"A few weeks ago. Recon. Didn't want any surprises."

"Didn't you say there's a spring?" Mason asked from behind him.

"There is. And a nice spot for pitching a tent, or a hammock."

For the first few miles, they chatted about hiking, Liam's last trip to Wyoming, and random facts about the flora and fauna native to the area. Mason asked most of the questions. Liam did most of the talking, but Emily chimed in every now and then.

He kept a close eye on her. She wasn't out of breath, her arm didn't seem to be bothering her, she wasn't struggling to keep up, and as far as he could tell, she wasn't freaking out as every step took them farther away from civilization.

TEN

Emily listened to the conversation between Mason and Liam, amazed by the depth of knowledge Liam possessed and the lack of attitude coming from Mason. She'd have to mention it to Liam later. They needed to make more efforts in the future to get that boy out of DC and into nature.

She had no idea what time it was, where she was, or how far they'd walked. But to her surprise, she didn't hate it. Not yet anyway. The fall weather was perfection. A hint of a bite in the air, blue skies that looked like they'd been streaked with marshmallow cream, and every now and then a breeze that flirted with her hair before disappearing behind the trees.

The hike had a few inclines, but nothing she couldn't handle. She'd been warned that this afternoon's hike would be moderate, but the hike planned for tomorrow was more strenuous.

She'd deal with tomorrow . . . tomorrow.

For now, her goal was simple: don't make them regret bringing her along.

As she walked, she lost count of how many times she reached for the phone that wasn't in her pocket. She didn't care about social media updates, but she did want to know what was happening with the investigation into the attacks. Not that there would've been much about it in the press. If anything, security was so tight that there was a good chance the wider world had no idea about the danger that had stalked the vice president's family this week.

It didn't make sense to her. Why attack the house when the vice president wasn't at home? Why another attack at the safe house? What was the goal? Was it to kill someone? If so, it was badly planned and poorly executed.

But what if death wasn't the goal? What if it was about distraction? What if it was about fear?

Emily couldn't see anything stopping the vice president's ascension to the White House. But if Mrs. Lawson was injured? Or if Mason was threatened? Would that be enough? Maybe.

If they were killed?

Honestly, she wasn't sure. She had no doubt the vice president loved his family. But he was ambitious, and he was closer than ever to realizing the ultimate achievement in his chosen profession. He might be zealous enough to use the tragedy to his advantage.

She rejected the thought as soon as it entered her mind. Not only because it was reprehensible, but because he simply didn't need it.

So, what other reason could there be? Had Mrs. Lawson ticked someone off? Emily could see that happening. The SLOTUS was no wallflower. To Emily's knowledge, no one had ever seen Heather Lawson lose her cool. She'd never snapped at a reporter. Never thrown a tantrum in front of her staff.

One of the worst-kept secrets in DC was that if the SLOTUS took a shine to you, she would throw her support behind your business, your charity, or whatever was meaningful to you.

But she was also famously intransigent. If she didn't like you, she would never be rude, but her silence about you or your cause said all that needed to be said.

Even the vice president knew better than to try to change her mind once she'd decided on a course of action. The only person who'd had any success over the years had been Macy, but without Macy running the show, had Mrs. Lawson's stubborn streak put her on the wrong side of some dangerous people?

Ahead of her, Liam stepped to the side of the trail and waited for Emily and Mason to join him. "We're about a quarter mile from the point where we'll leave this trail and head north-northeast for another mile. The path will become a lot more strenuous. There are a few places where we'll need to climb ladders and one stretch where the path is on the edge of an overhang, and you'll need to hang on to a rope for safety."

"Cool." Mason grabbed a branch and pulled it down to tap on the top of Emily's head. "I'm ready to get to our campsite so I can make fun of Emily trying to put up a tent."

"Congratulations, Mason. I never had a younger brother, and I used to think I wanted one. You've cured me."

They laughed, and Liam told Mason to take the lead and look for the point where the trail forked. Emily planned to fall in behind Liam, but he blocked her path. "Is something wrong?" She wasn't sure why she whispered her question, but it seemed appropriate.

"You tell me," he whispered back. "You've been awfully quiet. Everything okay?"

———

"Peachy." Emily winked.

"Baby, you have no idea how much I want that to be true, but I'm not sure I believe you. Is your arm bothering you?"

Emily shifted the pack on her shoulders, and now there was no humor or sarcasm in her voice. "My arm is fine. It was just a bad scrape, and it isn't hurting. Even if it was, I'm not sure I would notice. It's beautiful here. The weather is perfect. In this moment, I have no complaints. Although I do have some concerns about the rest of the hike and how the night will go, but I'm fine."

"But?"

"I just can't get my brain to turn off. I don't understand what's going on. Who is the real target? What is the motivation? I keep analyzing and rejecting each hypothesis because nothing makes any sense. And I can't bounce my theories off you because I don't think this is a conversation we need to have in front of Mason, and you probably wouldn't be willing to have this conversation with *me* anyway. So I'm stewing in my own conspiracy juices."

"Wow. That's a lot to unpack there."

Emily grinned at him. "Go on." She gave him a small shove, but he didn't move his feet.

"You go ahead of me. I'll take the rear."

She narrowed her eyes at him but complied without any fuss. Once she was a few feet ahead of him, he fell in step behind her. Mason wasn't so far ahead that they couldn't see him, but he was out of earshot if they kept their voices low. "First, I'm thrilled that you aren't miserable. I've been worried for the past hour that you were back here thinking murderous thoughts toward me and everyone responsible for you being here today."

Her only response was a shake of her head that told him she thought he was an idiot. He could work with that.

"Second, the night will be fine. I think you might enjoy it once you get over having to pee in the woods."

"Not likely to get over that part, Harper."

He couldn't stop himself from laughing, and when she looked over her shoulder at him, he was relieved to catch a glimpse of her gorgeous smile.

"Third—"

"There's more?" This time her body shook with laughter, but she kept walking.

"I told you there was a lot to unpack."

"Carry on."

"Third is that I'm wondering if you can read my mind, because our thoughts are traveling the same trail."

"I'm not surprised. Mason is probably having similar thoughts."

"Probably. And so, fourth, you're right. This isn't a conversation we can have with Mason, beyond listening if he wants to talk."

"Agreed."

"But why would you think I wouldn't want to talk to you about this?"

She moved to the side of the trail and turned to him. "I assumed it would be a violation of confidentiality to discuss it with me."

"I won't share any confidential information with you, but that doesn't mean we can't talk about what happened and brainstorm possibilities. Who knows? We might solve it before we get home. Being in nature is the best time to think deeply about all kinds of things. I almost never return from a trip the same man I was when I left, because at some point during the journey, I'll have a moment of clarity about an issue I've been working through or a decision I need to make. It's why I love getting away like this."

Emily had taken a step toward him while he spoke. He wasn't

sure if she realized she'd done it, but he wasn't complaining. They were standing two feet apart, and she was looking at him like—well, like she liked what she saw.

"You guys coming?" Mason's call interrupted the moment, but Emily didn't step back. Interesting.

"Right behind you." At his words, Emily turned to the trail, but Liam caught her elbow and leaned toward her. "We'll talk after we get settled for the night."

"Okay."

"Emmy?" That earned him a soft smile. Unless he was badly mistaken, she liked the nickname.

"Yes?"

"I'm glad you aren't hating the hike, but if you were, that wouldn't change the fact that I think you're an extraordinary woman."

ELEVEN

Four hours later, Emily couldn't stop herself from flushing with a potent combination of delight and embarrassment every time she remembered Liam's words, and the unhidden sincerity in his gaze.

Could any woman resist a man who treated her with such genuine affection and tenderness? Maybe.

Could she?

Apparently not.

She couldn't put her finger on when it had happened. Oh, the slide began months ago with the first conversation about DC food trucks. But now she had the sense that while she might wind up mourning this man, the risk was worth it if it meant she could have days, weeks, months, maybe years or decades with him.

She wasn't in love with him. She didn't know him well enough for that.

But she could be—someday.

And even more terrifying? She wanted to be.

Gil and Ivy were just weeks into their new relationship, and Gil had already bought a ring. He hadn't given it to her yet because he had plans for an epic proposal. But their love made Emily's heart clench—not with jealousy but with longing.

She'd gone to Raleigh to visit them last weekend. They'd

had dinner, just the three of them. Then they'd had a party at Ivy's place—Ivy's way of banishing the ghosts of the torture and death that had stalked her in September—with Gil doing the cooking and Gil's fellow Secret Service agents joining them for the evening.

Luke and Faith, Benjamin and Sharon, and the couple but not a couple, Zane and Tessa, had all been there.

And then there'd been her. Not that she'd minded. Much. No one had treated her like she was a third or, in this case, ninth wheel.

But it was different. In the past, she'd been Gil's person, and she knew she still was. Their bond was eternal. But it was a sibling bond. It wasn't an "I choose you to be my person forever" bond.

Gil loved her. Always had. Always would. But had he had much of a choice in the matter?

She wanted someone to choose her.

And if Liam wanted to choose her after dealing with her in the woods—with no electricity or running water and her wearing clothes that didn't belong to her and never would—then she was going to choose him right back.

"Are we ready to shoot?" Liam studied the target Emily had propped against a tree. "Will this thing stay still?"

"You'll have to hit it to find out."

"Oh . . . burn." Mason fiddled with the bow. "Want me to show you how it's done?"

"Knock yourself out." Liam chuckled.

Mason pinched his lips together in an attempt not to smile. "Please, please tell me that wasn't your attempt at archery humor."

Liam feigned innocence. "What?"

"You're too young to be making dad jokes."

Emily watched and listened, correcting Mason's stance, and

making sure he didn't injure the shoulder she'd spent months getting back in shape.

He hit the target twice.

Then it was Liam's turn. He looked at her, then the bow, then back at her. "You're going to have to talk me through this."

"With all the outdoorsy stuff you do, I would've expected you to be into primitive weapons."

"I hike and camp. I don't hunt. I'm not opposed to hunting, per se, but it's not my thing. Probably because after you bring down whatever animal you're hunting, you have to either drag it out of the woods or field dress it and pack the meat out. Which effectively ends your hiking trip. So no thank you."

Emily was 99 percent sure he wasn't lying to her about the hunting or about having skill with a bow. But there was 1 percent of her that suspected this was Liam's attempt at flirting.

If that's what it was, it was working for him.

"Give me the bow."

Liam complied and took full advantage of the fact that for the next few minutes, he had permission to watch Emily's every move.

She was graceful and confident as she nocked an arrow and talked him through the process of preparing to shoot. She might not know how to pitch a tent, but she'd done great following his directions earlier. She might not know how to start a fire, but she had tried and the attempts had been hilarious. She might not particularly want to be sleeping outdoors, but she hadn't complained once. She was an excellent teacher and clearly knew her way around a bow. She took aim and nailed the target before handing it back to him.

"Your turn. Let's see if you listened any better than Mason."

"Hey!" Mason yelped in mock outrage. "I bet he doesn't hit the target more than I did."

"I'm afraid you're going to lose that bet." Emily patted Mason's shoulder and took a seat beside him on a tree stump as Liam lined up to shoot.

"What makes you so sure?"

"He's an agent."

"So?"

"So, I'm guessing he has excellent hand-eye coordination and is no stranger to lining up a target."

"But a bow isn't a gun."

"No, but while I don't spend a lot of time at the range, and I'm better with a bow than a gun, I'm still a pretty good shot."

"Really?"

Liam was tempted to put down the bow and listen to their conversation. Anytime Emily volunteered information about herself, he wanted to drink it all in. But in this case, maybe it would be better to shoot so she could come back over and analyze his technique. They were burning daylight, and soon it wouldn't be safe to continue.

He took aim and released the string.

The arrow clipped the top right corner of the target. Nothing close to Emily's bull's-eyes, but at least he'd hit it.

"Not too bad, Harper."

He nocked another arrow, aimed, and missed.

Mason laughed so hard he almost fell off the stump.

"Third time's the charm." Emily watched him with a critical eye. "Wait." She stepped behind him and with a feather-light touch adjusted his stance. "Try it now."

He waited until she'd returned to her spot beside Mason and then let it go. "Yes!"

The arrow wasn't in the center, but it was solidly in the rings of the target.

"There's hope for you yet." Emily walked over and plucked the arrow from the target while Mason went in search of the arrow that had flown into the trees beyond. It took him several minutes to find it, and then Emily called a halt to the proceedings. "Let's save it for tomorrow. We'll have more time, right?"

"Oh yeah. Our hike tomorrow will only take part of the day. We'll make it back here with plenty of time to shoot or read or sleep or think deep thoughts."

Mason mumbled something that sounded a lot like, "I don't want to think."

Liam didn't push him to elaborate. He didn't consider himself an expert in dealing with teenagers, but he was reaching expert level when it came to dealing with Mason. If Mason was muttering, he *wanted* to talk, he just wasn't *ready* to.

If Liam tried to force it, Mason would shut down, but if he was left alone, he'd share. Eventually.

———

Twenty minutes later, the fire was crackling, the campsite was prepped for the night, and the sleeping bags were opened on small air mattresses that had delighted Emily.

She claimed to be high maintenance, but she wasn't. Oh, he had no doubt she was working overtime to keep the drama to a minimum this weekend. And he had no trouble believing that spending the night in the woods was not her idea of a good time.

But she wasn't a diva. She was sweet. Helpful. Genuinely curious. Able to laugh at herself about what she didn't know, but humble about the things she did know.

She had schooled them on the best sticks for roasting marsh-mallows, and only now that the sticks met her specifications did she and Mason take up positions around the fire.

Mason put his marshmallow all the way into the fire, then pulled it out, admiring the flames for a second before blowing them out.

Emily tsked. "What is wrong with you? First you bring me sticks that are two feet long because apparently you don't care if your eyebrows get singed off, and now you've flambéed that poor marshmallow and rendered it inedible."

"It isn't inedible." Mason pulled the gooey mess off the stick and popped it, whole, into his mouth, making his next words garbled. "It's perfect."

"Puh-lease." Emily continued to twirl her marshmallow in a slow spiral over the edge of the coals. "The key is to get the outside a crisp, golden brown while melting the insides. This is a process that cannot be rushed." She spoke about the marshmallows the way a wine connoisseur might speak about a particularly fine vintage, her accent a weird cross between British and Charleston.

It was obvious she was teasing, but at her words, Mason's face clouded, his shoulders slumped, and his chin dropped almost to his chest before he lifted it and looked from Liam to Emily and then back to Liam.

Emily abandoned her marshmallow masterpiece and went straight to Mason. "Honey, what is it? What's wrong?"

TWELVE

Emily's first instinct was to wrap Mason in a hug, but she was careful never to touch him unless it was part of his treatment. But right now, he needed reassurance, and standing a foot away from him wasn't cutting it. She squeezed his forearm and waited for him to make eye contact. "You can tell us. No matter what it is."

"It can't be rushed." Mason stared into the fire. "That's what she said."

"Who?" Liam had moved toward them. When Mason didn't respond, Liam clapped him on the back. "Mason?"

Mason continued to stare into the fire. They stood like that for thirty excruciatingly long seconds before Mason turned to Liam. His eyes held a million secrets, and he looked both very, very young and also very, very old.

"Lisa." Mason pulled away from them and paced the perimeter of their small fire, waving his roasting stick like a conductor's baton. "Last week." His gaze landed on Emily. "I, um, kind of snuck out of the house."

"You didn't." Emily expected Liam to laugh at Mason's outrageous statement, but he nodded in confirmation. "You did? Can I ask why?"

"I was bored."

Liam cleared his throat.

"Okay, fine. Earlier that day, Lisa had been going on all afternoon about some policy stuff Dad was dealing with, and she and Mom were holed up in Mom's office for hours discussing the strategy for Mom's next appearance and whether they wanted to bring it up or ignore it. You know how it goes."

After the last six months, Emily did. While it was the vice president's name on the ballot, Mrs. Lawson was his top advisor, and it was no secret in Washington that she was fully briefed on all policy issues.

Mason yanked three marshmallows from the bag and skewered them with more force than was required. "I honestly thought they were done when I went to Mom's office, and, before you say it, yes, I should have waited."

Liam gave Mason a commiserating smile. "Yeah. Definitely would've been better to hold off. Anytime you can choose the timing of the battle, you have an advantage."

Emily was in the house three times a week, but she wasn't involved in every aspect of Mason's life the way Liam was, so she didn't quite follow the discussion. "What did you do?"

Mason plunged the marshmallows into the fire, then pulled them out and waved his newly lit torch around a few times before blowing out the flaming sugar. "I asked if I could go to a movie."

Emily did know about this long-standing argument in the Lawson household. "Ouch."

"Yeah. Lisa didn't appreciate being interrupted or my request. You know the look people give Mom when they don't like how I'm behaving?"

"I might have seen it once or twice."

"Yeah. She was laying it on thick. But Mom told her they were done for the day. She and I went up to the private living room, and she wasn't mad." His grin was smug. "Said Lisa was driving her crazy, and she appreciated my interruption. But she still shot down my request to go to the movies."

"It's a security nightmare." Emily wasn't sure if Liam was telling her or reminding Mason, but Mason responded.

"I know. Doesn't mean I don't want to do it. I can't ask a girl out on a date because I know it will include a chauffeured ride in an armor-plated limo."

"I don't know." Emily couldn't resist trying to pull Mason from the gloomy pit he was wallowing in. "Lots of girls would enjoy a ride in a limo."

"Yeah? I bet they wouldn't enjoy having agents on either side of us at the movies or in the restaurant or, oh, I don't know, at her door when I drop her off. I can't hold a girl's hand without an audience. Much less kiss her."

He wasn't wrong about that.

"I've given up on dating until college. I'll figure it out then. But right now, I'd just like to say yes when my bros ask me to go to a movie."

Emily found all of this fascinating. And any other time, she would have been willing to help him brainstorm a way to make it happen. Because she was of the opinion that Mason should be able to do regular teenage stuff. At least some version of it.

But at the moment, she needed Mason to connect the dots between his teenage angst and a remark made by his mother's chief of staff.

"Anyway, I wasn't mad at Mom. It isn't her fault. I mean, it kind of is. If anyone could talk Dad out of running, it's her. But she's never going to do that. We all know she wants the White House as much as Dad does, which means this is my life, and I was just mad in general. So I decided to go for a walk."

That didn't sound particularly ominous.

"At two a.m."

Uh-oh.

"Alone."

Yikes.

"Dressed as one of the staff."

"Oh, sweet mercy, you didn't." Emily's eyes were huge, her mouth open, her expression a mixture of confusion and horror.

Liam snorted. "Oh, sweet mercy, he did."

Mason, for his part, had the decency to look ashamed.

When no one spoke for a few seconds, Emily prompted them. "One of you needs to start talking. What happened? How far did you get? When did you get caught? I need details, people." That last sentence was spoken with fake, but not entirely fake, frustration.

"It's Mason's story. He should tell it. I'll just say that I got a phone call at two-thirty a.m. asking me if I had any idea where he might have disappeared to. I was not amused."

"I should think not." Emily's outrage on his behalf was fun to witness. "Mason, honey, you cannot do that. You shouldn't do that under any circumstances. Whether you're living in the vice president's house or a tiny house in the middle of nowhere, sneaking out is never okay."

"I know. It's not an excuse, but sometimes I think I'm going to jump out of my skin if I can't get some peace and quiet and fresh air."

Liam was sorely tempted to rat Mason out to Emily about the late-night walk he took last night, but he resisted. Not for the first time, Liam wished for the power to smooth Mason's path. He'd been praying for months that God would use Mason's unusual upbringing to make him stronger. Wiser. More empathetic. Not bitter, jaded, or angry.

Emily picked up her roasting stick. "Mason, have you told your parents this?"

"Yes. Mom says she understands. And this might make you mad"—Mason glanced at Liam—"but Dad thought it was hilarious and said he wished he'd thought of it. Told me next time to let him in on the plan so he and Mom won't worry."

Counting to ten before speaking would not work. If Liam spoke at all right now, it would be bad. Emily, however, had no problem speaking. "Mason, you're going to give Liam an aneurysm if you keep sneaking out."

"I know. Dad was just joking. But he wasn't mad. Neither was Mom. And they were so cool about it that I didn't want to bring up what I had heard. I didn't want to ruin the moment. And I'd convinced myself that it wasn't what I thought I had heard. Until yesterday. Now I'm not so sure."

Liam had managed to get a grip on his temper with the knowledge that the VP wasn't planning to sneak out of the house dressed as the staff. "Mason, what did you hear?"

Mason went for another marshmallow. The kid was going to be on a sugar high for hours at this rate. Emily narrowed her eyes at him but didn't stop him, so Liam let it go. He took a marshmallow for himself and offered the bag to Emily. "If you don't get another one now, you might not get a chance."

She took a marshmallow and skewered it on her stick. Mason winked at Emily. "I'll try it your way if you'll try it mine."

"No thank you. I've had your way before. Bleh."

Mason flambéed his marshmallow while Liam joined Emily in the slow-roast method. "Mason," Liam said, "you're stalling."

"If I tell you, you'll flip. And if I'm wrong, a lot of people will get in trouble over nothing."

"I appreciate your perspective. However, I would like to point out that it's my job to protect you. Part of that includes investigating far-fetched efforts to harm you and your family, including a recent one where someone had the bright idea to fly over the house in a hot air balloon and drop grenades in the yard. How they thought they were going to get away, or get close enough to the residence, I don't know. The point is, we investigate every threat, including"—Liam paused and waited until Mason was looking at him—"anonymous ones."

Mason's shoulders slumped in obvious relief. "You won't say where you got the information?"

Liam worded his response carefully. "It's possible that at some point I may have to reveal the source. But I'll only do that if there is no choice. And I won't do it in a way that puts you or your family in greater danger."

"Okay. So Lisa was outside. Vaping." Mason made a gagging face. "She was on the phone, and the person talking was so loud that I could hear both sides of the conversation. She was mostly whispering, well, hissing really, but I was close enough, so I'm not guessing. I heard the person on the other end of the call say, 'You put this in play six months ago, and we're tired of waiting.' And let me tell you, she did not like that."

Mason pulled in a deep breath and continued. "She was so mad. She was half yelling, half whispering, and she said, 'It can't be rushed.'"

Liam had a bad feeling about where this was going.

"I was tucked against the house where the staff go for their breaks." Liam knew the spot. It was relatively private. Quiet. A nice spot to take a breather. He'd used it himself more than

205

once. "And I was in the corner, because, obviously, I was hiding. I wasn't hiding from her. But she didn't see me when she walked out. It was the middle of the night and completely dark, and I was stuck, because if I'd tried to walk past her, she would have recognized me, so I stayed put."

Emily gave a tiny grunt Liam took to mean "I get that" while she inspected her marshmallow.

"Anyway, after she said it can't be rushed, the guy on the other end of the line cussed a lot, so I won't say exactly what he said. But in between he said, 'The kid is the key. You said the kid was the answer, and we believed you. But your plan didn't work, so we're taking it in a new direction.'"

Mason met Liam's eyes then, unvarnished fear radiating from him. "I think, maybe, I should have told you earlier."

THIRTEEN

Emily almost choked on her marshmallow. Liam had gone preternaturally still, and she wasn't sure if he was in shock or if he was contemplating strangling Mason.

She'd had a sixteen-year-old brother once. Boys that age were wonderful, but their prefrontal cortexes weren't fully developed, and sometimes intelligent young men did incredibly stupid things.

This was one of those times.

For a long minute, the only sound came from the fire as it continued to crackle merrily, unaware of the bomb Mason had detonated in the middle of their campsite.

"Yeah. You should have told me before." Emily gave Liam full marks for saying those words without a hint of sarcasm or rancor. "But I'm glad you told me now."

Mason gave him a jerky nod.

"Finish the story. What else did you hear?" Liam's order held no frustration, but there was an edge to his tone that had Emily's neck prickling.

Mason got the message, and the words tumbled out of him. "She was mad. She said something about how they'd asked for her advice, and they'd regret it if they didn't follow it, and that she'd been clear about what she'd signed on for, and if they took it further, she wouldn't help them."

Mason stabbed his stick into the ground. "Then the guy said they didn't need her anymore. He kept talking, but she walked away and I couldn't hear any more. I waited another fifteen minutes, then I snuck over to the back deck and waited to be found there. And"—he looked at the ground and mumbled the rest—"that's why I lied about where I'd been hiding when you asked me. Because I didn't want her to know where I'd been."

Liam ran a hand through his hair, leaving it sticking up all over the place in a way that reminded Emily of her brother. Gil did the same thing when he was stressed out, and she had no doubt that Liam's stress levels had skyrocketed in the last five minutes.

They were in the middle of the woods, sleeping in tents, far away from solid walls, much less the armored shelter she knew Liam was wishing for right now.

And what she'd heard made her think someone had targeted Mason. They'd thought that by taking him on the camping trip, they were removing him from the danger, but they may have put him in greater danger than before.

Liam stalked to his tent and ducked inside. Emily and Mason stood by the fire, waiting. Should they move? Should they put out the fire? Mason was a huge target right now. Emily refused to consider her own target status.

Liam emerged with a satellite phone—something she only knew about because she'd seen Gil's—and three guns. He settled one into the now-visible holster at his hip, the other into the shoulder holster he'd unearthed from somewhere, and the third into an ankle holster.

"I'm going to step away and make a few phone calls." The Liam who had emerged from the tent was not the same one who'd entered it. There was nothing fun or lighthearted about this man. This man was a Secret Service agent through and through. He was tough. He was a warrior. He would protect Mason Lawson with his life.

This Liam Harper could die and leave her devastated. That should have sent her running, on an emotional level, as far away as she could go. But for the first time, she understood why anyone would choose to be in a relationship with someone who put their life on the line every day.

Because she wasn't afraid to care about him. Oh, she was terrified. She didn't relish the idea of being shot or blown up or whatever fresh torture was headed their way, but she was also bizarrely proud of Liam and intensely confident in his abilities to keep them safe.

Liam had been expecting more fear. Maybe Emily's eyes shining with unshed tears? Maybe Mason kicking trees or throwing his camping equipment around?

But no. Neither of them appeared to be overly alarmed. Did they not realize the seriousness of this situation?

No. They knew. But they weren't falling apart or freaking out, which was going to make his job much, much easier.

"I won't go too far. I'll be able to see you both. I'm going to check the perimeter and call in some reinforcements, and then we'll go from there."

"Yes, sir." And that was quite possibly the first and only time Mason had ever sincerely said those two words.

"Be safe." Emily brushed her hand along his arm as he passed.

He walked into the woods and dialed the number of the support team that had camped about half a mile away. That team of three agents was running random patrols in a perimeter around the campsite. If they'd noticed anything, they would've let him know. The fact that they hadn't? Could go either way. If there was nothing to see, then it was good news. If they hadn't seen something that was there, then it was bad news.

The leader of the three-man team, who had a real name but only ever went by the nickname Cobra, answered. "Harper? What's wrong, man?"

"Possible threat. Need you to run a wider perimeter and then a close perimeter. Then pack up your camp and join us."

"What aren't you telling me?"

"Details later, but it's possible Mason's the target."

Cobra turned the air blue in a blistering ten-second diatribe before he said, "On it."

It was a testament to how much Cobra trusted Liam that he didn't question him, and Liam appreciated the silent vote of confidence. "Check in every ten minutes."

"Done."

Liam walked in a slow circle around their spot, flashlight bright and brash in the darkness, with no effort at subtlety. There was a time for stealth, but this wasn't it. If someone was out there, he wanted them to know he was looking for them. If there was a trap, figurative or literal, he wanted to see it before it sprung.

He paused long enough to call Jesse, then kept walking, scanning the area.

"Didn't expect to hear from you, Harper. If the kid is hurt or has run off, I'm—"

"Mason may be the target."

"Come again?"

Without using Mason's name, Liam told Jesse what Mason had overheard. When he finished, Jesse was so quiet that Liam would've worried they'd been disconnected if he hadn't been able to hear the rhythmic tapping as Jesse typed something. "I'm sending reinforcements."

"I appreciate that."

"I'll handle the investigation on this end. But you're the expert where you are. Can you hike out in the dark?"

"Can we? Yes. Should we? No. There's a stretch about a half mile from here that requires holding climbing ladders that have been secured to the rocks and a small section with a rope to hold on to where the path follows the edge of a creek bed. If there's anyone out here with us tonight, we'd be serving ourselves up on a silver platter."

"Good point. Can you get yourselves into a more defensible position than where you are?"

"Where we are is already as good of a spot as there is. That's why I chose it."

"Talk me through it."

"We're near a creek, and the front edge of our site will be difficult to defend, but our tents are up against a low hill that offers some decent natural protection. It wouldn't be impossible, but it would be difficult to get the drop on us from that side. If they approach us, they'll have to come from the creek. We can set up a guard, stay alert, keep the fire going—all of which will make us a less appealing target than if we'd banked the fire and crawled into our tents for the night."

Liam paused. "When the team gets here, we can scout out a few places we can run to if we believe the threat is imminent. Small spaces, too small for us to stay in overnight but that would be easier to defend."

The tapping stopped, and the sound of a chair groaning filtered through the speaker. "I want to hurt somebody right now."

"You and me both, brother."

"Do we have anybody who can get to you guys tonight? And if the answer is no, I'm thinking about sending in some air support."

"The people who could find us are already out here with me. You could send an alert and see if anyone has knowledge of the area, but I wouldn't want to send anyone here unless they have specialized experience."

More than one agent had a special forces background and had never met an obstacle they couldn't conquer. They would be excited about the challenge, but it was difficult to justify sending them in over what could be an overreaction.

Not that he didn't believe the threat was real. He did. But whether the threat had followed them remained to be seen.

"Okay," Jesse snarled into the phone. "I don't like this, but I agree with your assessment of the situation. Sit tight. I'll get the ball rolling on our end, get people headed your way who will be ready to go at daylight."

"Roger that."

"I won't insult your intelligence by telling you how to handle things tonight. Do what you need to do. Keep the phone within reach."

"Will do."

"And Harper?"

"Yeah."

"I'm sending a chopper."

FOURTEEN

Emily didn't try to make small talk with Mason. When Liam left them, they both took seats on the rocks they'd been using as chairs. After five minutes of silent staring into the fire, she stood, grabbed the marshmallow bag, and silently offered the remaining few to Mason. When he declined, she rolled the bag tight and placed it back in their sealed food storage box.

"Next time we go camping," she said, "I'm volunteering to carry the graham crackers and chocolate. If I'm going to sleep in the woods, I want s'mores."

Mason huffed. "You're assuming we'll invite you next time."

"That was a low blow, Your Royal Hiney."

"Ah." He yelped like she'd hit him. "You play dirty. I'm gonna tell Mom you're calling me names."

"I bet she's called you worse."

"She has." Mason dropped his head into his hands, and she almost missed it when he whispered, "Emily?"

"Yeah?"

"Are you scared?"

"A little."

"Do you need a hug?"

"Yeah."

Mason stood and wrapped his arms around her. She squeezed him close. He released her after a few seconds and returned to his rock chair.

"Want me to pray for us?" Emily had no idea if the social faith she saw from the Lawsons had any roots in the love and forgiveness offered only through the gospel, but they weren't antagonistic toward believers. And if she had an opportunity to demonstrate what a real relationship with Jesus looked like, she didn't want to pass it up.

"Sounds like a good idea to me."

"Okay." She resumed her seat and dropped her head. "Lord, we have a bit of a situation here."

Mason snorted and muttered, "A bit?"

"Fine, Lord, we are in a mess, and we aren't sure how we'll get out of it. We don't want our friends, the agents who are here to protect us, and Mason's family to be harmed. Father, could you give us wisdom, protection, and confidence that you are with us and for us?"

Emily faltered for a moment. This was one of her biggest fears. She could keep it to herself, or she could lay it out there. Might as well be real. Fake faith never did anyone any good.

"Jesus, I don't know why you don't always choose to protect people, and I haven't always liked your decisions. Right now, I'm kind of scared about how this is going to go." A rustle in the leaves drew her eyes to the trees, and to Liam approaching.

She closed her eyes again and continued. "Could you please comfort us while we wait? Protect us from those who have violence in their hearts. Keep us in your peace. Give us confidence that no matter what the next few hours hold, you are with us and you will never leave us. We need you, Jesus. Please be near. We believe. Help our unbelief. Amen."

"Amen." Mason spoke from her left.

"Amen." Liam spoke from her right.

Emily jumped to her feet. "Well?"

"Yeah, don't keep us in suspense. Kinda waiting to find out how bad I screwed up."

Liam's smile was tense but genuine. "You did okay, man. But we're cutting our trip short."

"How short?"

"Going home at daylight, and I can't rule out the possibility that you'll be in a chopper."

Mason deflated in front of her eyes, but then a slow grin spread across his face. "While you were gone, Emily said the next time 'we'"—he put heavy emphasis on *we*—"go camping, she's carrying graham crackers and chocolate for s'mores."

"She did, did she?"

"Yep. I'm going to tell Mom I want Emily to come, and we can plan it for the spring. Deal?"

Emily's mouth opened and closed several times, but no sounds made it past her lips. Liam desperately wanted to finagle this promise from her. This guarantee of a do-over. But it wouldn't be fair. "How 'bout if we get home in one piece, figure out where the threats are, and get you graduated from physical therapy before we lock Emily into a binding contract that she spend more time with us?"

"Nah." Mason crossed his arms with a deviant twinkle in his eyes. "I want a promise. Now. For the spring. No matter what."

"Mas—"

"Deal." Emily held up a finger. "But I'm not camping in the rain."

215

Mason extended his hand toward Emily and she, crazy woman, shook it.

Mason turned to Liam. "You can thank me later, man."

Why that little—

"What's the plan?" Emily asked.

"The other team is headed our way." Liam explained the plan while an annoying voice in the corner of his mind screamed at him to find out what was going on with Emily agreeing to another camping trip. "When they get here, we'll set up a watch. We'll also discuss emergency procedures for what to do if we need to leave this area. After that, you two will try to get some sleep so we can make good time in the morning."

"What about what I heard Lisa say? What's happening there?"

"Being investigated as we speak."

"Do Mom and Dad know?"

"By now, I'm sure they've been notified."

"Mom will freak."

"Probably. But we can't do anything about that. What we can do is pack everything we won't need now, prep our bags, and be ready to roll as soon as we have sufficient daylight."

It took only twenty minutes, by which time the other team had joined them. Introductions followed, and then they spent another thirty minutes reviewing evacuation procedures that Liam prayed they wouldn't need.

When everyone was satisfied with the plans, Liam tried to send Emily and Mason to their tents.

Tried being the operative word.

"I'm not tired," Mason managed to say without sounding like a four-year-old. "I can pay attention, keep watch, whatever."

"I can help too." Emily came around the corner of the tent

with the bow in one hand and the arrows in their little case, whose name Liam had already forgotten, strapped on her back.

Liam pointed at Mason. "No." He pointed at Emily. "And no."

"You can't make us sleep." Now Mason sounded like a four-year-old.

Emily studied him for several long moments that became uncomfortable after the first three seconds. Was she going to blow? Pout? No, he didn't think she was a pouter. When she did speak, he was unprepared. "Mason, honey, we need to do what Liam has asked. He's facing a long night. If we get in our tents, he knows where we are and we're out of sight of anyone who might have ill will toward us."

He appreciated how she kept using the plural and not pointing out that there was one target here, and his name was Mason.

"If we do fall asleep, we'll be better rested for whatever tomorrow holds. If we don't sleep, we'll be able to give an honest evaluation of the air mattresses and sleeping bags—and at least for me, I'll know if we need to upgrade before the spring. Because if I'm doing this, I'm doing it right."

"Pretty sure your girl wants to go glamping instead of camping." Mason shook his head in mock sorrow. "She's going to make this very interesting. But for now, I need to use a tree so I can sleep. Does someone need to hold my hand?"

Emily smacked Mason's arm in faux outrage. "I really am going to start calling you Royal Hiney if you don't watch it."

"Sticks and stones." He grinned at her as Cobra approached.

"Did I hear something about needing a tree? I'll go with you, kid. Could use one myself."

Cobra and Mason walked to the far side of the campsite and into the woods, leaving Liam alone, or as close to alone as was possible under the circumstances, with Emily.

"Deep down," she said, "sometimes way deep down, he's a good kid."

"He's a menace."

"Are you saying you don't want me coming on your spring camping trip?" Emily smiled ever so sweetly and batted her eyes at him.

"You hate it out here."

"I never said that."

"You told us you don't like dealing with bugs, getting dirty, going without showers, or being too hot or too cold. Those very words left your mouth not twenty-four hours ago. What changed?"

"Nothing. Those things are all true. But I'm not miserable. It's lovely here. Peaceful and soothing." Her expression clouded. "Or it was prior to the threat of imminent death and/or dismemberment."

"That *will* put a damper on the festivities."

"Indeed, but until then, it wasn't so bad. I mean, except for that unfortunate spider situation on the trail, I haven't seen too many critters. And the fire is cozy. The tents are quite nice, and the little air mattresses are a revelation. I was prepared for nothing between me and the ground but the sleeping bag and tent floor."

She grinned. "I can't say I'm not a tiny bit relieved at the prospect of a shower tomorrow, but I think if I were planning to go camping and had my own clothes and supplies, I could make it work."

"I guess we'll see. You promised Mason."

"Yeah. I know. Promising anything to a kid is like swearing a blood oath. There's no getting out of it now." She pinched her lips together and looked up at him through her long lashes. "Do you mind?"

"Are you kidding? I'm thrilled. This guarantees me at least one more chance to convince you to go on a date with me."

"It won't take much convincing."

"You say that now, but we're talking six more months."

"Yeah, we are." She flushed the prettiest pink Liam had ever seen.

"Can I tell you how desperately I want to kiss you right now?"

Her pink turned scarlet, but she didn't back down. "I wish you would."

He groaned. "We have an audience, and when I kiss you for the first time, it will be just us."

"Drat you for being such a gentleman." Mason and Cobra returned from the trees, and Emily inclined her head in the direction they'd been. "I should probably find my own tree." Her disgust at the prospect was adorable. "Will Cobra go with me?"

"No. I don't want Cobra anywhere near you. I'll go." At her wide eyes, he couldn't stop himself from throwing an arm around her shoulders and pulling her against him. "I won't be close."

She allowed him to draw her toward their destination. "I should hope not. Talk about a mood killer." She frowned. "But why can't Cobra come with me?"

He didn't dignify that question with a response. His silence seemed to amuse Emily, but she stayed quiet as they entered the trees. She took care of business as quickly as possible and didn't speak until they were back in sight of the tents. "Before we go back, is there anything I need to know?"

"Sleep with your shoes on."

"I can do that."

"Try to sleep. Stress and fear are exhausting, and the hike back won't be the leisurely stroll we took today."

"I'll try." Her frown and tone highlighted her doubts about her ability to comply.

He walked beside her until they reached her tent, then reached for her hand and gave it a quick squeeze. "Sweet dreams."

"Good night, Liam."

FIFTEEN

Emily was certain she'd never be able to fall asleep, but she crawled into the tent and lay down on her sleeping bag. Two minutes later, she rolled over and pulled the bow and quiver from where she'd stashed them in the corner. One of the best things about a bow was that it was impossible to shoot yourself in your sleep. Armed to the best of her ability, she closed her eyes.

When she opened them, everything was dark.

Too dark.

Liam had told her they'd keep the fire going, but there was no flicker of orange filtering through the tent wall. Had they let it burn down to coals? Was someone headed to get fresh logs? Had one of the agents fallen asleep?

If she climbed out of her tent, what would she find?

Before she could make a decision, the scrape of the zipper against canvas sent a chill racing across her skin.

Someone was opening her tent.

She closed her right hand over the bow, her left over an arrow, and fought to steady her breathing even as her lungs threatened imminent hyperventilation.

She nocked the arrow. The zipper continued its sluggish trek. Her mouth dried out, her arms shook, her body hummed with dread. She could just make out a shape of darker dark as the canvas was eased open.

Then that darkness moved inside her tent.

"If you move one more inch, I'll send an arrow through your chest." It had been all she could do to utter those words through clenched teeth, her tongue stuck and her throat unable to swallow.

The shape moved back. "Emmy." The voice was barely a breath. "Don't shoot me, baby."

"Liam!" She lowered the bow and came up onto her knees.

He moved all the way to her, his arms pulling her against him, his mouth at her ear. "We have uninvited guests in the woods."

Emily nodded, her cheek brushing his lips.

"I need you to follow me. We're going to the creek."

She nodded again and climbed out of the tent, the bow clenched in her hand, the quiver over her shoulder, and her pulse pounding out a disturbingly rapid beat in her head. They'd gone over this earlier. The agents, all four of them, were familiar with the area, and they'd scouted two locations they could defend until the air support arrived.

No one had thought it would come to that, but here they were, scrabbling through the trees toward a dense thicket. Liam had her arm by the elbow, his grip uncomfortably tight, but she didn't squirm away. She'd rather have a few fingerprint-sized bruises than get lost in the woods.

Liam didn't release her until he'd squeezed her behind the wall of agents that surrounded Mason where he stood, leaning against a tree. His lips on her ear, Liam whispered, "Stay together. We'll get you home. Don't worry."

She nodded and wrapped her left arm around Mason's waist. In the faint moonlight, she could see his jaw clench and release, then repeat.

No one spoke.

Emily lost track of time. She shifted her weight from one foot to another. Raised and lowered her shoulders. Moved the bow from her right hand to her left, then back. Rolled her head in a slow circle. Counted to sixty. Again. And again. And again. Until she lost count of how many times she'd counted to sixty.

Mason twitched beside her, but he made no sound.

When they were back in DC, she would tell the Lawsons how extraordinary their son was. And she would volunteer to go with him to see the shrink she had no doubt Mrs. Lawson would insist they visit after this. And someday, when Mason was killing it on the PGA tour, she'd spend a small fortune to get tickets to the final round and heckle him until he called her Tiny Tyrant and threatened to throw a golf club at her. Maybe, if she was lucky, she would be with Liam and he—

All four agents grew impossibly more tense in front of her. What was happening?

Then she heard it. The *thwump, thwump, thwump* of a helicopter.

She'd kind of thought Liam was joking about the air support. Clearly, he was not. The chopper had a glowing spotlight that it flashed through the woods. And a loudspeaker.

"Walk to the creek with your hands above your head."

The chopper made a pass and turned around for another sweep. "US Secret Service. Go to the creek with your hands above your head."

She couldn't hear anything over the loudspeaker and the noise from the chopper. Were the bad guys complying? And why would they? Wouldn't it be better for them to run in the opposite direction?

And that's when she realized that while they wanted to know who was coming after them, the priority was Mason's safety.

Right now, what they wanted most was to get him out of here and to a protected location. They would hunt these guys to the ends of the earth, but they weren't trying to catch them as much as they were trying to run them off.

The chopper continued to make passes following the path of the creek, but it didn't appear that the bad guys were interested in enjoying the Secret Service's particular brand of hospitality.

The chopper was flying away and had reached the point where she'd come to expect it to turn around, when the air exploded with the sound of gunfire.

Were those idiots shooting at the chopper?

They were!

It was a lot harder to take down a military-grade helicopter than most people realized. And the pilot of this one was a combat veteran who had survived more than one close call. The piddly effort coming from these guys wouldn't be anything more than an annoyance, like having a swarm of gnats flying around your head. And the firepower the pilot had at his disposal had the potential to turn the shooters into roadkill.

One minute they were alone. And then out of the darkness, six guys, heavily armed, stood in front of them. They had retreated straight into the agents' hiding spot.

Cobra did what he was best known for. He struck, his fists and feet flicking out so fast and lethal that he had two men on the ground before the other four knew what had happened. Liam took the one on the right, aiming a punishing kick to the knee closest to him. It buckled, but this man was no military reject and he raised his weapon. Liam had already pulled his firearm from the holster at his waist, and he didn't hesitate to shoot.

His fellow agents responded to the threat as he'd known they would. Punches and kicks thrown. Weapons discharged. The air filled with grunts and the scent of burned gunpowder. Then silence.

Cobra flipped on a low-beam flashlight and bounced it across the six bodies on the ground. Two were bleeding profusely. Three were unconscious. One was dead.

Liam nodded at Yates, and he moved fast to block Mason and Emily from getting a good look before Mason closed his eyes.

Liam twisted to scan Mason and Emily. They were facing each other, Emily clutching the bow and murmuring a low, "Don't look, hon. You don't need that in your brain. Not now. Not ever. Just look at me."

Mason swallowed hard, his eyes locked on hers, his effort to be brave evident in the deep brown depths of his gaze. "You are very, very bossy, you know that?" His voice shook a little, and he cleared his throat. "Like, I thought it was just because you're a therapist, but this weekend has taught me that you really are a tiny tyrant."

"Deal with it, Hiney."

Mason was aghast. "I know you didn't."

"I did."

Liam put one arm around each of them and pulled them both against his chest, squeezing them into a three-way hug that was probably inappropriate, and he didn't care one bit. "You guys okay?"

"Yeah, man," Mason said, his head almost level with Liam's.

Emily's face was smooshed against his chest, but she nodded.

"Okay. I need you to stay right here. We'll get this sorted. But it will take a while."

"Yeah. We're cool." Something in Mason's tone made Liam

suspect that the Mason who walked out of these woods wouldn't be the same one who'd walked in.

Liam turned back to the six men lying on the ground. The two conscious ones had been restrained with zip ties. The three unconscious ones were being checked over. Two of them were losing so much blood that they could bleed out before medical help arrived. Yates had the most medical training, and he took the lead in trying to stabilize them.

Cobra joined Liam. "This is messed up, man."

"I think they were shocked to run into us. They didn't know where we were. My guess is they shot at the chopper to try to get it to back off while they retreated."

"Agreed."

"If we don't get him out of here"—Yates pointed to one of the unconscious men—"we may lose him. He took three."

"No vest?" Liam couldn't fathom these guys being without protection.

"He has one on, but one shot nicked his neck, one tagged him under his arm."

Liam's phone rang. "This will be Jesse. Let me give him a sit rep. Cobra, can you get the chopper pilot? See if they're equipped to get down here search-and-rescue style and collect this guy?"

"On it."

Liam answered the phone. "Harper."

"You'd better have good news for me, man."

"Six bad guys total. One dead. Two critical and unconscious. One serious and unconscious. Two tied up but not talking."

SIXTEEN

Emily stood beside Mason and listened to Liam's end of the conversation. He was reporting in, stating the facts with no embellishment or emotion.

Emily, however, was seething with emotion. What kind of horrible excuses for human beings would target a teenager? What was the objective? Because if the public's reaction to his shoulder injury was any indication, the entire country would lose their collective minds if Mason was targeted. They'd received so many get-well cards that the mail room staff threatened to revolt.

Emily wanted to scream. Or punch someone. If she kicked one of the guys who were conscious, that would be wrong, but some serious rage was pulsing through her right now. Was this a normal response to surviving multiple attacks in a thirty-six-hour period? Probably.

She tried to force her emotions from her thoughts and watched the agents handle the mess. All four were consummate professionals. Cobra was on one phone. Liam another. Yates worked on the bodies while Masterson walked in a slow circle, eyes out, gun drawn, on full alert.

And then one loud pop, and Masterson dropped.

Emily didn't think. She shoved Mason to the ground and hovered over his back, eyes frantically searching for what had taken down Masterson as Liam and Cobra dropped their phones and drew their weapons. Yates held his position on the ground by one of the bodies, scanning the area.

Emily looked behind, in front of, and all around them. There was a whole lot of nothing. In her peripheral vision she caught a flash of something that could've been an animal but probably wasn't. Not with all the commotion they'd been making. She nocked an arrow, shifted a fraction, and focused on the area where she'd seen the flicker of light.

Ten seconds later, and she could make out the shape of a person. She hesitated. She didn't want to injure an innocent— Oh, who was she kidding? No one out here was innocent.

When the figure shifted again, she let the arrow fly. Grabbed another from her quiver and rapid-fired the second arrow.

In the quiet, there was no mistaking the sound of the arrow making impact.

And then there was no more quiet as a man yelped in pain.

Cobra went to Masterson, and Liam sprinted around her and raced into the forest where the sound had come from. He came back moments later, dragging another member of the team. This one looked vaguely familiar.

And he had an arrow protruding from his rear.

It took all Liam's self-control not to punch the man he'd pulled to the tree that had become their base. This one was an annoying wannabe reporter who had a habit of making stuff up and posting it online to get reactions. He went by the name TruthTeller, but his real name was Wayne Rowland.

Wayne was also a former militia member and had some skill with weapons. He was a known potential threat but not one they'd considered to be a true danger. He was mentally un-stable, and an agent checked in on him every few weeks. How he was involved remained to be seen, but Liam couldn't wait to spread the news that Wayne had been taken down by an arrow to the butt.

"Anyone else we need to shoot?" Liam shook Wayne's shoul-der, and the man moaned.

"That's abuse, man. I'm gonna sue."

"Good luck with that, Wayne. You want to do yourself a favor here and talk? How many others are in your shooting party?"

"No one else. We weren't going to kill anybody."

"Really?"

"We just wanted to injure him bad enough to get the VP to back off."

"Back off what, specifically?"

"The presidency."

"Why?" The question seemed to throw Wayne.

"He's not who we want for president!"

"Who is *we*?"

Wayne chose that moment to shut up. He squeezed his lips together and shook his head, much like a tantrum-throwing toddler.

Liam glanced over to the spot where Cobra was tending to Masterson. "You'd better pray he makes a full recovery. And if anyone else comes out of these woods, I'm going to make sure the judge knows you endangered the lives of everyone present."

Wayne dropped his head. "There's no one else, man. You've ruined everything. It's all over. She's going to kill me now."

"Who is?"

"Lisa."

SEVENTEEN

The next ten hours were the most bizarre of Emily's existence. First there were the choppers. Plural. The one that showed up with well-armed men who rappelled down was super impressive. They hauled the injured guys out in baskets, like what she'd seen the Coast Guard do with water rescues, and flew away in what she assumed was the direction of the nearest hospital.

There was some chatter about sending her and Mason in a chopper too, but that idea was nixed. She and Mason were escorted back to their tents and told to rest. Like that was going to happen. They sat by the now-blazing fire, ate the rest of the marshmallows, and tried to stay out of the way. As daylight filtered in, more soldier-agent types descended on their campsite, having hiked most of the way in the dark and then traversed the last sketchy mile as soon as they could see.

A few were left behind to hold the scene of the shooting until the forensic teams could arrive to process it, which Emily thought was a significant waste of resources. They knew what had happened. But then she realized the political fallout was guaranteed to be ridiculous, and they would need to do everything by the book.

Around 10:00 a.m., Liam and Cobra led Emily, Mason, and the rest of the agents back the way they'd come, all the way to the trucks, where Heather and Patrick Lawson were waiting to smother Mason in hugs, kisses, and the kind of parental affection he normally eschewed but today tolerated quite well.

Emily was hugged, kissed, and generally hailed a hero, which she wanted no part of. The vice president told her she had an open line to him anytime she needed anything. She resisted the urge to say that what she needed right now was a shower and clean clothes, and if he could make that happen, then she would consider voting for him.

She probably wouldn't, but she'd think about it.

In fairness, she appreciated the sentiment. But her adrenaline had fled hours earlier, and it was all she could do to keep her eyes open. She could only hope she wasn't slurring her words. No one looked askance at her, so she assumed she was doing okay.

That didn't mean she didn't come close to crying in relief when Liam opened the door to a big, black SUV and helped her climb inside.

"I'll call you as soon as I can. I'm sure you'll have to come in for some interviews, but don't worry about any of that right now. I'll keep you in the loop. Okay?"

Wait. What? "Aren't you coming with me?"

"Sorry, baby." He ran a finger along her jaw. "I have to stay here."

She didn't have the energy to hide her disappointment. Liam reached for her hand. "Is it too soon to ask if you'd like to go to dinner?"

"Not too soon. And the answer is yes."

Liam grinned, tired but triumphant. "I'll call you."

One week later, Liam stood outside the door to Emily's apartment. He knocked, three short raps, and then dropped his hand. They'd talked only twice in the past week. His schedule in the post-attack aftermath had been brutal, and despite Mrs. Lawson's attempts to insist otherwise, Mason had missed all his therapy sessions for the week due to the increased security protocols in place.

As soon as Liam had been confident he had an evening free, he'd called Emily and set things up. He'd barely slept last night thanks to a combination of anxiety and anticipation that he couldn't remember experiencing since he was a kid on Christmas Eve.

Now that he was here, it was worse. If he botched this, he would never forgive himself. Emily Dixon was the kind of woman he could see being "it" for him.

Was this his last first date?

Would tonight be his last first kiss?

He sure hoped so.

Emily opened the door. "Hi!" She was radiant and energetic and completely calm. Apparently she was not the least bit affected by his presence.

Maybe this was just another first date to her. Or maybe she had extremely low expectations. Maybe he should rein in his imagination. If he wasn't careful, he would have them married with three kids and a golden retriever before the appetizers.

She pulled the door closed and settled her purse over her shoulder. "Are you going to tell me where we're going?"

"Nope."

Her grouchy face might have made him nervous if she hadn't been fighting a smile. "Are you going to tell me what's happening with Lisa Goldman?"

"There's not much I can share."

"I'd still prefer to hear it from you. The press has it all wrong."

"That they do." He held the car door open for her, and by the time he slid in behind the steering wheel, the nerves were gone.

Mostly gone.

Kind of gone.

Okay. Not gone but getting better.

In the confines of the car, he filled her in on what he was allowed to share. He wouldn't ever be able to discuss the changes to the security protocols or the fact that there was a well-documented paper trail showing the Secret Service had not approved Lisa Goldman's hiring due to discrepancies in her background check.

They had been told to stand down.

That was also well-documented.

Needless to say, the Secret Service didn't anticipate any issue with their vetting of future staff members.

He'd never tell her any of that, but he could give her more than what she'd been able to read in the papers.

"Lisa is, or was, great at her job. That was never in question. Her loyalties, however, were never to Mrs. Lawson. Bottom line, Lisa Goldman was planted by members of a wing of the party that does not appreciate the vice president's policies."

"How's Mrs. Lawson handling it?"

"Behind closed doors? I don't know. In the residence, she hasn't made any effort to hide how furious she is. In public, she's—"

"'Stunned, simply stunned,'" Emily said, mimicking Heather Lawson's intonation perfectly. "And so thankful for the brave agents who protected our family from this traitor."

"Yeah."

"Is she, though?"

"Stunned?"

"No, is she thankful to the agents? I can't believe Lisa Goldman's loyalties got past the Secret Service. I sense there's more to the story there. Which makes me wonder if she's embarrassed about her choice to hire Lisa, and if she's taking that out on the agents."

Oh boy. She was way too close to the mark with her suppositions. "Emily, if we're going to spend time together outside of work—"

"*If?*" That one word was so sharp, it could have sliced through concrete.

He grinned at her, unable to hide how much he loved that she did *not* appreciate his conditional statement. "Allow me to rephrase."

"Please do." Still sharp. Cutting him no slack at all.

If she was going to be that way, he figured he'd push it a little. "*Since* we will be spending *tons and tons* of time together—"

"That's more like it," she mumbled under her breath, and he gave himself a mental high five.

"We need to come up with a way for me to make it clear when I cannot talk about something."

"How about, 'I can't discuss that'?" She gave him a cheeky grin. "Although in this case, you've confirmed my suspicions without saying a word."

"I can't discuss that."

Emily's laughter filled the car. "See how easy that was? Now, what else can you tell me?"

"I can't get into the specifics, but someone"—he was careful not to put emphasis on the word *someone*—"was able to enter the residence with enough explosives to take out several walls. Which, by the way, the historical preservation people are losing their minds over."

"Oh, I can imagine. The residence is beautiful. It hurts to think of any of it being destroyed."

"Fortunately, the explosion was designed to be more bark than bite, but it was intended to injure Mason, and the long-term goal was to put so much heat on the Lawsons that they would withdraw from the race."

Emily's forehead wrinkled, and she turned to him. "What was the deal with the part Mason overheard? Did the same group that planted Lisa have something to do with his shoulder injury?"

"Do we have enough proof for court? Not yet. But yes. They staged the whole thing. The rabid social media fans that swarmed him, all of it. I don't think they intended to do him any real harm, but from what you've said about his arm, I've gathered that he might have been headed toward an injury and the attack exacerbated the situation. It's supposition on my part, but I don't think they intended to mess with his golf aspirations, but when it happened, they weren't sorry."

"Wow. You don't have to confirm or deny, but I bet Lisa Goldman is trying to get out of a harsher sentence by saying she didn't do anything to kill Mason, only to create fear."

Liam nodded but said, "I can't discuss that."

Emily chuckled. "Have there been any arrests?"

There had been. On top of the actual assailants, three of the individuals behind the attack had already been arrested. But that wasn't public knowledge. There were others under surveillance. The scheme had been in place for a while, but the walls were tumbling down around the conspirators. "I can't—"

"I get it. But please answer this. Is Mason safe? I know there's always a threat—but from *this* threat, is he safe?"

"I believe so."

"And is Masterson doing okay?

"Home from the hospital and expected to make a full recovery."

"Whew. So it's over."

"Yes."

"Can we change the subject?"

"Of course."

"Where are we going?"

EIGHTEEN

Emily couldn't have scripted a more perfect first date.

Two hours after they left her apartment, their stomachs full of chips, salsa, and what they both agreed was the best burrito in DC, Liam tucked her hand in the crook of his arm as they walked along the National Mall.

"I wanted to make our first date all about your favorite things. And you said you'd never met a mall you didn't like."

"I did say that, didn't I?"

"I think you also said something about pedicures, but I had to draw the line somewhere."

"This is perfect. Thank you."

He squeezed her closer. "I took a bit of a risk with the weather. It's in the fifties, not the seventies. But I figured if you were too cold, I could find a way to help you with that."

Emily bit down on her bottom lip to keep from grinning like a fool. "How, precisely, would you do that?"

She could feel the chuckle that rumbled through Liam's chest. He maneuvered them until they were walking deep in the shadows, and when there was no one in sight, he pulled her into his arms

She went willingly, her hands landing at his waist.

"I would start with this." The humor was gone and there was a husky quality to his voice.

"This is good." And it was. He was warm, his arms were strong and tight around her.

One hand released her, glided up her arm, and wrapped around the back of her neck. "Is this better?"

Emily decided she should save her air for breathing, but she managed a nod.

His thumb came around and brushed her lips. "Good . . . better . . ."

He lowered his head, and she went up on her tiptoes. When his lips touched hers, she squeezed his waist and pulled him closer. Their first kiss was gentle but not shy, mirroring their relationship that wasn't new but *was* entering new territory.

And that new territory was a place they both wanted to be.

The second kiss indicated that this was going to be an adventure.

The third hinted at the hope that this could be the love of a lifetime.

When Emily finally came down off her toes, Liam rested his forehead on hers and whispered, "Best."

EPILOGUE

Liam settled into the pew with Emily tucked in beside him. He had his left arm around her shoulders, and the fingers of her right hand twined with his, resting on his thigh. He lowered his head so he could whisper into her ear. "Just so you know, my presence here is evidence of how much I love you."

Emily pressed her lips to his jaw. "I know you love me, but what does coming to a wedding have to do with it?"

"Because March is perfect hiking weather, but I'm in Raleigh to attend the wedding of a couple I barely know with a group of people I'm not convinced actually like me."

Emily squeezed his hand. "They like you. They're just . . . protective."

He understood. Emily's brother was an agent, his friends were agents, and all of them seemed to believe that Emily was their sister and therefore it was their job to vet Liam thoroughly. They were doing an admirable job.

The problem wasn't so much that they didn't like him, but they hadn't really had a chance to get to know him. His schedule didn't allow for frequent weekends away. He'd squeezed in a quick trip to meet Gil and Ivy in Raleigh, which had turned into meeting almost everyone attending this wedding. Then Emily's parents had come to DC to meet him. Emily's dad was a typical papa bear when it came to his daughter, but he and Mama Dixon had been gracious and welcoming. Liam knew he had their approval as long as he continued to make Emily happy.

"Doesn't Faith look amazing?" Emily whispered to him.

FBI Special Agent Faith Malone was beautiful on any day, but she was a stunning bride. For a woman who reportedly tended to keep her emotions in check, she was letting them all out today. Secret Service Agent Luke Powell was a lucky man. Not only was it clear that his bride loved him, but it was also equally evident that he adored everything about her.

Liam didn't make a habit of attending weddings, but his mom had always told him that the person to watch at a wedding wasn't the bride. It was the groom the moment he saw his bride for the first time. She'd been right. When Luke had first seen Faith at the back of the church, his face had gone slack in absolute wonder. Liam hoped the photographer had gotten a good shot of Luke's expression.

As the wedding proceeded, Liam scanned the small wedding party. Emily's twin, Gil Dixon, and another agent, Zane Thacker, stood with Luke.

Faith's maid of honor, her sister, Hope Malone, was at her side. Tessa Reed, the only female Secret Service agent in the Raleigh office, stood beside her. A significant portion of the male population was sneaking glances at Tessa. Emily had told him that one of Tessa's cousins looked just like her and had been a Miss Universe not too long ago.

Tessa didn't appear to notice the attention of anyone in the crowd, but her gaze continued to lock with Zane's across the aisle. Emily had assured Liam that Tessa and Zane weren't a couple but had followed that with, "No one knows why." Based on what he was seeing, he'd bet their status was going to shift from "single" to "in a relationship" sooner rather than later.

Gil alternated between watching Faith and Luke with an indulgent smile and looking at his fiancée, Dr. Ivy Collins, where she sat to Emily's left. Gil and Ivy had a summer wedding on the horizon, and Emily was to be the maid of honor.

Which meant that in a few short months, he'd be back in this same church, attending yet another wedding. If things continued to go the way they'd been going since November, maybe the third wedding he attended would be his own. Although Faith's sister, Hope, and her FBI agent boyfriend, Charles, might beat him and Emily to the altar.

The pastor cleared his throat, and Liam returned his attention to the front of the church. "I now pronounce you husband and wife. You may kiss the bride."

Luke whispered something to Faith just before he took her face in his hands and pressed a gentle kiss to her lips. He followed that with a much longer kiss that broke right before it crossed the line from adorable to awkward.

The audience applauded and stood as the happy couple left the auditorium, followed by the wedding party. Ivy leaned toward Emily and whispered, "I've told Gil he can't kiss me for longer than five seconds at our wedding."

Emily shook with laughter. "It isn't Gil we need to worry about."

Ivy pursed her lips and then nodded in agreement. "Good point." She turned to Liam. "I may have to put you in charge of a diversionary tactic. Something that will make us not be gross in front of our friends and family."

Liam assured her that he was up for the challenge as a pleasant feeling slipped around his heart and squeezed. If Ivy assumed he would be at her wedding to Gil, then maybe they were beginning to accept him. He hoped so, because he had no plans to go anywhere.

Emily danced for hours at the reception. First with all the girls . . . Faith, gorgeous in white, Hope in a stunning deep teal that set off her hair and skin and stood out against the charcoal gray of her wheelchair, Tessa in the same shade of teal looking like a supermodel, and Ivy in a soft peach dress that Emily had insisted she buy because it did amazing things for her skin and eyes. They'd gathered in the middle of the dance floor and laughed through several songs before their various significant others had pulled them away.

That's when she'd danced with all the guys. A sweet dance with Luke where he told her that maybe Liam would do. Then Zane, who held her close and told her that if she loved Liam, she should hang on to him and never let him go. And then there was Gil.

He didn't have much to say at first. Then he squeezed her close and confessed, "I'm jealous of him, Em. You've always been all mine. I've never had to share."

She understood but pointed out, "I have to share you with Ivy."

"That's different. You've known her your entire life, and she's one of your best friends."

"So get to know Liam. Maybe he'll turn out to be one of your best friends too."

"I'll try. Is he still treating you right?"

"Of course."

"I want you to be happy. And I want you to have what Ivy and I have. What Luke and Faith have."

"I do have that, Gil. And I am happy. Deliriously happy."

He twirled her away from him and then back into his arms. "Good. You deserve it. I still reserve the right to hunt him like a rabid dog if he hurts you."

"Duly noted."

When the music slowed, she found herself pulled into what was more of a sway than a dance, Liam's arms gentle around her. She rested her cheek on his chest and closed her eyes.

"Thank you for coming to the wedding with me." She pulled back to look up at him, then rested her hand against his cheek. "I know this isn't how you would have liked to have spent your Saturday off."

Liam turned his head and pressed a kiss to her palm. "If I'm with you, I'm happy."

"I know." And she did. She felt the same way. "But I bet you'll be happier next weekend."

Liam grinned. "Maybe."

Six months ago, she never could have imagined that her life would be what it was now. There was so much love, so much healing, so much redemption all around her. She hoped it would spread to everyone in this group she loved so much.

In the midst of all the beauty, there was also a lot of change. Agents moving to new assignments, friends moving into new homes with their new spouses. New friendships being forged. New relationships growing into new lifelong commitments.

And perhaps the biggest change of all.

Emily was going camping next weekend.

And she couldn't wait.

Lynn H. Blackburn is the award-winning author of *Unknown Threat*, *Malicious Intent*, and the Dive Team Investigations series. She believes in the power of stories, especially those that remind us that true love exists, a gift from the Truest Love. Blackburn is passionate about CrossFit, coffee, and chocolate (don't make her choose) and experimenting with recipes that feed both body and soul. She lives in Simpsonville, South Carolina, with her true love, Brian, and their three children. Learn more at LynnHBlackburn.com.

CAUGHT IN THE CROSSHAIRS

NATALIE WALTERS

ONE

"Only six Thursdays left."

Panic squeezed Claudia Gallegos's stomach at Pecca's announcement. *Six Thursdays to what?* The tone in her sister's voice made it clear she should know this. Was it Maceo's birthday? Pecca's? Her own?

Claudia drove past the guard box at the end of the drive, giving a quick wave to Bruce as she drove off CIA property in Langley, Virginia. Could she blame her job for not remembering what was happening in six weeks—say she was busy saving the world? Of all people, Pecca would understand. Maybe.

A familiar ache throbbed in the scar on her arm. A reminder that kidnappings and gunshots weren't things people outside of the agency often understood.

"You don't know what I'm talking about, do you?" Pecca teased. "Worried you forgot my birthday or Maceo's?"

"Or mine." Claudia laughed.

"Thanksgiving. Only six Thursdays until Thanksgiving and you're in Texas with us!"

"Thanksgiving?" Claudia rolled her eyes. "Good grief, Pecca, not even being trapped in a tunnel in Libya with rats had me as nervous as you did just now."

"Ugh, some days I wish I was still oblivious to what you do in real life."

Guilt filled Claudia. "I do too. I never meant—"

"Stop," Pecca said, her tone softer. "I'm only sort of joking. Obviously you can't tell me the details of what you do, but I'm glad I can pray over you and the work you do to make the world safer."

She knew Pecca meant what she was saying, but it didn't erase what had happened to her and Maceo because of Claudia's career in the CIA.

"Oh, someone here's anxious to talk to his aunt."

"Aunt Claudia, it's me, Maceo." Claudia smiled at her nephew's need to remind her who she was talking to. "We got a new horse, and Dad's going to let me ride him in the rodeo—"

"That's not true." Pecca's voice cut in from the background. "We're still talking about it."

Maceo exhaled into the phone. "Dad says I can, but Mom's scared." His voice dropped to a whisper. "Dad also said you might teach me how to shoot, 'cuz Grandpa gave me his old rifle. Will you?"

"I think I can make that happen."

"Yes! Did you hear that, Mom? Aunt Claudia said—"

"Are you trying to win Aunt of the Year?" Pecca's voice replaced Maceo's. "I'm trying to keep my baby safe, and between you and Colton, Maceo's dream career is to ride bulls or become a Texas Ranger."

"Valid life choices." Claudia smiled.

"Hush. I need you on my side. Colton introduced him to *Walker, Texas Ranger*, and apparently that's more appealing than *The Great British Baking Show*."

"I'm going to have to go with Maceo and Colton on that one."

"Of course you would, because being a pastry chef isn't

exciting enough. You know, making tamales can be just as dangerous as catching bad guys."

Claudia barked out a laugh. "Only if you don't wash your hands after touching the red chile."

Pecca groaned. "My eyes still burn from that memory." She sighed. "I can understand why Mama always wanted us to have families and . . . oh, Claudia, I'm sorry. You know what I mean. She's just worried and—"

"It's fine. Look, I'm heading home from work and traffic's bad."

"Okay," Pecca said, her voice small, and Claudia imagined she was feeling guilty now. "Oh, we've got a pregnant mare due any minute, so expect a phone call from Maceo when it happens. He's so excited."

"He can call me anytime."

"Even at two in the morning?"

"Yes, even then."

Pecca laughed. "Okay, you're asking for it. I'll call you tomorrow."

Ending the call, Claudia was thankful for her renewed relationship with Pecca—even if it brought up old wounds. Or maybe not so old, given the hollow feeling in her chest.

Their mother had very clear expectations for her daughters, cultural expectations that they would get married and start families and . . . well, that wasn't the life Claudia had wanted for herself. Her choice to pursue a career was not well received by either of her parents when she left home after high school. Hurt and stubbornness created a divide that made it easier for Claudia to keep them in the dark about her job. After the incident in Georgia, Pecca worked hard to bring the family together and close that divide. Her mother and father were coming around, but Claudia still saw that hope in her parents' eyes that maybe she would get married and have kids.

That hope, combined with Claudia's immense love for her nephews and nieces, was beginning to make her wonder if she still believed she wasn't cut out for family life.

Her cell phone rang again, and Claudia clicked the button to answer. "It's on my calendar, Pe—"

"Miss Martina?" a male voice with a distinct accent spoke over her car speaker.

Claudia's adrenaline spiked at the use of her alias. She glanced down at the caller ID: UNKNOWN. "Who is this?"

"Radwan Al-Zahrani."

Claudia searched her brain for why the name sounded familiar. Radwan Al-Zahrani? Her career in the CIA had sent her overseas to the Middle East, but she was back in the US and *no one* would have her personal cell number.

"Miss Martina, please listen." The urgency in the man's tone was the only reason she didn't immediately end the call. "Prince Mohamed requested I call you. He trusts you and asks that you come to his residence. You have his address. Please. Come right away. We need your help. It is very urgent."

"What? I'm sorry but— Hello?" The line went dead. *Did he say Prince Mohamed?* The one person with that name stuck in her memory like a horrible song you can't seem to shake from your mind. Prince Mohamed bin Abdulaziz—the black sheep of the Saudi royal family.

That's why she recognized Radwan's name. She'd met Prince Mohamed and Radwan Al-Zahrani, the prince's head of security, in Dubai. And now his personal bodyguard was asking for her help. Again.

Not happening. Any communication with a foreigner outside the scope of a mission was prohibited.

A text message drew her eyes to the phone screen. An address.
A six-digit number. And a single word that set her spine tingling.

Hurry.

Working her jaw, Claudia came up with a dozen and one
reasons not to respond, the most important of which was not
putting her job in jeopardy.

We need your help.

What had the prince gotten himself into this time? Biting
the inside of her cheek, Claudia took the exit toward an afflu-
ent neighborhood in Virginia. What would it hurt to drive by
the house? Nothing unsanctioned about that, so long as she
reported it to her office.

A few minutes later, she found herself gawking at the ex-
pansive estates secluded behind acres of manicured lawns and
security gates. She pulled up to the address, a Spanish-style
mansion. There was a gate that probably required the six-digit
code Radwan had sent her.

Should she punch in the gate code?

Her conversation with Pecca came to mind, and Claudia
shook her head. Nope. Doing so could risk her job in the CIA,
one she willingly accepted when she thought it affected only
her, but the memory of her sister tied to a chair warned her that
the consequences were far-reaching when she broke protocol.

Her phone chirped again with a new text message. It was
from the same unknown number. She glanced up at the house,
wondering if they were watching her. She opened the message
to find a blurred image.

What is— A gunshot jerked her attention from the phone. Heart pounding, she searched the neighborhood, praying the sound had not come from the house she was sitting in front of. Shifting into drive, she pulled forward and punched in the code. The gate swung open as Claudia came up with the explanation she'd give. *I heard a gunshot and feared for those inside.*

She pulled her Mazda next to a bright-red Lamborghini and couldn't help rolling her eyes. Prince Mohamed bin Abdulaziz was never one for subtlety. At the front door she started to reach for the doorbell when she noticed the door was slightly ajar.

Claudia's nerves were buzzing. Something wasn't right about this. In Dubai, she'd seen the lengths Radwan took to ensure the prince was protected. His life depended on it. Pushing the door open, she called out, "Mister Radwan? It's Claudia." Nothing. "Prince Mohamed?"

Stepping inside, she saw that the door had an automatic locking system to keep unwanted guests out, but the door needed to be closed. Either the person who left it open was in a hurry to leave or they were still inside . . .

Where is Mohamed's security?

"Mister Radwan? Prince Mohamed?" Claudia's heels clicked against the Italian tile. Beer cans littered the floor. Her jaw grew tight. Trash, food, cigarette butts, puddles of liquid—nothing had changed. He was still the same guy messing around with the forbidden who she remembered from Dubai.

Claudia toed a beer can. The prince had luxury taste in everything but his choice of alcoholic beverage. He liked the cheap stuff. Beer that probably tasted as bad as it smelled. Like urine. Or maybe it *was* urine she smelled. She pinched her nose as she stepped down into the living room.

Her gaze stopped on the syringes and white powder on the coffee table. Cocaine? Agitation filled her. She backed out of the living room. If Radwan thought she was going to help Prince Mohamed get out of a drug charge, he had—

Claudia stopped cold at the streaks of red along the floor leading down the hall to her left. Her pulse pounded loudly in her ears as she followed the trail to a door. With her toe, she kicked it open and gasped. Her stomach churned at the sight of the royal Saudi prince lying faceup in a puddle of his own blood. Next to him, two women, their bodies splayed across each other.

Unable to take her eyes off the grisly scene, she dug in her pocket for her cell phone and cringed when she realized she'd left it in her car. Taking careful steps, she moved to the prince, wondering if she would find a pulse, but the gaping wound in his neck supplied the answer.

What about the gunshot? She stared down at the prince. Searched his body. No gun wounds. The others also had fatal stab wounds. So where had the gunshot come from?

Claudia needed to get out of here, call the police. She hurried to get back to the hallway, but her footing slipped in a puddle of blood and she lost her balance. She grabbed for a door handle nearby, pushing the door open just as she fell to her knees. The door led to a small room, and lying on the ground was Radwan—a single gunshot wound to his forehead. His empty eyes guaranteeing to haunt her sleep for weeks.

Claudia pushed herself to her feet, the knees of her pants soaked with blood. She had to get out of here. Hurrying from the room, she turned down the hall just as four heavily armed police officers burst through the front doors with their weapons trained on her.

TWO

Ari Blackman hit Send and leaned back in his chair, stretching his neck muscles. He checked his watch, surprised it was only a little after seven. He was done early. When was the last time that happened?

After shutting down his computer, Ari grabbed his wallet from his desk and stood. Time to call it a night. Maybe he'd actually be able to make it through more than one chapter of a book before sleep overtook him. He covered a yawn, annoyed that his body was already telling him there was a fat chance of that happening.

Maybe catching up on sleep was a better use of his early night.

Inside the elevator, his smirk reflected back at him. Thirty-four and excited to go to sleep. *Living the wild life.*

The elevator doors slid open to the first floor of the CIA headquarters. If he hadn't looked at his watch before he left his office, Ari wouldn't have known it was supposed to be the end of the workday, with the number of people coming and going in all directions. National security never slept.

But tonight, he would.

Ari's father used to tell him that nothing aged a person more than an irregular sleep pattern and contended that America was the worst at not recognizing the value of rest. *"Always in a hurry to prove something to someone.*" His father had brought that conviction with him, along with Ari's mother, to America from Israel fifty years ago.

Crossing to the glass doors, Ari made a mental note to call his parents before he went to bed tonight and figure out a time when he could visit them in Florida.

"Blackman."

Ari paused. He was only ten, maybe fifteen feet from stepping out of Langley and into freedom. Sighing, he turned and found Director Eisner hurrying toward him. His boss's clipped pace erased any hope of an early night or a phone call to his family.

"Yes, sir?"

"We've got a situation."

Ari pushed up his glasses. "You realize you sound like a movie cliché."

Director Eisner gave Ari a once-over before lifting his brows. "Says America's James Bond."

Ugh. Ari had earned that nickname during his two-year training with the CIA's clandestine operations after showing up to class in a custom-fitted suit. Or maybe it was when they found out how much he spent on a haircut?

"Did I forget something in my report?"

"Come with me."

Ari followed Director Eisner to the elevator and back up to the fourth floor. He did a mental sprint through the work he'd done over the last couple of days and the report he'd just turned in. Had he missed something?

"Your report was fine." Eisner crossed the office to his desk and grabbed a file. "A few hours ago, Prince Mohamed bin Abdulaziz was found murdered in a mansion in northern Virginia."

"The Saudi prince?"

"The one and the same." Eisner handed Ari the folder. "The prince's head of security, two bodyguards, and two women—yet to be identified—were also found dead on the scene. President Lawson has spoken with King Almansour and the Saudi ambassador. It's not good."

Ari didn't need to be told that. He sat down in front of Eisner's desk. A member of the Saudi royal family murdered in America was definitely a problem. "Are there any leads?"

"Not yet. But news has traveled fast, and at least two radical Islamic groups are praising the death as an act of justice against the monarchy."

"What about security cameras?" Ari surveyed the photos of the luxury home. "Surely a place like this has them everywhere."

"It does, but the system was cut. The FBI checked with the company, and there was no backup battery or digital storage."

"JTTF involved in this one?"

Eisner nodded. "The Joint Terrorism Task Force is handling the investigation, but our analysts are working with them to run down any leads that might indicate this was an act of terrorism against the royal family."

Any hope of walking out of work early in the foreseeable future vanished with that statement. "Am I headed to Saudi or . . ."

"Actually, I need you to head to the federal building."

"Federal building?" Was he working with the feds? It wasn't normal for the FBI and CIA to work together, but it did happen with high-level cases involving foreigners. "I thought you said there were no leads?"

Eisner handed him another folder, this one with the CIA's

emblem on top and the word *Classified* typed beneath. An employee file. Ari hesitated opening it. "One of our own?"

"Claudia Gallegos. She's a targeting officer."

Martina—aka novia de la agencia.

Ari opened the folder and scanned the dossier on Ms. Gallegos. The information was brief—basic profile information, years employed with the CIA, and her agency photo, which never looked good, but somehow this woman made her government photo . . . well . . . Ari shifted in his seat, his neck hot. She was very pretty. Very.

He focused on what was missing from the file of Martina, as most in the agency knew her by—the reputation she'd earned as a targeting officer who'd brought down several international criminals. So what did she have to do with Prince Mohamed's murder?

The question must've shown on his face when he looked up at Director Eisner.

"Ms. Gallegos was found at the scene when the police arrived. She was covered in blood."

"What? Is she okay?" His stomach clenched. Why had that been his first concern? *Because it's perfectly acceptable to inquire about the welfare of another intel officer.* Yes, that's what he hoped Eisner took from his question. "I mean, was she hurt?"

"No," Eisner said, not rattled at all by Ari's concern. *See, totally normal.* "According to the FBI, she received a call from Al-Zahrani, the prince's head of security, to come to the home. She found them dead when she arrived. May have even heard the gunshot that killed Al-Zahrani."

Ari closed the file. "Did she say why security called her to the home?"

"No."

"Has Ms. Gallegos worked with Prince Mohamed?"

Eisner nodded. "In Dubai. He interfered with an operation there, and she basically saved the kid's life."

Ari recalled images he'd seen of the Saudi royal family. None of the king's sons were under eighteen. "Kid?"

"Might as well be," Eisner said. "The *man* acts like an over-privileged frat boy, and the royal family's solution was to send him out of the country, where he quickly became the headache of those host nations. And now his death is ours."

"What do you need me to do?"

"This isn't the first time Ms. Gallegos has found herself in a . . . situation." Eisner rubbed a hand down the side of his face. "I need you to figure out how she's involved in this and whether we need to be concerned about Ms. Gallegos's allegiance."

Ari looked at the file in his hand. He'd heard rumors about something that happened in Georgia a while back—an officer who'd gone rogue. He looked up at Eisner. "Is this an official internal inquiry?"

"That depends on what you find out."

"Depends on what you find out." Thirty minutes later, Ari was still chewing on Eisner's words on the drive over to the DC FBI field office. That was his job as a special skills officer— use his expertise influencing governments, organizations, and people so they'd modify their behavior in a way favorable to the mission.

And now he was about to use those skills on a fellow intel officer to determine whether she'd compromised her oath to America in some way.

He followed FBI Agent Crenshaw through the halls of the federal building until he stopped at a door. Agent Crenshaw opened it to a room with a window and another door that led to a small conference room where Claudia Gallegos sat.

Ari took in her appearance. Dark blood stains smeared her white blouse, matching the ones on her gray slacks. Strands of dark chocolate hair had escaped the bun at the back of her neck and were framing her tired expression.

"Has she had anything to eat or drink?"

"We offered her something, but she only wanted water," Agent Crenshaw said. "She's a little shaken but has been very cooperative so far." He tipped his head to the camera positioned in the corner of the room. "I need to let you know that all conversations are recorded."

"Understood," Ari said and then stepped into the room.

He was ready to introduce himself but hesitated at Claudia's surprised expression. Or maybe it was the way the wariness he'd seen in her brown eyes just seconds ago morphed into a hardened stare.

"Ms. Gallegos, I'm—"

"I know who you are." She arched a brow, crossed her arms, and straightened in her chair. "I thought you'd be taller."

Ari frowned. They'd never worked together before, but from the tilt of her head and the critical look on her face, she seemed to know him. But that wasn't true, because he would've remembered her. "I'm six foot. Pretty average, actually."

"Average is not the way you're described by the women at Langley. *Playboy* is a word I've heard tossed around."

Heat clawed its way through his body, toes to ears. He'd spent nearly eight years in PSYOPS and now *his* job was to analyze situations and use psychological methods to gain the upper hand, but in one sentence, Claudia Gallegos had summed up every rumor about him—unfounded or not—catching him completely off guard.

"I've never put much trust in locker-room rumors." Ari adjusted his glasses and stepped the rest of the way into the room. "Shall we get this over with?"

Ari busied himself with the chair across from her and pulled out his cell phone to record the conversation in an attempt to shake his own surprise. His job put him in key positions of influence. Power and control. In the Army, his career as a PSYOPS officer had done the same, and he was good at it then and was good at it in the CIA, but he'd never been so shaken at the start of a conversation as he was now.

Schooling his features into a calm, practiced smile, he clicked his pen. "Why don't you tell me about your relationship with Prince Mohamed?"

Her eyes narrowed on him. "There was no *relationship*."

"So there was another reason you were at his home?"

"I was called there by Radwan Al-Zahrani. It's in the statement I gave the FBI."

Ari smiled. "And I'll read that, but how would you describe your relationship with Zahrani?"

"No relationship. Today was the first time I'd heard from him since Dubai."

"And how long have you been communicating with Zahrani?"

She sat forward. "I just told you, today was the first time he called me."

Ari watched the vein in her neck pulse. "And you gave him your cell phone number?"

"No."

"Prince Mohamed?"

"No." Her nose wrinkled. *So she didn't like the prince.* "I don't know how they got my number."

Ari frowned. "And yet you went to Prince Mohamed's home when Zahrani called. Didn't report the call, which is a security violation."

"Am I being investigated?"

Leaning back so as not to appear intimidating to her small frame, Ari shrugged. "No, I'm just here to ask a few questions and take a statement, and then you're free to go."

Her brows creased in suspicion. "I am?"

"The FBI's concerned about your relationship with the late Saudi prince, but they don't think you killed him. I'm just here to make sure you've been treated fairly. Have you?"

Claudia worked her jaw, her lips flattening into an expression she probably thought was intimidating but he couldn't help thinking was a little cute too. Ari swallowed, dismissing the thought immediately.

"I'm honored the agency felt the need to send you, Mr. Blackman, and your good looks and mind games might work on some women, but they mean nothing to me." She rose from the table and, bold as brass, gave him a once-over. "So you can take your psychological karate back to Langley and tell them the truth—I have no idea why Radwan called me or why he and Prince Mohamed and his entourage are dead."

Moving to the door, she looked over her shoulder. "I've got nothing to hide."

THREE

Did the CIA really think she was hiding something? *A relationship*. Ha. One look at her calendar and bank account would show them that the last time she'd been on a date was five years ago. The only relationship she'd been able to maintain was a working one, and now they were questioning her integrity.

The steering wheel shook beneath her hands, and Claudia tightened her grip until her tires found purchase on the slick DC streets. A quick glimpse at the speedometer displayed her accelerated frustration, and she lifted her foot off the gas pedal.

Thick sheets of rain hammered the city, driving the traffic off the streets. If Claudia wanted to give Director Eisner a piece of her mind, she'd need to slow down. They didn't need to send in Blackman to question her and imply some made-up relationship. She knew the rules about foreign and suspicious contacts, and she would've reported it had she not walked into a murder scene.

She shuddered, fighting the memory and the pull to look down at the blood stains on her clothing. Why had Radwan called her? She tried to recall his tone. It was urgent, but was it fearful? She had explained everything to FBI Agent Crenshaw and would've explained that to Ari Blackman, but he had to start with the head games. If the CIA thought she was hiding something, they'd sent their best.

She hadn't missed the way her words struck a chord with him. The man *did* have a reputation at the agency, and by the way he tucked his chin, *Mr. James Bond CIA* probably thought it was all about his chiseled good looks. Claudia rolled her eyes, her cheeks warming. Sure, she'd admit Ari Blackman had a sort of suave appearance, what with that custom suit his perfectly broad shoulders filled out, but his good looks didn't impress her—his reputation in psychological warfare did.

Missions were kept confidential, but every intelligence officer worth their weight had their nose in the news, monitoring the globe for potential issues arising in politics, economics, and terrorism, and Ari's name had been mentioned on more than one occasion when foreign policies shifted in favor of the US.

"Probably doesn't hurt that he's good-looking," Claudia muttered, agitation simmering beneath the surface. "And he knows it too. Super annoying."

Alone in the car, she thought her words made her sound like she was back in high school and facing off with Marcus McGregor at the JROTC Air Rifle Championship. Her insides tightened with the ugly memory of thinking he'd *actually* liked her when he asked her to sit with him at the banquet. Everyone thought he was so cute and charming with that stupid, perfect smile—and she had fallen for it too.

Claudia's pulse jumped when her cell phone buzzed with a text message. She came to a stoplight and hesitated to pick up her phone. *Pecca.* Claudia released a breath as she opened the photo and saw Maceo standing next to a brand-new baby foal.

Desi had her baby. Maceo named him Pasha.

The light turned green and she set the phone down, surprised by the unexpected emotion she felt from seeing the photo. Maybe it was Pecca's excitement about Thanksgiving and having the whole family together that was making her feel sentimental.

Not that long ago, Claudia would've cringed at the idea of going home to be with her family, but after tonight, the idea of a holiday with her sister and brothers, their families, and her mama's cooking . . . She inhaled deeply, her earlier agitation loosening its hold on her. Maybe Thanksgiving was just what she needed.

The scar on her arm began throbbing again and she massaged it, wishing she could massage away the memory associated with it.

The scrape of the wipers across the windshield pulled her focus back to the road and to the bright headlights in her rearview mirror. She reached up to tilt the rearview mirror, but the vehicle behind her quickly changed lanes and sped up next to her.

Great. Road rage was the last thing she wanted to deal with. She checked her speed. She was going a few miles over the speed limit. "Go around."

As if the driver heard her, they sped forward so fast it caused the back of their truck to fishtail on the slick surface.

"Idiot—whoa!"

The driver cut her off and slammed on their brakes, forcing her to hit hers. The back of her car slid side to side and she gritted her teeth, hands tight on the steering wheel. She yanked it left and nearly clipped the back of his tailgate. *That was too close.*

Her heart pounded against her rib cage as she changed lanes and accelerated, anxious to get away, but the growl of the truck's muffler told her the driver wasn't done yet. What had she done to tick this guy off?

She quickly took a left and then a right, heading down Constitution Avenue, which put her at a disadvantage with the National Mall on her left and the truck hedging her on the right so she couldn't take a side street to escape.

Another pair of headlights flashed in her rearview mirror. A second vehicle was cutting lanes to close in on her from behind. A chill skirted her arms. This wasn't a road rage case. She was being targeted. She pressed a button on her steering wheel. "Call 911."

A hit from the side sent her car careening to the curb, the jolt jarring her. Tightening her grip, she slammed on her brakes and tried to maneuver her vehicle behind the truck to get a look at the license plate, but the driver seemed to know what she was thinking and blocked her. She took a left at the next light.

"911, what's your emergency?"

"I'm on Twenty-Third about to enter Lincoln Circle, and someone is trying to run me off the road." She shot a sideways glance at the truck swerving toward her car again. "Black truck, older model."

"Ma'am, can you pull off the road and—"

The truck hit the side of her car, and Claudia fought to maintain control on the wet streets. At this speed, she was going to spin out or roll, but stopping was out of the question.

"I'm not pulling off the road with this lunatic." Claudia spun the steering wheel right, guiding her car into a U-turn. "I'm on Ohio Drive, the roundabout by Lincoln, and—" The car still followed, but the truck didn't make the sharp U-turn and instead jumped the curb, cutting across the greenway straight toward her.

Claudia glanced at the inky water of the Potomac on her right and then faced the blinding headlights screaming toward her. "He's going to send me into the river!"

"Ma'am—"

FOUR

The front of Ari's car nailed the curb overlooking the Potomac, but he didn't care. He'd been following Claudia since she stormed out of the FBI office, and he caught sight of the truck tailing her soon after. "I need an ambulance now!" he barked into the phone before throwing the car into park. He stared after the taillights of the truck speeding away, angry with himself. He should've acted sooner. Removing his glasses, he jumped out of his car and sprinted down the embankment toward the Potomac and Claudia's sinking car.

After toeing off his shoes, he jumped into the chilly water and swam toward Claudia's vehicle. *Please let her be okay*. The front of the car was already submerged, and the current was pulling them downriver. He kicked hard, trying to make his way around the front to the passenger door.

Ari was relieved to find the window broken, but not to see Claudia's body slumped in the seat, unconscious. Scrambling through her busted window, he worked to get her unbuckled and then gripped her beneath the arms to pull her out. With one arm wrapped around her, he used his free arm and his feet to swim them to the edge of the river.

There wasn't much of a shore along the Potomac, so he clawed his hand into the dirt and grass and mustered his aching muscles to push Claudia onto the ground. When he was sure she wouldn't slide back into the water, he fought to climb out, his feet slipping against the muddy surface slick from the rain.

"Come on, Claudia." He checked for her pulse and began CPR. Wiping away the wet hair from her face, he noticed how blue her full lips were. He breathed into her, watching her lungs rise, then sat back and began compressions again. "Lord, don't let her die."

The sound of sirens echoed from the Arlington Memorial Bridge above him. Ari continued compressions, praying for the woman who had both insulted him and intrigued him within the first few minutes of his meeting her. When she walked out of the interview room, he couldn't help but watch her. He'd had an instinctive desire to figure her out that had nothing to do with the directive to look into her involvement with a foreign national. Witnessing the driver of that truck mow her down didn't feel like a coincidence, and he couldn't help but wonder if it was connected to Prince Mohamed's murder.

Anger thrummed against his nerves as he breathed into Claudia once more. He hadn't been able to get in between the truck and Claudia's car, and it was going to cost her life. He pressed his hands on the base of her ribs and continued compressions until the EMT ran up and forced him away.

The police arrived, and an officer pulled him aside to ask a few questions about what he witnessed. Ari offered his name, a description of the truck, and the partial license plate number he'd managed to catch through the rain, but his focus was on the still form of Claudia Gallegos.

Ari raked his hands through his wet hair, rain dripping into his eyes. Between his career in the military and CIA, this wasn't his first time seeing tragedy or death, but he'd never witnessed someone he'd just been with—someone who'd managed to get beneath his skin—die right before him. He'd been embarrassed by her comment, sure, but he'd heard the rumors about himself, and what he really wanted to tell her was that he, too, had heard some things about her.

A retching noise snapped his focus back on Claudia. She was moving. Actually, she was vomiting. Muscles throughout his body he didn't know had been bunched finally relaxed. The sound of Claudia coughing pushed his gaze to the dark sky in gratitude.

After several minutes, Ari finished giving his statement, read through the report, and signed it. The cop looked over to where Claudia was being assessed by the medics.

"Is she your girlfriend?"

"No." Ari wiped rain from his brow. "I told you, I don't know her."

The cop's brows lifted, his gaze suddenly curious. "You look pretty relieved for someone who doesn't know the victim."

"Aren't you relieved she didn't die?" Ari turned the topic around. The officer was maybe ten years older than he was, had a well-worn wedding band, and bags beneath his eyes likely caused by the exhaustion of the job, children, or both. Ari played into that and tipped his chin at the medics and firefighters carrying Claudia toward the ambulance on a stretcher. "This could've ended much worse."

The police officer followed the movement with his eyes and gave a nod before tapping his pocket where he'd tucked his notebook away. "Thanks for the information on the vehicle. We'll be in touch if we need anything else."

"Sir?" A young EMT walked over with a blanket in his hands. "We'd like to check you out up at the bus."

"I'm fine," Ari said but still took the offered blanket and

wiped the water and rain from his face. He glanced up at the ambulance Claudia had just been loaded into. "Is she going to be okay?"

He nodded. "Appears so, thanks to you."

The lights from the bridge and along the street allowed Ari to find his shoes before he walked back toward the street. He could feel the EMT assessing him from the side. "Where will they be taking her?"

"I'm not sure. If you're family, I can ask and let you know."

Ari glanced at the officer from earlier, who was now taking a statement from Claudia, and forced himself not to walk over and listen. Even if Claudia knew who was driving the truck, he doubted she'd freely give that information to the officer. CIA protocol.

Ari handed the blanket back to the EMT. "Thanks for everything you did tonight. You guys saved her life."

His words hit their mark, causing the EMT to dip his chin in humility. "Just doing our job, sir. Are you sure you don't need any medical attention?"

"I'll be fine. I'm just glad she's going to be okay."

"Me too," the EMT said. "Be sure to go to the nearest hospital or dial 911 if anything doesn't feel right. Sometimes that happens, ya know, when the shock wears off."

"Yes, sir."

Ari walked to his car and got in. Using compliments and respect was the easiest and most harmless way to manipulate a conversation. PSYOPS 101. It would've been his tactic with Claudia, but her words had thrown him off his game. He backed his car between a fire truck and a squad car with the help of another police officer before driving around the bend and pulling to the side of the road.

He pulled out his cell phone and dialed the director's number, watching for the ambulance to pull away.

"You work quick, Blackman."

Ari reached into the back seat and pulled out his gym bag. "Normally, yes, sir, but not this time." He quickly explained his brief encounter with Claudia at the federal building while unbuttoning his wet shirt. "Something told me I couldn't let her just walk out." Ari pulled a dry shirt over his head just in time to see the ambulance drive past him. He waited a half second and—just as he suspected—a police car wasn't far behind. Would it be the same officer? He pulled out after them.

"Blackman?"

His boss's gruff voice pulled him back to his explanation. "I noticed a truck pursuing her vehicle. I tried to intervene, but it was too late. The truck rammed her off the road and into the Potomac. I'm following the ambulance to the hospital now."

"Will she be okay?"

There was genuine concern in the director's question, and Ari appreciated it. Oftentimes, intel missions superseded the welfare of those involved, making those employed in the agency appear callous. "Yes, sir, it appears so."

"It's a good thing you were there, Blackman. I don't have to guess that you think the incident might be related to Prince Mohamed."

"No, sir." Ari watched the ambulance ahead of him. "The FBI believes Claudia Gallegos isn't involved, but somebody else thinks otherwise . . . and I think they tried to kill her tonight."

FIVE

Claudia winced as her fingers gently touched the six stitches at her hairline. She checked out the rest of her reflection in the bathroom mirror. Her mascara had run beneath her eyes, and her long hair had curled into natural waves that would've looked beachy if she was wearing a swimsuit instead of a hospital gown.

She shuddered, and the involuntary movement reminded her of how sore her muscles were from the accident. No, not accident. What happened tonight was intentional. Someone wanted her dead. Again.

Her sister's and nephew's faces flashed to her mind. She needed to call them, make sure they were okay. Warn Colton.

"Ms. Gallegos," a female voice said along with a tap on the closed bathroom door. "I've got a gentleman here who says he's a friend, and he's brought you some clothes you can change into."

Gentleman? Claudia stared at her reflection, a wrinkle between her brows. No one knew she was here. She glanced around the bathroom as if she'd find something she could use as a weapon. Her gaze paused on the string next to the toilet that, if pulled, would send a nurse to her aid. Except there was already a nurse in the room. Was she under duress? She didn't sound like it. There was a tiny speaker, so maybe if she pulled the string she could have them send more help?

"Ms. Gallegos, are you all right in there?"

Facing the door, Claudia stepped closer. "Um, can you tell me who the man is?"

"Oh, well, I'm embarrassed to say I didn't ask his name."

What kind of nurse doesn't ask a strange man his name before letting him into a patient's room? She rolled her eyes and blew out a frustrated breath. "Can you describe him to me?"

"Sure, honey. He's tall, good-looking, and has a smile that weakens the knees."

Claudia glanced in the mirror again as if she needed her own reflection to confirm the absurdity of what she'd just heard. She didn't care what his smile looked like, she wanted to know if Mister Tall and Good-Looking was going to kill her the second she stepped out of the bathroom.

"Oh, he did ask me to tell you that you don't have to worry about any rumors at work because he was a total gentleman when he did CPR."

What? Claudia's eyes rounded as a horror-stricken look lined her face. *Rumors . . .* Ari Blackman? The EMTs told her a Good Samaritan had rescued her from the Potomac—but Blackman?

She closed her eyes and let her forehead rest on the door, forgetting about the stitches until it was too late. Sharp pain radiated through the tender wound as she lifted her head. She opened the door an inch and the nurse was there, holding some unfamiliar clothing in her hand. Blackman had brought that for her? Curiosity got the better of her, and she peeked into the room.

"Where is he?"

"He's in the waiting room," the nurse said. She was at least as old as Claudia's mom, but there was a youthful pep to her movements and voice that made Claudia think she really loved her job. Her eyes moved to Claudia's hair. "I can bring you a hygiene kit. There's a brush in there."

Claudia tucked a wayward curl behind her ear. "I was literally drowning in the Potomac."

Her terse tone only made the nurse smile. "But you're not now, and that handsome young man saved your life." She pushed the clothes into Claudia's hands. "I'll grab that kit so we can make sure he's all the more grateful he did."

"I don't—" But before she could finish, the nurse was already out of the room. Claudia huffed. Maybe it wasn't the career the woman loved but the meddling? She imagined her mother would fully support the nurse's dedication.

Claudia left the bathroom and dropped the clothes on the hospital bed, then went to the plastic patient bag sitting on the chair. Inside the bag was her purse, which a thoughtful police officer had delivered once they extracted her car from the river. They'd even been able to pull her keys from the ignition—too bad her car was totaled. Her purse and pretty much everything else inside besides her ID and credit cards were ruined and smelling a little . . . swampy. Claudia lifted a handful of hair to her nose and sniffed. Ew.

Maybe the nurse had good reason to go for that hygiene kit.

Digging through her purse, she found a hair tie and swept her hair into a bun, careful of the stitched area at her hairline.

At least the airbags had done their job. She rubbed her shoulder. The doctor had checked for broken bones and then told her she was very lucky—she was going to survive with only some bruising and the gash on her head.

Exhaling, Claudia eyed the clothing on the bed and then unfolded the shirt. "Uh-uh. No way." She ground her teeth and looked toward the door. Somewhere in the waiting room Ari Blackman was probably having a good laugh.

She stared down at what the shirt said. HE'S MY BETTER HALF.

There was also a pair of sweats that appeared to be her size— Wait! Did these items belong to Ari's girlfriend? Claudia cringed. No way was she wearing Ari's girlfriend's clothes. She'd rather walk out in a hospital gown. Or scrubs. Yes!

Claudia hit the call button on the bedside remote.

"You've pressed the call button. Can I help you?"

"Yes, I, uh"—she glanced down at the T-shirt and sweatpants—"my clothes were ruined when I was brought in, and I need something to wear out."

A knock on the door turned Claudia around. *That was quick.* "Come in."

Her nurse walked in with a smile. "Those don't work?"

"Well, the gesture was nice, but, uh, I'm not sure I'm comfortable wearing them." Claudia bit her lip, hoping her request would not require further explanation. "Do you have something else? Scrubs?"

"We can't supply you with hospital scrubs. They make us pay for those now." She walked to a cabinet and pulled out a flat package. "But we have paper scrubs. They're huge and not comfortable and . . ." She looked out the window. "Well, you're probably not going to want to wear them in that."

Claudia turned to the window and the rain that was still sliding down the glass. *Great.* The last thing she needed was to wear paper scrubs in the rain. She'd turn into a papier-mâché mess. "No, that's okay."

"I'm sure your boyfriend is just happy you're okay."

"He's not—"

But once again, the nurse was out the door. *Man, she's quick.*

Begrudgingly, Claudia put on the clothes Ari had brought, grateful at least that they wouldn't disintegrate in the rain. She signed her discharge paperwork and was walking down the hall with pain meds and wound care instructions for her stitches when she recognized his familiar form leaning against the wall, chatting with a female nurse.

Nope. Claudia knew the visual cues lighting the woman's features—the way she bit her lip and batted her eyelashes, and ooh, the fake laugh. Classic. Annoyance burned in her chest.

Blowing out a breath that hurt, she continued toward him not because she wanted to but because she had to pass him to get to the hospital exit. Each step closer caused emotion to build in her. Except it didn't just feel like annoyance. When the nurse put her hand on Ari's arm, it was a flare of jealousy that fanned the heat rising to Claudia's cheeks.

She must've *really* hit her head hard. There was no way she was jealous. Hurt, maybe a little. After all, he was supposed to be here for her . . . Wait. Was that true? Had the CIA sent him here to check up on her? Find out why she was targeted?

"He was a total gentleman when he did CPR." Her nurse's words came charging back, and Claudia came to a dead stop. She stared at Ari, his back to her, realizing he was no longer wearing the fine-fitting suit from earlier. Instead, he sported a pair of workout shorts and a T-shirt that stretched in all the right places. That poor nurse didn't stand a chance against Ari's muscles.

"Don't mind her." Claudia jumped at the voice suddenly next to her. Her nurse was standing there, a mischievous smile playing on her lips. "Jenny flirts with everyone, but she's harmless."

"I don't . . . he's not . . . we're not . . . he's just a—"

"Hey there, Andretti."

Claudia turned to find Ari in front of her, the nurse back

behind the nurses' station, busying herself with some paper-work even though her gaze was still fixed on Ari. *Harmless?* Claudia wasn't so sure. According to some of her coworkers, it was pretty easy to fall under Ari's spell.

"How are you feeling?"

Ari's gentle words called her focus back. "Um, fine. Just a bump on the head."

"You're lucky."

His eyes moved to her wound, a tenderness in them that made her stomach feel light. Or maybe that was a side effect of a concussion. Had to be.

"I wasn't sure what to expect when I found you."

Found me. "My nurse . . ." Claudia twisted, but her nurse had disappeared. She was beginning to think the woman was a figment of her imagination. The doc said she didn't seem to have a concussion, but Claudia was starting to wonder. "My nurse said you did CPR, that you pulled me from the river?"

Ari's expression grew serious, those dark brown eyes searching her face again. "I tried to intercept the truck before it happened, but it—" His Adam's apple moved as he swallowed. "It was too late. He hit you and I thought you were going to roll, but—"

"I turned into the hit."

"Yeah." Ari nodded. "You were quick. It probably saved your life."

"Actually, I think you did that." Claudia couldn't explain the lightness moving through her chest, so she ignored it. "Thank you."

He dipped his chin, and Claudia appreciated the simple humility until a smug grin began pulling at his lips. Then he was full-on smiling at her.

She wrinkled her brow. "What?"

"Next time you don't have to go to such drastic measures for a first kiss."

Claudia's eyes bulged. "What! You really must think you're something if—"

"Come on." Ari laughed. "I'm joking."

She was so disjointed by his comment that she hadn't realized his hand had found its way to her elbow, his fingers warming her skin and ringing alarms in her head. She started down the hall, anxious to step out of his touch as naturally as possible.

From the corner of her eye, she could see Ari looking at her. "What?"

He chuckled. "You're wearing the shirt inside out."

Claudia cut a side glance to him. "I did it on purpose. You might be someone's better half, but you're not mine. No matter what that nurse thinks." She mumbled the last part.

"What?"

"When I get home, I'll make sure to wash your girlfriend's clothing and get it back to you."

Ari's lips pulled into a funny smile. "The clothes belong to my sister. She left them here after a visit a while back and I was supposed to send them to her, but"—his eyes moved over her—"I figured you could use them."

"Thanks," she bit off, her skin tingling under his gaze. She reached for her cell phone so she could call for an Uber to take her home and end this day, but her hands found nothing. She groaned. Her cell phone was probably at the bottom of the Potomac.

"I can drive you home," Ari said.

Her eyes flashed to him.

"I'll call an Uber, thanks."

"The agency insists. They want to make sure you get home safely."

Or keep an eye on me. If she refused Ari's ride home, what would they think? That she had something to hide? Was going to meet someone? If she was in their position, she'd probably think the same. Then she'd follow herself to make sure, which meant Ari would follow her home anyway.

"Fine."

They walked through the automatic sliding doors of the hospital emergency room. Ari reached for her arm again, his gentle touch pausing her.

"Let me get the car and bring it around."

"It's only stitches. I can walk." To prove her point, she stepped out of the alcove and into the rain that had slowed to a drizzle.

"My car's this way."

She looked back to where Ari was walking—in the opposite direction of where she was headed. Without a word, she changed course and followed him to an older Honda Accord. The horn beeped and the lights flashed when he unlocked the car, and before she could grab for the handle, he was there opening the door for her.

Climbing in, Claudia surveyed the clean interior and was surprised there was no lingering scent of cologne. Not that she would notice Ari's cologne if he wore any, but the absence of it was unusual. At least according to her expectations of who she'd imagined him to be.

When he got in, Ari asked for her address and typed it into his cell phone before pulling out of the hospital parking lot. She shifted in the silence, trying to avoid giving in to the desire to peek at him.

"I expected you'd be driving some fancy sports car."

"Some playboys prefer dependability over speed."

Claudia looked over at him. His attention was solely focused on the road, but she noticed a tightness to the tiny lines at the corner of his eyes. Her earlier comment about his reputation had really struck a chord. "I'm sorry about what I said earlier. I guess I was ticked the CIA would think I was involved, and I took it out on you."

"Don't worry about it."

Ari dismissed her with a shrug, his tone telling her it was no big deal, but Claudia couldn't shake the feeling wedged between her ribs that she'd really hurt his feelings. And it bothered her that it bothered her.

"I, uh, can you tell me what happened?" she asked, wanting to shift the attention back to neutral ground. "I mean, I know I was rammed off the side of the road and into the Potomac, but the police officer didn't have very many details outside of that."

"We don't either. The agency is working with Metro PD." He gave her a sideways glance. "You didn't recognize the vehicle or the driver?"

The only way Ari would know that was if he'd already read the police report. And if he had done that, it meant that his purpose for being at the hospital wasn't entirely for her well-being—she was still under suspicion.

"No." A quick look from Ari told her he'd caught the coolness in her tone. "I have no idea who ran me off the road."

"Do you think it had something to do with Prince Mohamed's murder?"

Claudia blinked. It could be connected. But why would they be coming after her? There was no good reason that she could think of. One peek at Ari and she could see the lines of doubt all over his pretty face.

SIX

The rest of the ride to Claudia's townhome in Fairfax was silent. Ari kept casting quick glances over at her, curious if she was trying to figure out a way to answer his question. *Was tonight's accident related to Prince Mohamed's murder?*

Ari pulled into a parking spot outside Claudia's townhome and cut the engine. "I'll walk you to the door."

Claudia turned in the passenger seat, the car's interior light casting just enough light on her face to show the lines of frustration pulling her brows together. "Does the CIA really believe I'm hiding something?"

Claudia's tone held not only animosity but also exhaustion, and it reminded him of everything she'd been through in the last several hours. He chose his words carefully. "You know it's standard procedure to follow up on any situation where an intelligence officer is involved with a foreigner."

"There was no involvement of any sort," Claudia said, holding his gaze before turning to open the car door. "I can walk myself to the door."

He cringed when she slammed the door shut. This wasn't at all how his night was supposed to go. Quickly getting out of the car, he caught up to Claudia at the steps of her home. "My car might be old, but it's paid off and I'd like to keep all the doors on it if I can."

She ignored him, pulling her keys out of the plastic hospital bag.

"Today you walked in on the murder scene of the Saudi prince, and hours later a truck drove you into the Potomac with the intention, as you said, to kill you." He took a step, pivoting so he was in front of her door. "I'm not the only one with a reputation at the agency. You don't think I've heard about novia de la agencia? The CIA officer who *mailed* Hector Perez, the Valle Colombiano cartel boss, back to the United States for prosecution a few years ago?"

The tilt to her lip did funny things to his stomach. Claudia Gallegos was a legend in her own right—and she knew it.

"You can't expect the C—" Ari tilted his head when something grabbed his attention from his peripheral. He angled his head to a row of cars parked along the back edge of the parking lot. Nothing unusual . . . except his gaze dropped to the ground near the vehicles, where he spotted a discarded cigarette butt next to a piece of trash and some leaves. It wouldn't have stood out but for the orange ash glowing.

His eyes flashed to the vehicle, and even in the darkness he could see a shadow move. "Go!"

"Move!" Claudia yelled at the same time.

Wrapping his arm around Claudia's shoulder, he shoved her through the front door she'd just opened.

Pfft. Pfft. The crack of wood and breaking glass echoed with every shot being fired at them.

"Get down!"

"What do you think I'm doing?" Claudia said, dropping to her knees and putting her hands over her head.

Ari placed himself over her and used his heel to swing the

door shut. He was grateful to see Claudia had a double bolt, so he reached up and locked them both.

"I'm pretty sure that wasn't a ticked-off squirrel chucking acorns at us."

She was making a joke? His eyes caught on her stitches and then traveled down to the slight glimmer of fear he saw in her gaze. "Not unless your squirrels are trained by Rambo."

Ari held his breath as he tried to slow his pounding pulse. The shooting had stopped, but that didn't mean whoever was out there wasn't watching them, waiting for them to move. To his left was a sitting room with a window. The curtains were pulled back and the blinds open. If he could make his way over there, he could see if the shooter was still outside.

"Do you have any weapons in the house?"

"In my room. I have a safe in my closet."

He glanced back at a coat closet nearby. Opening the door, he was glad to see it wasn't overstuffed with items. With a sweep of his arm, he cleared out the boots and shoes. "Get in here and wait while I check the rest of your place."

The moonlight coming through the transom window over her door revealed her defiant expression. "I'm not hiding in the closet. I know how to fight back, Ari Blackman."

"I just want to check to make sure the shooter is gone. I don't need both of us getting shot."

"This is my house—"

"If the next line is, *I have to defend it*, I'll walk out and face the shooter right now."

"*Home Alone* is a good movie." The humor in her words sounded forced, like she was using it to keep herself calm.

"Now is not the time to explain why there was no way Kevin McCallister could defend his home, and I'm pretty sure we're not dealing with Marv or Harry." He pulled his cell phone out of his pocket, unlocked it, and handed it to her. "I just need to check if they're still out there. Will you wait here, call 911, and let me do that, please?"

Claudia pressed her lips together for a second and then took the phone from him. "Fine, but I am not hiding in the closet."

Ari detected through her tone that she wasn't used to giving in. He wanted to explain that this wasn't some patriarchal power trip. Claudia's past successful missions made it very clear that the woman could take care of herself, but when he pulled her limp body out of the Potomac, some protective instinct in him shifted.

Staying low, he moved to the window and peeked out. The spot where the car had been parked was empty. Behind him, he heard Claudia giving 911 her address. He released a breath, but it didn't unknot the tension bunching his shoulder muscles.

Someone had tried to kill Claudia. Twice.

Rising to his feet, Ari backed up and turned, misjudging the distance, because he was suddenly very close to her. Close enough he could feel her sudden intake of breath. Her eyes met his, and for a long second neither of them moved. What was he doing?

Claudia reached for the light switch, but he stopped her, putting his hand over hers.

"I didn't see the shooter's car out there, but that doesn't mean they didn't move locations. Let's hold off on the lights until the cops get here."

"If you wanted to hang out in the dark with me"—her lips curled into a smirk—"you could've done it in a less dramatic way than with a shooter, you know."

It took him a second before he got it—maybe because she was still standing so close. He sidestepped, giving himself the space he needed to get his brain working again. "Ah, okay, because of the whole first kiss thing I said earlier. Ha. Ha."

Claudia reached into a basket on the floor inside the closet and pulled out a flashlight. She tipped it up at her face and clicked it on, casting what would've been an eerie glow had her smile been more sinister and not . . . *really nice.*

"Come on," she said. "Let's check the house."

Ari noticed Claudia's nervous humor ended when the police arrived a few minutes later and searched her home again. She was detailed in the report she gave them and accepted their assurance that they'd do their best to find the shooter. Ari didn't doubt they'd try, but it wasn't enough to keep him from having a conversation about Claudia's safety with Director Eisner. Thankfully, he agreed . . . and now Ari just needed to let Claudia know she would be going to a safe house for the night.

The knots in his stomach tightened. In the very brief time he'd known her, there was no denying her stubborn streak—and that she didn't seem to care for people telling her what to do. How would she take being told she had to leave her home and remain under his watch until they figured out who was behind the attempts on her life?

"If you give me a few minutes"—Claudia checked the locks on the slider in her kitchen before pulling the curtains closed—"I'll grab some clothes and my toiletry bag."

His face must've given away his surprise, because she quirked that eyebrow. "Seriously, Ari, you know I'm in the CIA *with* you. Trained. Sat through the procedures class."

The tips of his ears burned. He cleared his throat. "Right, no, I know that. I was just, uh . . ." He pushed his glasses up his nose. "I was expecting more of a fight."

Claudia shrugged. "What would be the point?"

Ari watched her disappear down the hall. *Get it together, man.* He shook his head, hoping it would dispel whatever fog he was in. He needed to focus on Director Eisner's parting words: *"Get her to talk."* According to Eisner, the news was already reporting on the suspicious death of Prince Mohamed and speculating as to how the Saudi royal family was going to react and how this would affect US–Saudi relations. The CIA station chief and the US ambassador in Riyadh were already seeing an influx of conspiracy-related chatter.

He glanced around Claudia's living room, noting the bland décor that didn't reflect the personality he'd already gotten a peek at. The generic knickknacks and artwork were what anyone would find in a home furnishings showroom, but nothing inside this space told a visitor about the person who lived here. No books. No discarded clothing with her alma mater on it. No photos.

Be careful, his inner voice warned when he recognized the lack of personal belongings. The townhome was functional—served a purpose—and whether Claudia Gallegos realized it or not, it revealed something about her that others might miss. She was a professional—trained and ready to disappear at a moment's notice.

SEVEN

I never thought I'd find myself in a safe house on American soil." Claudia looked around the large master bedroom inside the Crystal City penthouse apartment. Large floor-to-ceiling windows on two walls gave her a spectacular view of the Pentagon and the familiar outline of the monuments in the distance. Her gaze moved from the Lincoln Memorial to the spot just behind it where a truck had plowed into her.

She remembered hitting the frigid river but nothing past that. Her fingers traced the stitches at her hairline. If Ari hadn't been there, she would've drowned.

Claudia shuddered and pulled on a pair of fuzzy socks. She was grateful to have her own clothing to slip into—a measure of comfort to dispel the chills. She threw a sweatshirt over her long-sleeve thermal top, hoping the layers would warm her up.

Stepping out of the bedroom, she found Joy Mullins, an intel analyst from the CIA, sitting on the couch in a well-appointed living room that separated one-half of the large apartment. On the other side was a chef's kitchen, where Ari was . . . standing in front of the stove, stirring a pot of whatever was filling the apartment with a tangy aroma that caused her stomach to give a low growl.

Claudia let herself watch Ari. The way he moved in the

kitchen told her he wasn't in uncharted territory—and why that made her smile, she wasn't sure.

"He's promised to save me some for lunch tomorrow since I've already eaten," Joy said, snapping Claudia back from checking out Ari. He looked up from the pot and smiled, which caused her cheeks to burn and the chills she'd felt a second ago to suddenly melt away. "Will you make sure he keeps his word?"

"Uh, sure." Claudia swallowed and stepped aside so Joy could go into the bedroom. "Are you sure you don't want to eat with us?"

"I'm going to call my husband. Our son had a football game tonight, and I want to see how he did."

Claudia felt bad. It wasn't agency protocol to send an officer to stay overnight, but Claudia had insisted. She didn't want any rumors to set the ladies' locker room buzzing.

Her attention drifted back to the kitchen. Was it possible that seeing Ari with a towel draped over his shoulder made him more attractive? It was silly. What woman didn't like a man who could cook? Did he know that? If it wasn't for the delicious aroma wafting from the pot he was stirring, she would've assumed it was an act to catch her off guard.

"So, you cook?"

Ari smiled at her. "Why does every assessment you make of me sound like a surprise?"

Crossing the living room, Claudia glanced at the television, which was on but muted. She paused. A man in a plaid shirt, knit beanie cap, and full beard was doing some kind of construction on a cabin. "You're watching a home improvement channel? Or did Joy put this on?"

"No, me." Ari tapped a spoon on the rim of the pan and pointed it at her. "See? Surprise."

She couldn't resist matching his smirk with one of her own. "Can you blame me?" She looked back at the television. "Are you planning on building a cabin? Going off the grid?"

"Maybe one day." He turned and opened a cabinet to pull out two bowls.

When he didn't offer any more, Claudia slid the cuffs of her sweatshirt over her knuckles and hopped onto a stool at the kitchen island. "What did you make?"

"Red lentil soup, but I didn't make it. I had Joy pick it up from one of my favorite restaurants."

The oven timer went off, and he grabbed a pair of oven pads before opening the door and pulling out a tray of naan. She tried to school her surprise, but he'd seen it and shook his head.

"I am more than good looks, ya know?" He set the warm bread on the stovetop.

Claudia arched a brow. "See, now here I was thinking maybe he's not so egotistical, and you go and say something like that."

Ari smiled—and, boy, was it a nice one. She could definitely see why he was a frequent topic of conversation among the women of the CIA. His dark eyes flashed to hers. "How are you feeling?"

His concern appeared genuine, and it caused something to flutter in her chest. Ignoring it, she nodded. "Good, for now. I took the painkillers the doctor gave me to get ahead of the headache he said would come."

Ari turned his attention to ladling soup into the bowls. "You'll probably be pretty sore tomorrow."

"Yeah, he said that too." Claudia inhaled the aroma of the meal Ari placed before her. "It smells delicious."

"Tastes good too." Ari walked around the island and sat on the stool next to her. He reached across for the naan, and

CAUGHT IN THE CROSSHAIRS

Claudia couldn't help noticing the way his back muscles pulled beneath his T-shirt.

Wow. Was she seriously checking him out? *Ever since I stepped out of the bedroom*, her own voice echoed in her ears. Blinking, Claudia grabbed her spoon and ate a mouthful of soup. "H-hot!" She closed her eyes, cringing as she forced the hot liquid down her throat. When she opened them, she met Ari's amused expression. "What?" she croaked over her burned tongue and throat.

"It's soup." He lifted a spoonful and blew on it. "It's hot."

"*I know*." Claudia was careful to blow on the next few bites. "I didn't realize how hungry I was."

"Nearly dying takes it out of you, I suppose." He tore a piece of naan and chewed it. "Maybe as much as the person saving your life. Twice."

"I'll give you the river, but I think it was *me* who pushed *you* into the house."

His eyes grew wide. "You're not serious, are you? I saw the glowing cigarette butt, the guy in the shadows. I'm the one who pushed you."

She shot him a look, and he snickered before he ate a bite of soup and winked at her. "Maybe we should just stick to figuring out who's so interested in killing me."

Even though she had tried to add humor to the words, Ari's serious expression said he wasn't buying it. "Tell me what you know about Prince Mohamed."

"Very little, actually." Claudia ate some more soup, wanting to be careful about what she said. "I crossed paths with Prince Mohamed when I was working the Colombiano mission during the Dubai Formula 1 Grand Prix. He was a real piece of work. Women, drugs, parties—he loved pushing the limits but crossed a line when he took the wrong girl back to his hotel. No amount of money was going to buy his way out of the beating headed his way. Even if the prince deserved it, that kind of trouble would've compromised my mission, and I'd worked too hard for that to happen. So I stepped in and leveraged Prince Mohamed's shares in their family's F1 racing team."

A look of admiration filled Ari's face. "You are quite the woman, Claudia Gallegos. It wouldn't surprise me if, with enough time, you could brokerage a peace deal across the Middle East."

He couldn't help but ooze charm and— Wait. Claudia jerked her attention back to her bowl of soup. Was this a game? Get her to let down her guard so he could get information from her?

"I can see why you've earned your nickname, Mr. Bond. But you don't need to wield your slick charm on me. I'm telling you everything I know." She narrowed her eyes on him, expecting a rebuttal, but he stayed silent and it made her uncomfortable. "Which you can pass on to Director Eisner."

Ari's expression sobered. "You can't think of any reason why Radwan would call you? Maybe the prince had gotten himself into trouble with the Colombiano Valle cartel again and wanted you to use your mad skills to get him out of it?"

"I don't know." She answered honestly and hoped Ari would accept it. "But from the scene I walked into, I don't think he's changed much. I'm sure he's ticked someone off." A thought occurred to her. "You wouldn't happen to have a computer with you?"

He frowned. "Yes, why?"

"The only way I can stop you from looking at me like I'm hiding something is to figure out what Prince Mohamed got himself involved in that might've led to his murder. The best way to figure that out is on the internet."

Surprising her, Ari crossed the room and pulled out his laptop. He set it on the island, logged in, and turned it to her. "Go ahead."

Claudia quickly searched Prince Mohamed's name on several sites. Some were already mentioning his death, but one caught her attention immediately. "Look at this."

Ari leaned in, and she caught a hint of his cologne. So he did wear it. The smell was a bit sweet and . . . familiar. *Sandalwood.* And she only knew that because she had a candle in her townhome with a similar scent.

She cleared her throat, annoyed that somehow her brain was turning to mush in his presence like some lovestruck teenager. Claudia had worked too hard and sacrificed too much to be anything but professional.

"It looks like Prince Mohamed had an altercation three days ago." Claudia clicked on a link that started a cell phone video of the prince and another man in a heated argument inside a nightclub. "There's no sound on the video, so I can't tell what they're saying or fighting about." She sat back. "What do you think? Does that man look angry enough to kill Prince Mohamed?"

Ari reached in front of her and hit the key to play the video again. "He certainly doesn't look happy. You don't know him?"

"He's not any member of the Colombiano Valle cartel that I recognize, but we need to find out who he is and what the fight was about."

"We're a bit limited in what we can do. This is the FBI's case. Not ours. And in case you missed the memo, they're not really keen on agency interference."

Claudia thought of Pecca and Maceo. She didn't care what the FBI was keen on—if there was a remote chance they could be in danger again because of her, she would do what was necessary. "I don't plan on interfering." She eyed him. "But I have an idea. Can I borrow your phone?"

Ari set down his spoon and wiped his mouth with a paper towel. He pulled his cell phone from his pocket, unlocked the screen, and handed it over to her.

She dialed her brother-in-law's number and let it ring twice before ending the call. She repeated it twice more. The third time, she caught Ari leaning on his elbows watching her. Waiting for the phone to ring, she looked up. "It's late, and he won't recognize the number. Three calls right after one another will let him know it's me."

He simply nodded.

"Claudia?" Colton's voice was a mixture of concern and grogginess. "Everything okay?"

"Yes." Her throbbing head called her a liar. "I'm sorry to call so late, but I need Ryan Frost's personal number."

"Sure, okay." She grabbed a pen from the basket on the island and wrote the number Colton gave her on a piece of paper towel. "Are you sure everything's okay?"

Claudia bit her lip, her gaze moving to Ari before he stood and cleared their bowls. "Um, actually, Colton, some things have happened and I need you to keep an eye on Pecca and Maceo for me."

Several seconds of silence ticked off, and Claudia closed her eyes, hating herself for what she was putting them through again.

Finally, Colton said, "They'll be fine here. Promise you'll be careful."

Emotion burned her throat, and she managed a yes before promising to call as soon as she could. She ended the call and set Ari's phone down next to her.

"You okay?"

Claudia swallowed, forcing the emotion back. "Yeah, and now I have the number for the man who can help us work the case."

"What makes you so sure?"

"Agent Ryan Frost works on the FBI's Joint Terrorism Task Force, and if he thinks my sister or my nephew might be in danger, he'll help."

Ari frowned. "You think your sister and nephew are in danger?"

"You said it yourself, someone tried to kill me—twice. The last time someone wanted me dead, they went through my sister and nephew to get to me." The scar on her arm burned. "Which is why I'm not going to just sit here and do nothing."

EIGHT

The last time someone wanted me dead . . ." Those seven words haunted Ari's sleep until he finally gave up tossing and turning sometime after three. He'd used the building's gym before coming back for a shower and was now watching the sunrise over the DC skyline, his emotions on edge from the night before.

He ran a hand through his damp hair, staring at his reflection coming off the floor-to-ceiling window in his room. He heard stirring from the room next door where Claudia and Joy had slept. Hopefully, better than he had. A light tap pulled his attention to the door. He walked over and opened it.

Claudia stood there with two travel mugs of coffee in her hands. "Billy Adler."

He frowned and pointed to himself. "Ari. Blackman." He smothered his laughter when he saw her confusion and looked her over before meeting her narrowed gaze. The olive-green sweater she wore complemented her skin tone. "We should take you back to the hospital. You might have amnesia."

"Very funny." She rolled those beautiful eyes at him. "Agent Frost called this morning to let me know the man in the video is Billy Adler. He works for Tidemark Technology, and we're going to his office."

Ari blinked, still stuck on why he was so quick to describe

Claudia's eyes. They were definitely lovely, but was it really important to make note of that? He checked his watch. "It's kind of early."

"It's nearly eight, Blackman. You don't need any more beauty sleep." She handed him the coffee and turned back to the kitchen. "You get any more good-looking, and the agency will need to send you to the surgeon to make that handsome mug of yours a little more covert."

"Did you just call me good-looking and handsome?" He followed her into the kitchen. "In the same breath?"

Claudia paused by the island and lifted her own cup of coffee to her lips. "Don't let it go to your head. I'm not blind . . ." Her gaze traveled over him, and he noticed a bloom of pink color her cheeks when their eyes met again. She cleared her throat. "I've been trained to be suspicious of handsome men."

Her words stung, and from the way Claudia snapped her lips closed and the apologetic look in her eyes, she knew it.

"I'm sorry, I didn't mean—"

"I get it." Ari huffed out a small laugh. "You're a highly trained professional, immune to tactics of the enemy." He pointed to himself. "Me, being on that list."

"No, I-I didn't—"

"It's fine." He cut her off again, losing hope that he had any chance to change her impression of him and frustrated with the growing desire that made him want to change it in the first place. He grabbed his keys from the counter. "Do you have an address for Tidemark?"

"Yes."

"Then we should go." He turned on his heel and headed for the door.

Claudia stood rooted to her spot for several seconds before

he felt her following him. They rode the elevator down to the parking garage in silence, which gave him time to bring his focus back to the case.

Late last night after contacting Agent Frost and Director Eisner, an agreement was made that Claudia and Ari could assist the JTTF in gathering information pertinent to Prince Mohamed's murder. The sooner they got this done, the sooner he could be back at his office, avoiding further insults from the woman whose words seemed to strangely have a direct line to his heart.

Ari had hoped a new day would provide a fresh start for him and Claudia. A fresh chance to prove to her he was not the playboy she seemed to think he was. Maybe it was easier to just let her keep believing whatever she wanted.

At his car, he opened the passenger door for her and ignored the still-surprised look he caught in her expression. Good grief, were the men she dated that thoughtless? He walked around his car as a strange sensation snaked through him at the thought of Claudia dating. Or maybe it was the idea they were all untrained in the art of good manners.

Ari climbed into the driver's seat, pushing the bothersome thought away, and punched the address for Tidemark Technology into his car's GPS. It wasn't his concern who Claudia dated or whether they had good manners. His concern was helping the JTTF figure out who killed Prince Mohamed and keeping Claudia Gallegos from getting under his skin.

They were several minutes into their silent car ride when he felt her eyes on him. "Something wrong?"

"Look, what I said last night, the whole playboy thing—"

"Don't worry about it." He gripped the steering wheel. "I know what people say about me. It's not a big deal."

"It seems like it is."

His eyes flashed to her and she lifted her eyebrows, a dare lingering there to refute her words. He looked back to the road. "It's a nickname. If people want to read more into it than that and believe something about me that isn't true, it's not worth my time to change their mind."

They drove in silence for a few more miles until she spoke again.

"When they first gave me the nickname novia de la agencia, the agency girlfriend, I took it as a compliment." The softness in her voice pulled his attention from the road, and he caught her rubbing her arm again. "I was dedicated to my job, and I was glad people saw that . . ."

"But it's not who you are," he supplied. "Not wholly."

Claudia turned and their eyes met for a brief second, but it was enough for a mutual understanding to pass between them. She offered a tight-lipped smile before looking away, severing their connection.

"I'm sorry about what I said last night and this morning. I won't judge you on your devilish good looks if you don't judge me on my crackerjack skills and dedication to the job."

A burst of laughter bubbled out of him. He glanced over and saw her smiling. "I wanted to believe that was an actual apology, but now I'm unsure if it was a backhanded compliment to yourself."

Her laughter sliced through the tension like a warm knife through butter, and he found himself enjoying the sound of it and the way it seemed to unravel the knots of stress in his muscles. That hope from earlier returned. Maybe this wouldn't be so bad after all.

NINE

'm so sorry, but you just missed Mr. Adler."

Claudia narrowed her eyes on the young woman batting her fake lashes up at Ari as if she were trying to cast a spell on him. Ten minutes ago, they'd arrived at Tidemark Technology, an information and technology company, and now they were being stonewalled by a twentysomething named *Ember*. What kind of name was Ember?

"I spoke to you earlier, *Ember*, and you said Mr. Adler was here."

Ember blinked, looking startled as if she'd forgotten Claudia was standing there. "Well, he was, but then he left."

"Can you tell us where he went?" Ari said, his tone smooth as chocolate. "We really need to talk to him."

"I'm sorry. I can't give you that information, but"—she smiled seductively, tossing her hair over her shoulder—"I can make an appointment."

Oh, can she?

Ari smiled, his posture tilting toward Ember. "What time will he be back?"

"Not for the rest of the day. He had me cancel all his appoint—" She closed her lips. "I'm not sure when Mr. Adler will be back, but if you give me your card, I can call you when he returns and set up that appointment."

Claudia didn't like the sound of that, and from the look on Ari's face, he didn't either. At least they were on the same page.

His attention went back to Ember. "So he's headed out of town for a few days?"

The woman's doe-eyed expression was full of surprise. "I didn't say that."

Ari smiled at her. "The only thing that would cause me to cancel my schedule is an unexpected trip. Vacation?"

Claudia didn't know if it was his smile or charm that sent Ember's lashes into flight, but she worried the woman would lift off. This was getting old. "Em—"

"It's really important that we talk to Mr. Adler," Ari said. She narrowed her eyes on him, but he didn't notice and it bothered her a little. "Can you tell us which airport he's flying out of?"

"I really can't tell you anything," Ember whined.

Claudia had had enough. Her hand went instinctively to her pocket for her cell phone . . . that wasn't there. Drats. She tapped Ari's arm. "Give me your cell phone. I'm going to make a call to the FAA and get Mr. Adler's flight grounded." She turned her narrowed gaze on Ember. "Then you can explain to your boss why his trip was delayed and to the FBI why you're hindering their investigation."

"Investigation?" Ember's eyes rounded, moving between Claudia and Ari, where they stayed—*naturally*. She swiveled in her chair to face Ari. "I'm not trying to be difficult. I just don't want to lose my job!"

"I understand, and we don't want you to lose your job either." Ari's expression turned sympathetic. "But there's no harm in letting us know what airport he's flying out of, right?"

Ember bit her lip, looking more flirtatious than worried. "I—"

"You wouldn't be breaking any privacy rules with your boss, because as my partner said, we can make a simple phone call and get the aircraft information ourselves. But you'd be helping us out *and* protecting your boss."

"I would?"

Claudia's temper was rising, and it didn't help when she saw Ari flash another flirtatious smile. It was enough to make Claudia sick. Actually, it kind of was making her sick, but not in the way she expected. Ari was doing his job, and as she watched the woman scribble down the name of the airport, it shouldn't have bothered Claudia how he got the information . . . so why was her stomach churning with something that felt like jealousy again?

"Thank you for your time and help," Ari said before he and Claudia walked back to the elevator. When they stepped inside, he looked over at her. "Everything okay?"

"Yeah, why?"

"You just look . . . upset."

"I'm annoyed," Claudia said. "She wasted our time. Adler is on the move, and in the time it took us to get the name of the airport, he could already be gone."

The elevator doors slid open and they stepped out, heading toward the parking garage.

"She was just doing her job." Ari unlocked his car and opened the passenger door for her. "She doesn't quite have the cracker-jack skills you do, but she's dedicated."

Claudia's annoyance peaked at his playful turn on her words from earlier. "I guess I can see why they call you Bond, Ari. So good with the women."

Ari clenched his jaw, his gaze shifting from her to the ground as he closed the door for her. Guilt washed over her, and as she watched him walk around the front of the car, it struck her that it wasn't Ari or Ember she was annoyed with—it was herself. Somehow she'd allowed Ari to get into her head.

When he climbed into the car, he unlocked his cell phone and handed it to her. "Call Agent Frost and let him know we're on our way to the Kensington Airfield. Maybe he can do something about holding the flight."

His straight-to-business instruction silenced the apology she wanted to offer him. She took Ari's phone and dialed Ryan's number, wanting to avoid the heaviness of her earlier comment twisting her stomach into knots. *"But it's not who you are."* He had spoken those tender words to make her believe she was more than her nickname, and all she'd done in the last several hours was reinforce the nickname Ari was quietly dispelling.

Ryan answered her call, delaying the apology she owed Ari. She quickly explained their brief encounter with Ember, and when she finished the call, she set the phone in the console between them.

"I told Ryan we're headed to Kensington Airfield, and he said he's going to work on getting the flight information, but delaying the plane is likely going to require a warrant and more evidence than a viral video of an argument between Adler and the prince."

"Makes sense." Ari nodded, following the GPS directions. "So, this Ryan, he an old friend of yours?"

Claudia glanced over at Ari. The way he'd said *old* made it sound like he was asking more. Was he? "Not really. He's actually a friend of my sister's who I met after . . ." Her hand moved to the spot on her arm. Her sweater was too thick to feel the scar, but she didn't need to feel it to know exactly where it was. The memory of that day still caused her throat to thicken with nausea.

"Did you take the medicine the doctor gave you?"

She clasped her hands in her lap. "Oh yeah. I mean, I'm sore. Woke up feeling like Mike Tyson used my body for a punching bag, and my head still stings a little bit."

"What you said last night about them going through your sister to get to you . . . how badly were you hurt?"

"Some damage to my back muscles and a gunshot wound to my arm."

From the corner of her eye, she caught the muscle in his cheek as it popped. "I don't know many people who could go through what you did who'd be out here working the field the next day." He looked over at her. "You're as tough as they say."

"Novia de la agencia, remember?"

"No." Ari shook his head. "That's not it. I know people who give their lives to the agency are fully committed, but—please don't take this the wrong way—your commitment is next level."

She heard the hesitation. "I appreciate your attempt to say I don't have a life outside of my work."

"Do you?"

Claudia's cheeks warmed. She swallowed, unsure how to answer. If she was honest, no. But then that would confirm what Ari and everyone else believed about her. "Up until a few years ago, I would say I was exactly who people said I was. I worked hard to get into the agency and wanted to prove I deserved to be there. Prove it was worth the sacrifice."

The last words slipped from her lips and she prayed Ari hadn't heard them. Joining the CIA had been an easy decision, one she'd made without care to the cost it might have on her relationship with her family. Now, twelve years later, she was beginning to wonder if it had been worth it. If maybe there wasn't something more she'd given up by saying yes to her career.

"My father's brother, David, worked for Mossad," Ari said. "When I told my father I was applying to work for the agency, he was concerned. Worried the job would make me choose between it and my family."

Claudia sighed. "The agency doesn't make it easy."

His quick glance over caused her to avert her gaze. "No, but I think it's possible to find balance—to have a life, relationships, that exist outside of our careers. My dad says it's all about keeping a healthy dose of humility at the forefront."

"What does humility have to do with intelligence?"

Ari shrugged. "Everything. There's nearly twenty-two thousand of us, and yet none of us possess a single skill that makes us irreplaceable. We leave or get injured"—he looked over—"they'll have someone there to take our place. Humility is understanding that at the end of the day, we're just another employee in a company. Humility is recognizing that our value and worth don't hang on the promotions or successful missions completed— though what we do is valuable as a whole, God can take care of it without us, just like the CIA can. It's wise to remember that."

Claudia, unsure how to respond, turned her attention to the scenery outside of the car.

"Surprised?"

She swung her gaze around and met his eyes, a tease in his expression that was infuriatingly attractive. "What? No. No, I'm not surprised." He raised a brow at her. "Okay, so maybe a little. I didn't peg you for philosophical or religious."

"I'm neither." Ari chuckled. "I'm just repeating the words my father spoke to me and standing in faith—not religion—that God is who he says he is."

Not in a million years would Claudia have guessed she'd be sitting in a car with Ari Blackman, talking about God—and yet, his gentle words came from a place of sincerity, and for some reason it made her want to know more.

"We're here." Ari drove past a sign that read Kensington Airfield and steered the car down a long, landscaped drive. "Fancy, huh?"

He parked in between a Jaguar and a Mercedes, and they got out of the car. Claudia glanced around at the other luxury vehicles as they walked through the parking lot. "I have a feeling we won't find an abundance of humility here."

"You could be surprised," Ari said, holding open the glass door to the two-story building. As she passed by him, he leaned down so his words tickled her ears. "Humility can be found anywhere—even in handsome CIA officers."

TEN

nhaling deeply, Ari pushed the breath from his lungs and shook his head. Why had he said that? It had slipped out, was totally unprofessional, and likely only further fueled her belief about him.

"I can see why they call you Bond, Ari."

He wasn't like Bond at all. His charm played a role. One that kept him safe, just like an alias did when operating overseas. So why did her words bug him so much?

He'd never cared much when others called him Bond or joked about his supposed playboy status, but hearing it come from Claudia felt different. Maybe it was the guarded expression in her eyes whenever she looked at him.

Their steps echoed against the marble flooring guiding them into Kensington Airfield.

"Wow."

Ari heard Claudia whisper his thoughts just as a large security guard rose from behind a counter. The stern frown stitched across his forehead said he knew they didn't belong there.

The place was the stuff movies were made of, with its art deco–designed interior. Vintage posters from TWA, Pan Am, and other American airlines lined the mahogany walls, but the pièce de résistance was the twenty-foot water feature showcasing chrome jets intersecting at the top with glass contrails trailing behind them.

"May I help you?" the guard said, giving each of them a quick glance as though assessing their threat level.

"Good morning." Ari stepped forward. First impression said the guard wasn't going to freely give them information, which meant he was going to have to break CIA protocol. He pulled out his wallet and flashed his badge. "We're looking for a passenger scheduled to depart from here."

Ari watched Claudia cross to the double glass doors that separated them from the passengers inside the lounge.

The guard stepped in front of her. "You're not allowed in the lounge unless you're a member or an approved guest of a member."

"We need to speak with Billy Adler. His secretary told us he was flying out this morning. We promise not to disturb him or anyone else and to be quick."

"Not quick enough." The guard looked over at Ari. "Mr. Adler's flight is leaving now."

Ari glanced to the wall of floor-to-ceiling windows that overlooked the length of the airfield and woodland backdrop of Great Falls Park. A private jet was beginning its taxi down the Jetway.

"We have to stop him." Claudia's words pulled his and the guard's attention to her. "He's running."

"You can't go out there either unless you are a registered traveler." The guard's eyes flashed to Claudia. "No exceptions."

"Thank you." Ari walked toward the window, putting himself between Claudia and the glass doors leading to the airfield just in case the guard had good reason to be concerned.

She tapped his arm. "Can I use your cell phone again?"

He unlocked his phone and handed it to her. "What are you doing?"

"We need to let Ryan know that Billy Adler is potentially running. Maybe he can pull the flight plan and find out where he's going. Have authorities stop him there."

Claudia stepped away to make the phone call, and Ari's attention returned to the plane taxiing away.

Behind him, he could hear Claudia explaining the situation to Agent Frost. There was still something unsettling about the icky feeling playing games with his mind regarding her seemingly platonic relationship with the FBI agent. Ari shoved away the thought. It wasn't worth exploring, given her very strong opinion of who he was—or at least who she thought he was.

Ari squinted, bringing his face closer to the glass door and the scene unfolding beyond it. The jet Billy had boarded had stopped and was sitting in the middle of the runway. The airstairs descended and a female flight attendant hurried out of the plane, running toward the building. *What the—*

Before the security guard could stop him, Ari pushed through the door and ran in the direction of the plane. An alarm sounded behind him, but Ari kept pushing forward until he met one of the pilots at the base of the steps, panic etched into his face.

"What's happened? What's wrong?"

"He's dead." The pilot ran a hand over his face, eyes glazed. "He just died."

"Who?" Claudia asked, breathless from her run over. "Who's dead?"

Ari stepped around the pilot and climbed the airstairs into the jet and found a second pilot and a male flight attendant standing over Billy. "What happened?"

The male flight attendant looked over at Ari, his face as white as a ghost. "I-I don't know. He asked for a bottle of water, said he wasn't feeling good, and then he . . ." He looked down at

Billy and back. "He started gasping for air and—" He covered his mouth and shook his head.

Claudia bumped into him from behind. "He's dead."

Ari looked back at her, but he could see she wasn't asking a question. "Call Ryan back and tell him Billy Adler isn't going anywhere."

ELEVEN

Claudia stared at Billy Adler's vacant eyes and suddenly became dizzy. "I, uh . . ." She hitched her thumb toward the door. "I'm just gonna step outside for a second."

"Are you—"

She didn't wait to hear the rest of Ari's question. Anxious to get out of the stagnant air closing in around her, she headed for the plane's exit. Was she having a panic attack? Stepping down out of the aircraft, Claudia sucked in deep, slow breaths.

"Hey." She felt Ari's warm hand gently brush against her shoulder. "Are you okay?"

This was so embarrassing. Billy Adler was not the first dead body she'd seen, nor was it the most gruesome scene—that distinction solely belonged to Prince Mohamed's house, and she wasn't keen on it becoming a challenge. Still, her chest squeezed at the energy it was taking for her to breathe.

"Yeah, I think so." She turned and flinched when a hole appeared in the fuselage next to Ari's head. The crack of gunfire sent them both scrambling to take cover.

"Here." Ari directed her behind the airstairs, using his body to shield her from the pops of gunfire still coming at them.

Claudia peeked around the steps toward the building.

"If Billy's dead, why are they still shooting?"

Ari kept her tucked into his side, his troubled expression revealing his answer.

"Me." The nightmare from the night before returned. "They're shooting at me." The metallic pinging of bullets hitting the aircraft had her gritting her teeth. "He's going to hit the fuel tank. We've got to get out of here or this thing is going to explode."

Ari was on his cell phone telling who she assumed was the emergency operator that the shots were coming from the wooded landscape next to the airfield. She held her breath, listening, but there were no more shots. Instead, the noise filling her ears came from the sirens on the police vehicles racing toward them.

She glanced back at the woods, her eyes scanning for some kind of figure with a gun trained on them. *On her.* There was no doubt in her mind. She jumped when Ari rested a hand on the small of her back, his knee on the ground. She swallowed at the warmth of his touch, internalizing the crazy amount of comfort it was providing her.

"Are you okay?"

"Physically, yes. But I'd really like to know why I'm being shot at."

Ari waited until three patrol cars had pulled up to the plane before gently leading her out from the cover of the airstairs. His jaw was tight. "We're going to figure that out."

Three hours later, and Claudia had stopped noticing the rancid scent of old coffee that permeated the little county police station. Great. She sniffed her sweater and wrinkled her nose. She couldn't smell it because she'd become one with it. Gross.

She dropped into the chair, regretting it the second her bruised muscles hit the seat.

"Do you need more pain medicine?" Ari's brown eyes were laced with concern, and it caused her to dip her chin, unwilling to give her brain space to imagine ridiculous scenarios that included Ari. "Claudia?"

"I-I'm fine," she answered through clenched teeth. First it was the panic in the plane, and now her pulse was playing games every time Ari's arm brushed against hers. He'd removed his jacket, and his shirt sleeves were rolled midway up his muscular forearms. "The headache is mostly gone."

And had been replaced with errant thoughts of how many times she had sneaked a look at him without being noticed. *Seven.* She was beginning to think dealing with the headache was safer, but it was easier than thinking about someone wanting her dead. Her fingers touched the still-swollen stitching on her scalp. "I wish Ryan would hurry up."

"Are you sure you're okay?"

She hadn't noticed Ari had been watching her. Dropping her hand to her side, she nodded. "Yeah. Just trying to make sense of everything."

"Maybe I can help." Ryan Frost walked in carrying a laptop and a file. He brushed a hand over his strawberry-blond hair before setting up the laptop on the table. "Billy Adler was poisoned."

Ari moved closer to her. "How?"

"The initial reports say cyanide." Ryan logged into the computer. "Likely consumed, but the flight attendants hadn't served him anything yet, which means he was poisoned before he stepped on the plane. The bartender at Kensington served him two glasses of Tripp's whiskey."

"It was the bartender?"

"Yes," Ryan answered Claudia. "But also, no. According

to the bartender, Billy Adler is the only member who drinks Tripp's whiskey. When Adler asked for it, the bartender said the bottle was empty, which was unusual because, again, there's only one person who drinks it."

Ari nodded. "The one who's dead."

"Right." Ryan continued to work on the computer as he talked. "Since it's not a common bottle, the bartender was afraid they wouldn't have any extra bottles in the back, but a delivery had been made an hour before Billy Adler showed up for his flight."

"Let me guess." Claudia exchanged a look with Ari. "There was a bottle of Tripp's Whiskey in the delivery."

"The bartender is adamant that he did not order an extra bottle and showed us the purchase order, which confirms he didn't." Ryan typed on the computer, and a surveillance video filled the screen. "This is the video of the delivery earlier today."

Claudia leaned in at the same time as Ari, their shoulders brushing, but Ari either didn't notice like she did or didn't care. She forced herself to pay attention to the video. After watching the short clip, she looked up at Ryan. "That's it?"

"Yep," Ryan said on an exhale. "Whoever delivered the poisoned whiskey knew the location of the camera and kept somewhat out of view."

"What about the delivery truck?" Ari leaned back. "Get a license plate?"

"There was no license plate, and the box truck wasn't from the distributor. The whole thing was a setup."

"Just to poison Billy Adler." Claudia sighed. "Someone went the distance to ensure he died."

"Which doesn't explain why we were shot at." Ari's jaw muscle ticked as he glared at the paused video.

"Unless I was the secondary target." Claudia voiced the worry that had been weighing on her mind. "I just wish I knew why."

"You're sure Zahrani didn't tell you anything?" Ryan asked. "Anything you might've missed?"

Claudia shook her head. "No. Just that weird photo from the text he sent me."

"We're working on getting the image cleaned up for you," Ryan said.

"Thanks." Claudia's gaze moved to the paused video. She squinted, leaning closer. "Is that a tattoo?"

Ryan slid the computer in front of him, fingers flying over the keyboard for a few seconds before pushing his glasses up on his nose. "Looks like it." He smiled at Claudia. "You have good eyes. I'll add that to the profile and see if we can get a hit."

Ari shifted in his seat next to her. "Any word from Tidemark Tech?"

"Evelyn Bellamy, the CEO, wasn't very helpful. She confirmed Adler worked for her company as a procurement contractor, and if we wanted any more information, we could get a warrant."

Claudia tucked her hair behind her ear. "You think they're hiding something?"

"At first glance, nothing looks suspicious," Ryan said. "But we're going to continue digging."

"So what do we do now?"

"There's not much to do but wait until we find something." Ryan closed his laptop. "And after what happened at the airfield, I think you need to hang low for a while."

"I agree." Ari stood. "We should head back to the safe house."

"No way." Claudia's nerves thrummed with agitation. "There has to be something else or someone else we can check."

Ryan looked between her and Ari. "There's really not. It's the process."

She knew the process. Hated the process. "We need to find the man with the tattoo. He's out there killing our leads." Her eyes met Ryan's. "He can't get close to . . ."

"I know." Ryan nodded, understanding in the unspoken words. "I've already spoken with Colton."

Claudia swallowed, unable to voice her gratitude over the emotion balling in her throat.

Ari placed a gentle hand on her shoulder. "Let's go get something to eat, and we'll check in with Agent Frost after."

"That's a good idea," Ryan said. "At a minimum, I won't have anything for a couple of hours, but I'll call you the second something comes in."

"Fine." Claudia stood, feeling the effects of her hunger. She eyed Ryan. "Call the second you hear anything, or I'll call my sister."

Ryan's blue eyes rounded as he drew a cross with his finger over his heart and gave her a teasing smile. "I promise."

"And you'll make sure they're safe."

"Yes," Ryan said, nothing humorous in his tone or expression, and Claudia believed him.

Leaving the police station, Claudia searched the surrounding area. If the tattooed man was the shooter, they needed to find him before his next bullet found her.

TWELVE

I t's going to be okay." Ari spoke the words, hoping to calm the woman sitting in the passenger seat of his car. Claudia hadn't stopped fidgeting since they left the county police station. "Ryan is going to call us as soon as he identifies the man with the tattoo."

"What if it's too late?"

He glanced over at her. Claudia was no longer rubbing the old wound on her arm but was squeezing her arm instead. Without thinking, he reached over and placed his hand on hers, threading his fingers between hers. He was surprised that she yielded her grip until he was able to cup her hand in his. Her skin was soft and cool to the touch.

"Are you worried about your family?"

His question sounded silly as soon as he said it. Of course she was worried about her family. She slipped her hand free of his. Claudia fidgeted in her seat. "If I've ever doubted my ability to be a parent someday, this job has made it clear I can't do it. I took this job to keep people safe, and I can't even keep my family safe."

"What do you mean?"

"I'm supposed to keep people safe, and all I've done is bring harm to my family. What kind of a person would I be if I decided to get married and have kids? It's ridiculous."

315

"You're probably right. Most people don't assess their parenting abilities by how well they deal with a psychotic drug lord."

Claudia stared at him. "Is that one of your mind game tricks, Blackman? Agree with me until I see the absurdity of my statement?"

"You said it." He shrugged. "And I don't know what you've heard about me and my supposed mind games, but I can promise you it's probably ten percent accurate."

She folded her arms and sent him a serious side-eye. "You didn't swing the vote in Villa Celeste? Or negotiate the release of missionaries in Baraka? Or—"

"I cannot confirm"—Ari tilted his head—"or deny those rumors."

"Except that smirk on your lips tells me they're not rumors at all." She smiled, and he was glad to see it. "At least you don't try to pretend to be someone you're not. Wait a minute. I'm sorry to ask again, but—"

"I don't even know why I'm carrying it anymore." Ari entered his passcode and handed his cell phone to her. Her fingers brushed against his, sending a tingle straight through him. "What are you going to do?"

"I have an idea." They drove in silence for several miles until she said, "Bingo."

"What?" He glanced over in time to see her look up and point out the windshield.

"Stop. Pull over there, please."

Ari looked at the rock outcropping near a grove of trees overlooking the Potomac. He flipped his blinker on and pulled into a small parking lot for the nearby trail. He parked his car. "You want to go on a hike or something?"

Claudia smirked, then opened the door and got out, leaving him wondering what in the world she was doing. He got out of the car and followed her. She had the camera app opened on his phone.

"Stand over here." She directed him to a spot near some trees. The deep green foliage was speckled with a few leaves beginning their transition to bright fall colors that contrasted against the dark, jagged façade of a high-walled cliff of rock. Holding his phone up at different angles, she took a step forward and glanced over at him. "This spot is perfect."

"Perfect for what?" he asked even though he did as she asked.

"Okay, now turn and face this way."

He frowned at her as she held up his phone again, aiming it at him. Ari put his hand up. "Are you taking my picture?"

With one hand, she swiped his hand down and moved the phone around. She blew out a sigh. "Okay, hold on." She set the phone down and took a step closer to him. "Just a little tweaking."

Claudia put her hands on his shoulders and gently angled them, then brushed his hair off his forehead. The touch tickled and sent a streak of heat coursing through him. He held his breath as her fingers moved down the side of his face, pausing at the edge of his jaw. His heart hammered loudly against his chest, and when her gaze met his beneath those dark lashes, he was sure she could hear it too.

He swallowed and tried for a teasing smile. "Um, you do this professionally?"

His voice came out rough, and she blushed before withdrawing her hand and stepping back. She forced a laugh. "No. But I've seen enough fake poses. I think this will work."

"Fake poses?"

"Okay, now don't move, and I want you to kind of look off into the distance and laugh."

Ari made a face. "What?"

"Just trust me." She laughed. "And don't make that face again. Makes you look like Daffy Duck when Elmer Fudd gets him."

He laughed. "I can't even tell you how long it's been since I've heard those names."

"The last of the great cartoons," Claudia said, not missing a beat. "Now tip your chin up a little."

"Like this?" Ari lifted his chin. "If you told me what we're doing, that might help."

"In a minute," she said, and he heard the click of the camera app. "Okay, now pretend to laugh."

He looked down at her, but her wide-eyed expression pushed his attention off to the distance. "How does one pretend to laugh?"

"I just need you to smile but not look like you're trying to smile too hard, and relax your shoulders. A little less presidential, Blackman."

He laughed.

"Got it!"

"So I can move now?" He gave her a sideways glance.

"Yes." She walked over. "Give me a minute and . . ."

A breeze lifted the hair around Claudia's face, framing it as she typed on his phone. His fingers itched to brush the loose strands back, but he made the smart decision to shove his hands into the pockets of his jeans.

"So? What're you doing?"

"Making you an Instagram account."

"What?" Ari stepped forward, reaching for his phone. "You can't do that. We're not—"

Claudia deftly moved her hand and his phone out of his reach, turning so that he was behind her, close enough to catch the soft fragrance of her shampoo. "Don't worry. I know the rules. You are Floyd Weatherbee."

"*Floyd Weatherbee?*" Ari scoffed. "Who is Floyd Weatherbee?"

"He's a model, he has a dog named Cheeseburger, and most importantly"—she looked over her shoulder and his eyes moved to her lips—"he's single and muy caliente."

"And all of that matters because . . ."

"Because"—Claudia tapped on his phone and then held it up to him—"you are going to slide into the DMs of Charmaine Barlowe."

Ari took the phone and saw the photo Claudia had just taken of him along with multiple photos of a golden retriever and another one of him he hadn't realized she'd taken. It was a candid shot of him looking at the ground, almost contemplative, except . . . he'd been thinking about her.

"Who's Charmaine Barlowe?"

"The argument between Prince Mohamed and Billy Adler took place at a club called Pegasus. They have an Instagram account and a hashtag that people use when they post their photos. I went through all the photos from that night and found this one."

Claudia held up his phone. The image showed a blond woman with too much makeup, too little clothing, and a drink in one hand smiling coyly at the camera like she'd just heard the funniest joke. After what Claudia told him, he had to assume it was posed.

"Look at the person sitting on her left."

Ari looked, but the person was cropped out of the photo,

so only a portion of his right side was in the image. He was about to ask Claudia what he was supposed to be looking for when he saw it—

"The tattoo."

"Looks like the one from the surveillance video, doesn't it?"

Ari nodded. "His face is cut off, but I bet Ryan can get access to the club's security cameras."

"We could, but I have a feeling we'll run into the same issue we have with Tidemark Tech with the warrants. Let's just see if my idea works."

"And that is?"

"You'll have to wait to see." Claudia started walking back to his car. In two long strides, he made it to the door, their hands landing on the handle at the same time. She looked up at him. "You don't always have to open the door for me, you know."

"I know. But my father taught me to."

Claudia eyed him, and he couldn't help but notice her suspicion. He had to know. "Please tell me the men you date open the door for you."

She blinked, something dimming the brightness in her eyes for just a second. She shrugged. "It's been a long time since I've gone on a date."

And that was it. She didn't say anything else as she climbed into the car. He closed the door and walked around, his curiosity growing. "Why not?" he asked as soon as he got in.

Claudia fiddled with her seat belt, clearly uncomfortable with his questioning—and why wouldn't she be? It wasn't his business, and if he'd been asked the—

"Do you date?"

"Uh." He started the car. "Not currently."

"Me either."

A few seconds of silence ticked between them before he looked at her. "I'm sorry, I shouldn't have asked. It's none of my business."

"It's fine."

She shrugged as if it didn't bother her, but there was a sadness in her tone he wanted to understand. "Can we just talk about the name you gave me? Floyd? I sound like I should be in my seventies."

"Most women with social media accounts like Charmaine screen their followers. Floyd is not a common name, which means she likely clicked on your account to make sure you weren't a creeper, or at least I can hope she did. She would've seen the photos I took of you just now, maybe been distracted by your handsome profile photo, your obvious love for your dog, and would likely assume Floyd is a family name passed on, which would make her believe you're not a threat to her."

"And Weatherbee?" He looked at the graying sky. "Came up with that because of the weather and you saw a bee?"

"No. Mr. Weatherbee is from my favorite comic book. *Archie*."

Ari's gaze landed on her again, and she blushed. "Now I think you're the one surprising me. And Cheeseburger the dog was your—"

"Favorite meal. The cheeseburger, not the dog," Claudia corrected. "Guess I was thinking of food when I named your fictional pet."

"And on that note, we should go get some lunch."

"Good idea." She smiled. "Marty's on F Street and 13th."

THIRTEEN

Based on the looks of Ari's trim figure, Claudia hadn't been sure if he would appreciate the greasy diner she chose, but when he added extra cheese and bacon to his burger, she knew he was in for a treat. As they sat in a booth inside the eclectic diner decorated with random items left by customers, it was like a junk store had exploded around them.

"So, people just leave their stuff here?" Ari asked, looking up at the wall above their booth. Sitting on the shelf was a *Miami Vice* cassette tape, a red Teletubby with its face covered in marker, a Styrofoam cup from a pizza place in Texas called Shorty's, and an old cigarette lighter from a car.

"Sort of." Claudia sipped her water. "I think the story started when a traveler was stranded in the city and couldn't pay for his meal, so the owner asked them to leave something of value." She pointed to the pair of military dog tags hanging in a frame behind the counter. "Those belonged to Ernesto Carbajal. He was taken prisoner in the Battle of Bataan and was forced to labor in a coal mine for three years before he was liberated."

"*That* I can understand having significant value, but"—Ari's eyes flashed to the items next to them—"that doll is going to give me nightmares, and I'm not sure what value a cigarette lighter has. Is everything in here from someone who couldn't pay?"

The waiter delivered their burgers, and Claudia inhaled the

delicious aroma before sticking a fry in her mouth. She finished chewing and placed her napkin on her lap.

"I think some of the items are from those who couldn't pay, but I think Carbajal's story inspired customers to reevaluate what's significant in their lives. To us, that child's toy might be creepy, but to the child, it might've been their favorite doll. The thing that got them to sleep, made them feel secure. Perhaps the cigarette lighter forced someone to stop smoking, and they lived a longer life with their family."

Ari's brown eyes landed on her, and a spark of something lingered in them that made her stomach feel like jelly.

"Do you make up a story for all the items?"

She smiled. "I do."

Ari took a bite of his burger and raised his brows, eyeing the Styrofoam cup. "Shorty's?"

"The location of the most romantic proposal," Claudia said around her bite.

He smiled around his own bite and finished chewing. "And the *Miami Vice* soundtrack?"

"Just good music." She winked, and Ari's smile deepened in appreciation. "What?"

"I didn't peg you as one for nostalgia."

Ari's cell phone rang, snapping their attention from each other, and Claudia could breathe again. Why was he so unnerving? Probably because she felt like she had to be on guard with him. Was he analyzing her? It didn't feel like it, and yet he seemed to be able to read things about her. How did he know about her insecurities? A good guess, or was she just that obvious?

Ari looked over at her. "That was Ryan. He said you need to call your sister."

323

Panic choked her, and Ari must've seen the fear in her eyes, because he quickly held up his hand to calm her. "It's okay. Ryan didn't sound concerned, just said that your sister called him and asked that you call her back."

Claudia exhaled and then cringed. "My cell phone. I'm sure she's been trying to call me."

Ari handed her his phone, and she dialed her sister's number. "Hello?"

"It's me."

"Claudia, what's going on?" Pecca said, her voice high-pitched. "Why aren't you answering your phone?"

Ari slid from the booth, pulling out his wallet and mouthing the words "I'm going to pay." She reached for her wallet, but Ari shook his head and walked off.

"It's a long story, but everything is okay." Claudia took one last bite of her burger. "I lost my phone last night and haven't had a chance to replace it."

"How did you lose it?" There was suspicion in her sister's tone—and for good reason. "And why won't Colton let me or Maceo out of his sight?"

"Uh . . ." Claudia's lunch suddenly felt heavy in her stomach. "It's just precautionary until I figure some things out."

"Like what? Are we in danger again?"

"No," Claudia answered quickly. "I don't think so. Look, I can't give you details, but I'm doing my job and I promise you and Maceo are safe." She dropped her gaze to the laminate table, hating that she really could not keep a promise like that. Especially after what happened in Georgia.

"Just give it a few days and let Colton take care of you. He's a protector. Let him protect."

"Oh, I don't mind *his* protection, but you realize we're hosting a few of his battle buddies, which means I have *all* their protection on me. It's like living with our brothers at home all over again."

Claudia made a face. "That wasn't good for any of us."

"Just made you tougher," Pecca teased. "Got you ready to take on the real bad guys."

The softness in her sister's voice tugged at her heart. Their lives were so different. Pecca was a mother. She hadn't come to motherhood the way their parents had hoped, having gotten pregnant before marriage, but that didn't stop them or their whole family from loving and adoring Maceo. Claudia had to keep her sister and nephew from harm.

"Promise me you'll stay safe, Claudia. Promise me you won't do anything extra to put your life in danger."

"*Pfft*, me?"

"I'm serious."

And the absence of lightheartedness in her sister's voice told Claudia she was being very serious. Rubbing the spot on her arm, Claudia nodded. "I know, and I promise I'll do my best."

There was no sense in telling her sister everything that had just taken place. It would only incite more fear, and she wouldn't put Pecca through that again.

"Everything okay?" Ari was at her side.

"Yeah." She handed him his cell phone. "My sister was worried about me."

"Did you tell her what happened?"

"No. I explained to her husband, Colton, that he might want to keep an eye on her, just to be sure. Until we know if I'm a target or just caught in the middle of this mess, it's better to be safe than sorry."

"I agree." Ari gestured to the door. "The bill and tip are already taken care of."

"Thank you." Claudia opened her wallet. "I didn't intend for you to pay for lunch."

"Seriously?" Ari didn't accept the money she held in her hand, so she put it away. "It's really not that hard to accept a kind gesture. You just smile and say thank you. Try it."

She raised an eyebrow and pulled on her coat. "Thank you." Claudia wrinkled her nose, then pulled her lips into a showy, fake smile that made Ari laugh and roll his eyes.

"That hard, huh?" He stretched out his hand and she placed hers in it, and then he gently pulled her from the booth. "I'm going to have to work on that."

His voice was breathy and his gaze lingered under thick lashes, moving over her face before stopping on her lips, then flashing back to her eyes.

"That's, uh, gonna be hard to do," she said, taking a sidestep to put some space between them.

"Why's that?"

Claudia started for the door. "I'm afraid it's been ingrained in me to take care of myself. It's going to require more than your good manners and a few days together to get me to—" She stopped talking. *Trust.* That was what she was going to say, and it surprised her.

She narrowed her eyes on Ari as they left the restaurant. "You're good."

His brows pinched. "What do you mean?"

"The way you get people to talk. I can see how you've earned your reputation."

Hurt flashed in his eyes before he looked away. He unlocked the car door and opened it. "We might not be together long enough for me to earn your trust, but I do hope I can at least change your opinion of me. I am more than my reputation."

And with that, Ari shut the door. Claudia released a sigh. This was why she avoided relationships. They were hard to figure out, and the last thing she needed was someone who could read her.

FOURTEEN

Ari hated the harshness in his words to Claudia. Hated that in the short time he'd been in her presence, she'd managed to needle her way into his psyche and draw out emotions he wasn't sure were healthy.

Claudia was attractive, smart, and surprising. But falling for a woman who struggled to trust was a recipe for disaster.

His cell phone pinged, but it wasn't a call or a text.

"It's a notification," Claudia said. "May I see your phone again?"

He handed the unlocked phone to her and watched her make a few swipes with her finger before her lips curled into a smile.

"Way to stay predictable, Charmaine."

Ari started to lean in to see his phone but decided against it. "What happened?"

"You want to take a drive to Georgetown?"

He waited for a car to pass and then pulled into traffic. "What's in Georgetown?"

"Charmaine, in predictable fashion, just posted a selfie and tagged her location, which she does around this time every day. My guess is she lives somewhere in the area."

"And she posts that information publicly?"

"No, but you—or, rather, Floyd Weatherbee—slid into her DMs."

He glanced over. "And it worked?"

She smiled. "And it worked."

Ari headed down K Street toward Georgetown. "So everything was okay with your sister?"

"Oh yeah." Claudia looked up from his cell phone. "She's too smart for her own good. Figured out there was something up when Colton and his friends were less than subtle about watching her and Maceo."

"How's she taking it?"

Claudia glanced at him, and the softness in her gaze revealed how much she loved her family. "As well as she can. She's worried about me."

Ari's gaze drifted to the stitches near her temple. Even though she brushed her hair over them, he could still see the purplish bruise peeking out. "You didn't tell her what you've been through."

"No." Claudia huffed a breath. "There is a reason I've stayed away from my family. They're safer not knowing."

"But then you're missing out," Ari said. "God intended our lives to have balance. Don't you miss your family and friends?"

Claudia checked the photos on Charmaine's account, seemingly comparing them with the area they were driving by. Or avoiding his question.

He turned onto M Street. "Is that why you don't date?"

"Are you trying to psychoanalyze me, Blackman?"

"I'm trying to get to know you." Ari glanced over, their eyes meeting, and he wanted more than anything for her to hear the truth in his words. "Truly."

Her lips softened into a sad smile. "I don't date because I'm afraid of falling in love, because if I fall in love, then I'll want a family, and if I want a husband and a family, then that means my mom was right and that maybe I've wasted a lot of years trying to prove she's not."

Ari swallowed, not expecting her honesty. "You don't date to prove your mom wrong?"

Claudia released a small laugh and shook her head. "Well, when you say it like that it sounds silly, but I can't do my job well if I'm afraid of someone I love getting hurt."

"There are many excellent intelligence officers who have families."

She held his gaze for a second before releasing a sigh. "Being a mom and a wife comes with expectations that I can't meet. Believe me, my mom tried to teach them to me, but at the end of the day, I'd let her down, and that's painful enough. Letting down a husband and my own children . . ." She rubbed her arm. "I think taking a bullet would be less painful."

Did she really believe that about herself? It made him sad, but it also ignited a desire in him to prove her wrong. Ari had caught glimpses of her kindness, and he had no doubt she'd make a wonderful wife and mom one day. That last thought lodged itself in his chest. He could see her being someone's wife, yes, but there was a growing part of him that was bothered by the idea of her married to another man.

Claudia looked up from the phone. "You're going to take a left at the street coming up."

Ari took a left and drove down Prospect Street. He didn't want to push her, but he hoped that when this was done, maybe they could be friends.

"Is there an address we—"

"There." Claudia pointed to a woman pushing a stroller with a little girl in it up the driveway of a stately home.

Ari pulled in behind her, and a woman who looked nothing like the one in the photo faced them. "Are you sure that's Charmaine?"

"Exchange the yoga pants and oversized sweatshirt for a skintight dress and makeup, it's her." Claudia unbuckled her seat belt and opened the door. "Charmaine?"

Ari followed Claudia up the drive and discovered the woman was a lot younger than he'd expected. But he finally saw the similarities from the photo.

"Yes?" Charmaine took a step, putting herself close to the baby in a protective way that instantly bumped up Ari's opinion of her. "Can I help you?"

"My name is Claudia, and this is Ari. We're with the government. We'd like to ask you a few questions if you have a minute." Claudia looked at the baby squirming to be released from her stroller. "We can go inside if it's easier for your little girl."

"Oh, she's not mine." The little girl in the stroller began to whine, kicking to be released. Charmaine unstrapped her and lifted her to her hip. "I'm the nanny."

Claudia held out her hand, and Ari unlocked the screen of his cell phone and handed it to her. She showed Charmaine the photo. "This is you at the Pegasus a few nights ago."

Charmaine leaned over the phone, the little girl's chubby hand trying to grab for it, but Charmaine pulled her hand back. "Yeah, so?"

"Can you tell us who you were with?" Claudia asked.

She looked at Claudia, then at Ari. "Why?"

Ari noticed the way Charmaine's shoulders bunched. Stress. Anxiety. Nervousness. "There was an incident at the club that night involving a foreigner and a man named Billy Adler. Do you know him?"

"You're the police?"

"No," Claudia answered. "We're working with the FBI."

Charmaine cursed, and Ari was grateful the little girl in her arms was too young to understand the word. "I didn't hear much. The music was loud, and it was over quickly. I think the bouncers escorted them out of the club."

"What did you hear?" Claudia pressed. "Anything will help."

"I really don't know. Something about a car or oil." Charmaine looked around the neighborhood as the little girl in her arms gave a tired squeal. "I need to take her back inside."

"Wait." Claudia held up the phone again. "Who were you with?"

"I'm sorry?"

"At the club that night, the man with a tattoo on his wrist."

Charmaine narrowed her eyes on Claudia, confusion in them. "Who?"

"The guy with the tattoo sitting next to you." Claudia's tone was short. "The one whose hand is near your leg."

Charmaine looked at the photo again, then shook her head. "I don't know who that is."

"You seem awful cozy with him."

Indignation flashed over Charmaine's face, and Ari stepped in. "You're not in any trouble, Ms. Barlowe." He kept his tone calm but firm. "But if you'd be more comfortable talking at the police station, we can do that."

"I thought you weren't the police."

"We're not," Ari said. "But we're investigating the argument that took place there, and we'd appreciate you helping us."

A car drove by, and Charmaine's gaze tracked it before meeting his. "Look, I don't know who that guy is sitting next to me. He came over to talk with—" She swallowed. "To talk with the man I was with."

"And who was that?" Claudia asked.

Charmaine pressed her lips together, giving the neighborhood another look. It caused Ari to take a quick survey of their surroundings too. Would the shooter show up here?

"We're not here to get you into trouble," Ari said for the second time today. "But that man with the tattoo killed another man, and that means whoever you were with that night could be next."

Charmaine's face paled. "Am I in danger too?"

"I hope not," Ari said. "But we need to find the man with the tattoo as quickly as possible."

"I can't lose this job," Charmaine said to Ari, eyes pleading. "If they found out . . ."

"Are you having an affair with a married man?"

Claudia's question was one he had wanted to ask himself but wasn't bold enough to. He kept his focus on Charmaine, who looked less surprised and more agitated by the question.

"Why is that any of your business?"

"Look, Charmaine, if you give us the name of the man you were with, I promise we will not mention you at all," Claudia said. "We want to keep you safe."

Charmaine reached into the stroller and grabbed a toy for the squirming baby. "Dennis. Dennis Richardson." She switched the baby to her other hip and started to push the stroller to the front door of the house. "I need to go now."

The wheel of the stroller turned, catching on an uneven crack in the walkway, and Charmaine struggled with it. Claudia stepped forward to help and lifted the stroller over the bump.

"Charmaine, you're a lovely girl. You don't need to settle for a married man who isn't going to leave his wife. No matter what he tells you."

The woman gave a tight smile before continuing into the house.

Ari walked next to Claudia back to his car. Had she slowed her pace so he could get to the door before her?

"That was nice what you said to her."

Claudia shrugged as she stepped back so he could open the door for her. "If she's having an affair with a married man, I don't think me judging her is going to give her the confidence to do the right thing."

Ari couldn't help the growing flare of admiration for Claudia and the way she no longer looked up at him with guarded apprehension. He couldn't be sure, but he thought—hoped—that what he saw lingering in the depths of her brown eyes matched the attraction he could no longer deny was taking root within him.

FIFTEEN

Claudia's gaze followed Ari as he walked around his car. He flashed her a smile, and it caused her insides to flutter with . . . anticipation. Was she beginning to feel things for America's Bond?

Ari paused by the door to answer a call, and it gave Claudia time to calm the burn in her cheeks. Shame filled her. Ari was nothing like the rumors. Sure, he was handsome and had the kind of confidence that might be read as arrogance, but anyone who spent time with him would find a genuinely kind, smart, and funny man. Traits that only enhanced his good looks.

She glanced out the window and saw his handsome features transform with a look of concern. He ended his call and got into the car. "Everything okay?"

"That was Ryan." Ari started the car. "He wants us to head to his office."

An image of Pecca and Maceo popped into her mind, sending her pulse jumping. "Something wrong?"

"He didn't say, but"—his eyes rested on her—"if it was something about your family, he would've told us."

"Yeah, you're right." Claudia swallowed against the emotion building in her throat. "Um, did you tell him about Dennis Richardson?"

"I did, and he said he'd run a check on him."

"Okay."

Claudia forced herself to breathe for the fifteen-minute drive to the federal building where Ryan worked. She nearly asked Ari to drop her off at the front door but kept silent as he pulled into a visitor space and parked the car. She was reaching for the handle when Ari's voice stopped her.

"It's going to be okay."

She looked at Ari, and if his tone wasn't enough, the determined assurance resting in his gaze made her want to believe him. His hand reached for hers and she kept still, a small part of her needing to feel his touch. But he pulled back at the last second and left her feeling hollow.

Ari grabbed his keys and cell phone. "Uh, Ryan said he'd wait for us in the lobby."

"Right."

They took the elevator to the first floor and met Ryan there.

"Thanks for coming in," Ryan said, handing them each a visitor ID badge before ushering them to another set of elevators. "Everyone in Texas is safe."

Claudia released a breath. "Thank you."

After they took the elevator to the third floor, Ryan led them to a medium-sized conference room. Two other agents stepped out as they entered, and Claudia's attention went straight to the two large whiteboards covering the walls. They were filled with photos, names, information, and notes. Her eyes landed on images of two familiar faces: Prince Mohamed and Billy Adler.

"Our inquiry into Tidemark Technology grabbed us some attention from the Saudi Ministry of Economy and Planning," Ryan said. "In the past nine months, Tidemark and several new information and technology companies have moved into the region."

"Is that unusual?" Ari folded his arms over his chest. "Isn't Saudi Arabia trying to offer their citizens free enterprise?"

"Yes, to a degree," Ryan said. "The Saudi monarchy still maintains supreme control of their economy and the companies allowed to operate in their country."

Claudia studied the notes on the board. "That seems hypocritical."

"It does, and it's only one of the many charges against the royal family. There are several groups opposed to the monarchy for their . . ." Ryan made a face. "Let's just say their extravagant lifestyle, which has included forbidden activities like gambling, drinking, and womanizing that go against the religious principles of Islam."

"I can see the concern," Ari said. "And Prince Mohamed's lifestyle only solidified their opinion."

"How does that tie to Tidemark?" Claudia looked at Ryan. "And Billy Adler?"

"After Adler's family was notified of his death, we contacted Evelyn Bellamy, Tidemark's CEO, and when she learned what had happened to Adler, she was a bit more forthcoming in her answers." Ryan pointed to the map of Saudi Arabia. "According to her, Adler had secured a contract to bring Tidemark to Saudi Arabia, but when we checked with the ministry, they said the approval had not gone through the appropriate channels for permission."

"It requires a lot of paperwork to bring an American company overseas." Ari frowned, roughing a hand over the scruff that had been filling in since Claudia first saw him the night before. "How did Tidemark get past all of that?"

Ryan tilted his head. "The Saudis suspect Adler got the contract for Tidemark illegally through corrupt government officials, and that leads me to my next point." He walked to the board and pointed to two names written there. "A few weeks ago, we learned about a private meeting that took place in London between major oil corporations from Norway, Venezuela, and Saudi Arabia, with *someone* pretending to represent the Saudi minister of energy. America relies on oil from Saudi Arabia, but the US has alternative sources through Venezuela and Norway, so a meeting between these countries raised red flags. However, Saudi Arabia depends on the exportation of oil to maintain its economy, and they assured our State Department that no such meeting happened."

"Did it?" Ari shifted on his heels.

"Yes." Ryan exhaled. "And the concern is that either Saudi officials are lying to us or—"

"Someone is lying to them." Claudia rubbed her temples, studying the information in front of her. She searched her brain for the briefing she'd been a part of a few months back. "The major threat against the monarchy comes from radical Islamist religious groups opposed to the way the royal family's lifestyle goes against their groups' religious standards. They openly criticize the royal family and broadcast charges against them that continuously fuel violent riots and attacks. There's always been suspicion that they've got a network working within the government—and if Saudi Arabia is telling us the truth, then there's no better way to undermine the monarchy than by disrupting the Saudi Arabian commerce and economy."

Ryan ran a hand through his strawberry-blond hair. "That kind of interference in the current regime's system would likely cause confusion and give the implication of instability."

"Exactly," Claudia said. She looked between Ryan and Ari.

"What if Prince Mohamed figured that out?" Her eyes moved to the photo of the Prince. "And was killed for it."

"You don't think he could be behind it?"

Claudia scoffed at Ryan's suggestion. "No. He knew where his bread and butter came from. And besides, as much of a playboy as he was, he loved his family. I think secretly he played the part to hide the hurt of being cast out by them. He was more than what people believed him to be."

Ari's gaze flashed to hers before looking away, and her cheeks warmed at the mistake. She'd once used the same word she'd associated with Prince Mohamed for Ari, and they could not be more different.

"At least this would explain why Charmaine overheard something about oil the night Prince Mohamed and Adler argued at the club," Ari said. "Did you find anything on Dennis Richardson?"

"JTTF has been monitoring suspicious intel coming out of Iran about a group of Saudi military veterans who have been funding violent protests, riots, and attacks." Ryan held up his hand as if he read the question in Claudia's expression. "Yes, veterans. They were forced to fight Russia during the Afghanistan War. When the war was over, they returned home to unemployment and impoverished living conditions that left many of them jaded. A group of them have become staunch fundamentalists who are anti-Saudi and anti-US, and with their expertise in small arms and explosives, it makes them a serious threat to the current Saudi regime."

"And the perfect group to do the bidding of those who want to see the monarchy overthrown," Ari said. "Do you know who's funding them?"

"Well, once you gave us Dennis Richardson's name, we did

some digging and learned that he is the president of International Banking and Investments here in DC. Thanks to some quick work on the CIA's part"— Ryan looked at Claudia—"we found a link from IBI to a money laundering case in which money was sent to a terrorist group in Iran."

Claudia's nerves began to buzz with adrenaline. "Dennis Richardson is laundering money to Iran in an attempt to overthrow the kingdom."

"A coup."

She nodded at Ari and looked back at Ryan. "We need to speak to Dennis Richardson."

"We're working on that right now," Ryan said. "JTTF is trying to fast-track a warrant—"

"There's no time." Claudia paced to the board. "The best recruiting method for terrorists and dictators is to give people what they lack. Food, security, money. A majority of the population in Saudi Arabia don't have this, so if someone brings in American corporations like Tidemark, with jobs and technology, it will appeal to the crowds. And if Richardson is laundering money to terrorist groups interested in seeing the royal family dethroned, they can raise up an army to start a revolution like we've seen in other countries. If Prince Mohamed figured this out, we can assume he was killed to keep him quiet, and maybe Adler too. We need to get to Richardson and find out who he's laundering money for and where it's going, before he's killed next. He's our last lead."

"I get that, but we don't have a team ready or—"

"I'll go to the bank," Claudia said. "I'll talk to Richardson and find out who he's laundering money for. Send me."

"What?" Ari swung his gaze to her. "You can't go in."

Claudia stiffened her spine. "Why not?"

Ari's wide-eyed gaze moved from her to Ryan and back again. "Someone, maybe Richardson, wants you dead. You show up to the bank to talk to Richardson and you might as well put a bigger target on your head."

Claudia's stomach twisted. "If Richardson's not the one behind the murders, then we can at least find out if he's funding terrorists."

Ryan swallowed. "I can probably get a team ready within an hour to *monitor*"—he made air quotes—"you."

"Claudia, you can't do this. Let the FBI do this the right way. We've done our job, and—"

"And I'm going." She turned to Ari. "With or without you."

SIXTEEN

With." Claudia had barely heard Ari whisper the word, and yet it had turned her insides into a tangled mess of emotions. In the FBI conference room, a female agent slipped the wire through Claudia's shirt as Ari and Ryan talked with two other agents about what would happen when they walked into the IBI building to find out who Dennis Richardson was laundering money for.

Not only did they need to find out who killed Prince Mohamed and Billy Adler, but they also had to prevent a coup that could have a devastating ripple effect on US–Saudi relations. America didn't just rely on Saudi Arabia for its oil; it was also a strategic military location for the US.

She was doing the right thing, right? One peek at Ari, and she couldn't be sure.

"Okay, I'll do a mic check when we get to the bank," the female agent said before walking to the table—but Ari intercepted her reach for the Kevlar vest. She looked back at Claudia. "We'll be ready in fifteen minutes."

Ryan and the rest of the agents left her and Ari alone in the conference room. Ari picked up the vest and walked toward her. "Here."

Claudia found herself holding her breath as Ari slipped the bulletproof vest over her head. He leaned in and grabbed the

Velcro strap, his face so close to hers that she could smell the faded scent of soap on his skin. She turned her head so that her lips were close to his neck and breathed in.

Ari lifted his head back and pressed the strap around her waist. "Is that too tight?"

She swallowed and gave a small shake of her head. "No, it's fine. Thank you."

His dark gaze lingered on her and she searched his face, wanting . . . his approval.

"Please don't be upset with me."

He blew out a breath. "I'm not upset, but I can't say I understand why you're putting yourself at risk for him."

Claudia tried for a teasing laugh, but it came out sounding nervous. "It's part of the job, right?"

Ari remained silent as he adjusted the straps, making sure the metal plate was centered over her vital organs. "I hope he's worth it."

Claudia blinked up at him. "What do you mean?"

"You were so quick to defend Prince Mohamed to Ryan. I just hope he's worth the risk."

Her defenses rose. "I was just suggesting that maybe it was easier for Prince Mohamed to pretend he was who everyone believed him to be than to try and prove he'd changed."

Ari huffed. "I'm not buying it. The man had no problem living the extravagant life. He was murdered in a twenty-million-dollar mansion and had two Lamborghinis and a Maserati parked in the garage. Not to mention the drugs and possibly innocent women caught in his mess. Seems like the only expectation he refused to accept was to be a decent human being."

"And yet, his last moment on this earth was spent reaching out to me and asking for my help. He was killed trying to protect his family," she said, unable to refute Ari's analysis. "I'm not saying he was a saint, but I wonder if living up to the expectations of his family was too much." Claudia thought about her own childhood. While she had not grown up in privilege like Prince Mohamed, she did understand a thing or two about familial expectations—not to mention the ones she lived with at work. "I would think you would understand that better than most."

Ari blanched. "I am *nothing* like him."

"I know." Claudia reached for Ari's arm, but he stepped back. She desperately wanted to take back her words or explain herself. "I didn't mean—"

"You know what really gets me." Ari took a breath. "You were so quick to suggest he might be more than his reputation, yet you continue to look at me with mistrust, like I would do anything to hurt you."

Claudia held his gaze, wishing she could convey everything her heart was feeling right then, but she didn't understand it. How, in such a short time, had her heart made space just for him?

"I know you wouldn't." She sighed, her eyes moving to the floor. "My whole life, I grew up trying to avoid becoming what my mom and dad wanted me to be, what my culture wanted me to be. I bucked the system at every chance. To the point it nearly cost me my family. They couldn't understand how I would want to do or be anything else, and so I felt like I had to make a decision. I could be who they expected me to be, a mom and a wife, or I could follow my heart and make my own path. Have a career that I love and . . ."

"You don't have to prove your mom wrong anymore, Claudia." Ari's statement was filled with strength—a gentle command—and it drew her gaze to his. "You don't have to keep living in this belief that it's only one way or the other. You can be a kick-butt intel officer and still share your life with someone you love, have a family." His stare intensified. "There's only one thing I've witnessed in the short time with you that lights up your eyes quicker than work talk—your family."

"I'm afraid for them. For my sister and nephew, what I've put them through."

The doubt on Ari's face matched what she heard in her own words. "You said yourself that her husband is capable of protecting them. So is it fear for them, or are you recognizing that maybe your sister has something you want?"

Claudia dropped her gaze to the floor, fearing he'd read the answer she was afraid to voice. She wanted to blame his PSYOPS skills, but the truth was that he was right. Ever since her time in Georgia, Claudia had felt like something was absent from her life. She discounted it as just missing family, but maybe Ari was right. She was beginning to want more. Balance.

"Whatever you decide, Claudia, I want you to know that I will support you. I'm just saying . . ." His pause drew her eyes to his. "I hope you can believe that it doesn't have to be a choice. You can have both."

With a boldness that surprised her, she took a step toward him and closed the distance he'd put between them. "Do you mean that? You wouldn't think I was just giving in to the expectations?"

The side of his lip turned up in a half smile, dark eyes sparkling with amusement. His fingers brushed against her cheek, warming her skin as he moved a piece of hair from her face. "Claudia Gallegos, you defy expectations."

She didn't know if it was the tightness of the vest making it hard to breathe or the intensity in Ari's gaze, but she wanted to believe him more than anything else. Her eyes moved to his lips. Maybe she could show him—

"Y'all ready?" Ryan's voice was like a sledgehammer. His eyes bounced between them. "We're all set."

"Yeah." Claudia tugged on the collar of the vest to find her breath. Ari's assurance to be there for her was unexpected, and at the same time, it spoke to something deep inside of her that she wanted. "Just one second." She reached for Ari's face, a mixture of surprise and anticipation radiating in his eyes. "I'd like our first *official* kiss to be while I'm conscious."

Ari started to grin, but she pulled him to meet her lips, and as he wrapped one arm around her waist and the other around the back of her neck, he kissed her for several seconds with such intensity, it caused her to forget they had an audience until Ryan coughed.

As they stepped apart, Claudia's cheeks burned with desire, and a quick glance at Ari confirmed he hadn't been ready to end the kiss either.

"Let's get this over with." Claudia marched out of the office, trying not to look at Ryan's shocked face. But she did hear his words.

"When this is over, we're gonna circle back to that whole unconscious kiss thing."

Claudia glanced over her shoulder and met Ari's playful smirk with a wink, and they laughed.

The interior of the bank made Claudia feel like she'd stepped back in time. She and Ari were escorted past the line of bank tellers helping customers behind a polished oak counter. Their brass partitions and Tiffany-style sconces highlighted the grandeur of the neoclassical architecture.

They'd entered the bank under the assumed aliases of Mr. and Mrs. Cartwright, a wealthy couple ready to invest the millions sitting in the fake account the FBI set up for them. They followed the branch manager, a woman in her fifties, to the back, where they would be convinced to invest their money here at IBI. Claudia did a quick survey of those inside the bank. Her gaze landed on a little boy, maybe nine or ten, standing with a man who looked old enough to be his grandfather.

Maceo.

A gentle jab to her ribs brought her attention to Ari, who motioned with his eyebrows to the two men nearby, both in suits that barely stretched over their broad builds to conceal their sidearms. Not the kind of security guards typically found in a bank.

"I guess I can be sure my money is safe here with armed guards like that," Claudia said, sure Ryan and the other agent would get the point. "Those two are certainly not rent-a-cops."

The woman looked back at them. "They're new and a little unnerving, if you ask me." She sent the guards a tight smile, holding her ID up and then scanning it over the keypad.

"It seems like they're protecting what's back here more than what's out there," Claudia whispered to Ari as they were escorted down a hallway. "Or keeping someone from running."

"Mr. Richardson has one appointment before yours, but he will see you shortly," the branch manager said as she led them to a small, private room with two chairs, a Keurig machine, a television, and some magazines. "Make yourselves comfortable."

"We're in," Ari said to the agents listening once the woman had left. He turned so he was facing the window overlooking the interior of the bank's main lobby. "Did you get a good look at the guards?"

Claudia looked at the tie tack that had a camera in it and heard the agents confirm they were running the guards through facial recognition software. She glanced through the other window to the offices that lined the opposite side of the hallway. They were individual offices that led to a large one at the end of the hall separated by glass and belonging to the IBI's president, Dennis Richardson. The fifty-seven-year-old looked just like the photo Ryan had pulled—white hair, trim build, a friendly face. He didn't look like the kind of man who'd be involved in laundering money for terrorists.

"Claudia."

"Richardson's in his office. He—" She stopped talking when she saw the deep concern on Ari's face. His jaw muscle flexed, and his once-comforting hand suddenly felt heavy on her shoulder. She started to twist so she could see what he was looking at. "What is it?"

He stilled her with his hand. "Don't turn. It's the man with the tattoo." His lips barely moved. "He's sitting in a chair in the lobby. There's a bag near his feet."

"Big enough to hold a gun?"

Ari nodded.

Claudia glanced around at the busy bank. There had to be at least twenty or so people inside the building, including the grandfather with his grandson. She turned to where Richardson was in his office on the phone. "We need to get to Richardson before he does."

"It might be too late," Ari said. "I think he's the first appointment."

This time Claudia turned to see the woman who had sat

them down talking to a man in a suit. He tugged his sleeve, but Claudia caught the edge of the tattoo. He grabbed his bag and rose to follow her.

Claudia stood up. "You stop him." She started for the door. "I'll get to Richardson."

Ari looked torn, but she squeezed his hand. "I'll be okay, Ari. Go."

He squeezed her hand back, and it felt like a reminder of what was waiting for her when this was all over. She turned and rushed down the hall toward Richardson's office. She was just about there when an alarm blared. A strobe light flashed from a fire alarm overhead. She looked back and saw Ari next to a wall-mounted alarm, winking at her before stepping into the lobby.

She peeked over to where the man with the tattoo had been. Everyone was moving toward the exit, escorted there by the two guards from earlier. But the man was gone. She turned and bumped into someone.

"Oh, I'm sorry, ma'am." Strong hands held her steady. "Are you okay?"

Claudia looked up into the eyes of Dennis Richardson. "Yes, I'm sorry. The fire alarm startled me."

"Well"—he looked over her head—"I don't think it's a test, so we should probably head out."

"Yes, we should." Claudia searched the area around them as Richardson locked the door to his office. "Would you, uh, mind walking with me? I'm afraid I've gotten turned around."

His eyes widened a fraction with concern. "Of course. Yes, come with me."

Claudia let him lead her down the hall, but just as they were ready to turn the corner, she pulled short, seeing the man with the tattoo ahead of them. His eyes locked on her, and she saw his hand reach into his coat. Claudia looked back and saw the emergency exit. Shoving Richardson backward, she pushed him through the door, setting off the alarm just as a gunshot echoed behind her.

"Wh-what's happening?" Richardson asked, stumbling into the alleyway.

"Stay down and keep going." Claudia scanned the alley that served as an employee parking lot. "There."

She led him around the front of a pickup truck and pushed him toward the ground just as the metal door slammed open. Peeking beneath the truck, Claudia watched the gunman step out, no doubt looking for which direction they had gone. Sirens were headed their way, and if they could just stay hidden long enough—

He started walking in their direction. "We need to go," she started to whisper to Richardson, but when she looked back at him, she saw he was already standing. "What are you doing?"

"I'm sorry," Richardson said, and he looked like he meant it. "I had no choice."

Dread filled her, coiling around her middle. She heard footsteps and turned slowly to see the tattooed gunman standing over her, the gun in his hand aimed at her.

SEVENTEEN

o you see her?" Ari scanned the street, feeling panic crawl
through his chest. After pulling the alarm, he'd stepped into
the lobby to follow the man with the tattoo, but he'd disappeared, and when he went back to find Claudia and Richardson,
they were gone too. "Ryan."

"I'm looking." Ryan's voice was breathless. He'd jogged over
from the van where he and two other agents had been monitoring the situation. "I've called in backup, and we've accessed the
security cameras. I'm waiting for them to give us a direction."

Ryan had been ushered out of the bank with the staff and
customers. Three fire trucks had arrived and were keeping
everyone out until they verified what Ari and Ryan had told
them—it was a false alarm set off because of the gunman. *The
one missing along with Claudia.*

The police were already on scene too, and . . . Ari looked to
his left. "Ryan, get agents to the back of the bank."

"Wait!" Ryan called out, but Ari sprinted around the side of
the building to where a long stretch of alley had been turned into
a parking lot for employees. He started down it and stopped
short when he heard her voice.

"You don't want to do this," Claudia said.

Cutting to the edge of the building, Ari pressed himself
against it as he advanced. "Ryan," he whispered, "if you can

hear me, the gunman is at the back of the building. He's got a gun on Claudia. Richardson looks fine for now. I'm moving in."

Using the vehicles to shield himself, Ari kept moving forward until he was about ten yards from the gunman. His back was to Ari, and he hadn't noticed or heard his approach. That was until Richardson looked straight at Ari. The gunman turned, and Ari charged at the same time Claudia did.

A gunshot echoed when Ari's shoulder collided with the gunman's ribs as they crashed to the ground. They rolled, Ari getting in two quick jabs to the man's kidneys before taking a hit to the jaw that had him seeing stars.

Ari slammed his fist into the side of the man's head, which gave him just enough time to twist out from under the man and free his legs. Jumping to his knees, he saw the gunman reach for the gun, and Ari lurched forward, tackling him to the ground. He ignored the sharp pain in his ankle and clamped his arms around the man to keep him from reaching the . . . where did the gun go?

"Don't move!" Claudia's demand stopped the gunman, but Ari didn't let go. They both looked up to find her aim targeted on the man. He started to make a move and Claudia pulled the hammer back. "That would be a big mistake."

Ari winced as the paramedic wrapped his sprained ankle. Next to him, Claudia was being checked out by another paramedic. "I really thought you were going to quote *Dirty Harry*, 'Go ahead and make my day.'"

"I wouldn't have pegged you as a Clint Eastwood fan."

He chuckled. "Actually, I'm more of a *Die Hard* or *Lethal Weapon* kind of guy."

"Ha." Claudia laughed. "Eastwood can take Willis any day of the week, right?" She turned to the paramedic for his opinion, and Ari laughed when the man wisely chose to agree with Claudia.

Ryan walked over. "Sounds like you two are going to make it."

Ari shared a look with Claudia, his heart rate increasing just enough that it caused the numbers on the pulse oximeter to rise. He quickly pulled it off even though the playful smile Claudia sent him said she saw it.

"What did Richardson say?" Ari asked Ryan. "Did he admit to his role?"

"He did. Someone reached out to him about three months ago and threatened his family. He has a daughter, and they were explicit in what they would do to her if he didn't comply." Ryan's jaw flexed. "No father should have to hear that."

"It doesn't excuse what he did," Claudia said, pushing herself out of the ambulance. "Does he know what terrorists do to women and little girls in the Middle East?"

Ari studied Claudia, his heart swelling with pride over her fierce determination to protect others. He had no doubt it would one day make her an excellent wife and mother.

"And Hashim Al-Hakim?" Ari looked at the tattooed man sitting in the back of an unmarked vehicle. "Who's he working for?"

"He's not talking, but we found a message on his phone with a photo of you on it." Ryan looked at Claudia. "There was a text about getting something from you."

Claudia froze, her body stiffening. Ari put his hand on her back and felt her lean into him. "What?"

"Did Prince Mohamed or Radwan give you anything? Tell you anything?"

"No," Claudia said, her tone pitching. "If I knew something, I would tell you."

Ryan pulled out his phone. "Will you take another look at this?"

Ari peeked over Claudia's shoulder as she took the phone. He frowned at the distorted image. "What is that?"

"That's the image from the text Radwan sent me." She looked up at Ryan. "I still don't know what it is."

Ryan nodded. "Okay, what about after you look at this photo?" He scrolled to another one. It was a clear photo of Prince Mohamed standing next to an F1 race car with the spidery grid structure of the W Abu Dhabi hotel behind him.

"That's from the Abu Dhabi Grand Prix at Yas Marina in UAE." She looked between Ryan and Ari, confusion stitching her brows together before a light of recognition filled her eyes. She scrolled between photos. "They're the same photo."

"Our computer tech couldn't really get a clear image from the photo on your phone, so we sent agents back to the house and they found the photo on a shelf near where Radwan's body was. Given that he sent it to you seconds before he was shot, it could've been a mistake."

"No," Claudia answered, shaking her head. "Radwan called me for help. Said it was urgent and that he trusted me. I don't think he accidently sent me that photo. I think it was on purpose. A final message. And I think I know why." She looked at Ryan. "You said the Saudi government fears someone is organizing an overthrow from within . . . someone with powerful connections to push through permits or request meetings with some of the world's biggest oil companies."

Ari looked Claudia over, finding something intensely attractive about watching her mind work, and he was here for it. He'd admired her career from afar through the stories spoken within the walls of Langley—but now he longed for more.

"You have someone in mind?"

"Basheer Al-Farouk," Claudia said. "Prince Mohamed's cousin. There's always been tension between the families because Basheer believes his father is the rightful heir to the Kingdom of Saudi Arabia. He was there in Dubai with Prince Mohamed, and after the situation with the girl in his hotel room, we learned that his cousin had set up the date."

Ari looked at her. "You think Prince Mohamed's cousin is behind the coup?"

"Basheer owns multiple F1 race cars, and one of his main sponsors is"—she held up Ryan's phone so the picture of Prince Mohamed was visible and pointed to the IBI logo all over the car—"International Banking and Investments. It was the perfect opportunity to set it up. They just had to distract Prince Mohamed to keep him from finding out."

"You're brilliant, Claudia." Ryan looked at Ari. "You know she's brilliant, right?"

"I do." Ari winked at Claudia, who rolled her eyes but was still blushing. "Are you going to look into Basheer Al-Farouk?"

"Yep, right now." Ryan took his phone back from Claudia. "I'll keep you two posted, but my director and Director Eisner asked me to deliver a message to you both." His gaze bounced between them, and Ari frowned. "You are to go home and put in your request for a two-week vacation. And if you show up at the office one minute before the two weeks is up"—Ryan's gaze stopped on Claudia—"you can expect a desk assignment in Greenland."

Ari cringed. "No thanks."

"Why do I feel like that was directed toward me?"

Ryan raised his eyebrows at Claudia. "Pecca's told me you can be difficult."

"Who, me?" Claudia spun to face Ari, a dare in her teasing stare. "Am I difficult?"

"Not at all."

"See." Claudia looked at Ryan, and Ari made a face at him, giving an emphatic nod. "I know what you're doing, Blackman."

Ryan started backing away. "I'm going to leave you two to sort that out." He mouthed "good luck" to Ari.

"Hey!" Claudia tried to slug him, but Ryan was fast.

"I was just saying, good *job*." Ryan turned and jogged over to the other FBI agents working the case.

"Well, another successful mission, Blackman."

"Indeed." He stretched his arms. "I think that's the third time I've saved your life. I might have to reconsider dating you. Seem a little high maintenance."

Claudia turned on him, a sparkle in her eyes. "Reconsider dating me? I don't remember you asking me out for a date."

Ari reached for her hand, his fingers intertwined with hers, and that magical zip of electricity pulsed through him. "We've already had two kisses, Ms. Gallegos. I'm pretty sure that means we're dating."

"The unconscious 'kiss' does not count." Claudia made a face as she wrapped her arms around his waist. "But I'm willing to make up for it."

Ari brushed a strand of hair off her forehead, his eyes looking at the stitches there. So much had happened in the last forty-eight hours, and he couldn't explain how they had gotten to this place. "Claudia, I want you to know that I'm not in this just for fun. I don't date casually and that usually scares women, despite what the locker-room rumors are."

Claudia smiled up at him, gently pulling his head toward hers, her invitation clear. He found her lips with his, the kiss deep and passionate.

Pulling back, Claudia ran her fingers down his cheek, the light in her eyes sparkling with truth. "I don't know if you've heard, Blackman, but I don't scare easily."

EPILOGUE

The US Embassy, Saudi Arabia Security Message for US Citizens

In recent weeks, there has been an increase in the frequency and intensity of security incidents in Saudi Arabia, particularly in the greater Riyadh area. Extremist rhetoric on social media sites has advocated the targeting of businesses and economic infrastructure in protest to the arrest of Basheer Al-Farouk.

The Embassy reminds US citizens in Saudi Arabia to review their personal security plans and remain alert to their surroundings at all times. The Saudi Arabian government has deployed a significant number of soldiers and police nationwide to maintain a peaceful environment and is advising all citizens to adhere to the law of the monarchy. As rumors circulate about the disappearance of Basheer Al-Farouk, US citizens should exercise caution when discussing political issues as they relate to the monarchy, the royal family, and the criminal trial of Basheer Al-Farouk.

Due to the possibility of violence and as a matter of general practice, US citizens should avoid areas where large gatherings may occur, as even events intended to be peaceful can become confrontational and escalate into violence.

Y ou ready?"

Claudia glanced up from the security message that was recently sent out to all US residents living in Saudi Arabia. She smiled at Ari. "Yeah."

Ari stepped around the partition separating her desk from the other intel analysts on Langley's ninth floor. He walked up behind her, his fingers just brushing the small of her back so that she'd feel them but not enough to draw the attention of anyone else. "Our flight leaves in three hours. You're not changing your mind, are you?"

"No." She closed out her files and locked her computer before shutting it down. "Did you read the security message from Saudi?"

"I did." He pushed his glasses up, and she saw his serious gaze. "You think Basheer's dead?"

"He hasn't been seen in person since they arrested him." Claudia grabbed her purse. "Not every country has the same due process as America."

Ari helped Claudia into her jacket. "Which is why the lawyers for Hashim Al-Hakim worked so hard to keep him here in the US to stand trial for the murders. He's probably a lot safer in Guantánamo than returning home to face Saudi Arabia's apparently swift justice."

Claudia buttoned her jacket. "I'm just glad it's over and now we can think about the next assignment."

Worry flashed in Ari's eyes. "Next assignment?"

"Aren't you tired of me yet, Blackman?" She laughed as they walked to the elevators. "We spent two whole weeks together. Binged all the Clint Eastwood and Bruce Willis movies to prove Eastwood would hands down take out Willis." Ari bumped her shoulder playfully. "Aren't you ready for me to leave?"

"No, but if it's what you want . . ."

His answer was so truthful, it made her feel bad for teasing him. They stepped into the elevator. "The only assignment I'm looking forward to is the one in which you survive Thanksgiving with my whole family."

"*Pshh*. If I can survive you, I'm sure I can survive them."

"I don't know," Claudia teased. "My brothers aren't even your biggest problem. If you can make it past them, there's Colton and his army of military friends who will put your PSYOPS tactics to the test, and then you have my sister, and she might be the worst because she'll immediately be planning our future."

"Is there anything wrong with that?"

A flutter erupted in Claudia's midsection at his question. "And if you can make it past her, there's my parents, who won't torture you with questions or demand to know your intentions . . . they'll take you out with food."

"Food?" Ari laughed.

"Don't laugh, Blackman. If you've never been to dinner with a Hispanic family, you have no idea what you're up against." She patted her bag. "I've made notes and packed antacids in my suitcase."

"You've thought of everything, haven't you?" Ari stepped close and wrapped his arms around her. His eyes zeroed in on her lips, and she quickly held up a hand.

Her eyes flashed to the camera in the upper corner of the elevator. "They're watching us."

A playful smile filled his face. "Let's give them something to talk about."

Natalie Walters is the author of *Lights Out* and *Fatal Code*, as well as the Harbored Secrets series. A military wife, she currently resides in Texas with her soldier husband and is the proud mom of three. She loves traveling, spending time with her family, and connecting with readers on Instagram and Facebook. Learn more at www.nataliewalterswriter.com.

Lynette, Lynn, and Natalie would like to thank Kelsey Bowen and Amy Ballor for their editing expertise. We would also like to thank the entire team at Revell who worked so hard to bring this project to life.

Lynn would like to thank:

Lynette and Natalie for being such amazing coconspirators on this project.

The experts who wish to remain anonymous but without whom I wouldn't dream of attempting to write about the US Secret Service.

My amazing family—Brian, Emma, James, and Drew—for helping make my writing dreams a reality.

Nikita Wells and Brennan Townsend for checking my archery terms.

Dan Case for the physical therapy that fixed my ankle and gave me the idea to make Emily a PT.

The Light Brigade for praying me through.

And always, my Savior, the Greatest Storyteller, for allowing me to write for him.

If you loved *On the Run* by Lynette,
make sure you catch the related books in the

DANGER NEVER SLEEPS SERIES

If you loved *Deadly Objective* by
Lynn, don't miss any of the other books in the

DEFEND AND PROTECT SERIES

If you loved *Caught in the Crosshairs* by
Natalie, don't miss any of the other books in the

HARBORED SECRETS SERIES

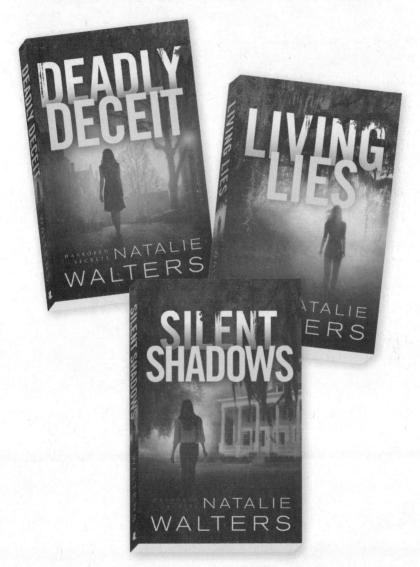